PLOUGHSHARES

Spring 2007 · Vol. 33, No. 1

GUEST EDITOR
Edward Hirsch

EDITOR
Don Lee

MANAGING EDITOR
Robert Arnold

POETRY EDITOR
David Daniel

ASSOCIATE FICTION EDITOR
Maryanne O'Hara

FOUNDING EDITOR
DeWitt Henry

FOUNDING PUBLISHER
Peter O'Malley

PLOUGHSHARES, a journal of new writing, is guest-edited serially by prominent writers who explore different and personal visions, aesthetics, and literary circles. PLOUGHSHARES is published in April, August, and December at Emerson College, 120 Boylston Street, Boston, MA 02116-4624. Telephone: (617) 824-8753. Web address: pshares.org.

EDITORIAL ASSISTANTS: Laura van den Berg and Kat Setzer. BOOKSHELF ADVISORS: Cate Marvin and Fred Leebron. ASSISTANT FICTION EDITOR: Jay Baron Nicorvo. PROOFREADER: Megan Weireter.

POETRY READERS: Simeon Berry, Kathleen Rooney, Autumn McClintock, Heather Madden, Julia Story, Elisa Gabbert, Maria Halovanic, Chris Tonelli, Zachary Sifuentes, Jennifer Kohl, Pepe Abola, and Meredith Devney. FICTION READERS: Laura van den Berg, Jim Scott, Kathleen Rooney, August Hohenstein, Simeon Berry, Chris Helmuth, Sara Whittleton, Vanessa Carlisle, Steve Himmer, Chip Cheek, Leslie Busler, Eson Kim, Wendy Wunder, Cam Terwilliger, James Charlesworth, Emily Ekle, Hannah Bottomy, Elizabeth Browne, Leslie Cauldwell, Laura McCune-Poplin, Dan Medeiros, Patricia Reed, Jason Roeder, and Gregg Rosenblum.

SUBSCRIPTIONS (ISSN 0048-4474): $24 for one year (3 issues), $46 for two years (6 issues); $27 a year for institutions. Add $12 a year for international ($10 for Canada).

UPCOMING: Fall 2007, a fiction issue edited by Andrea Barrett, will appear in August 2007. Winter 2007–08, a poetry and fiction issue edited by Philip Levine, will appear in December 2007.

SUBMISSIONS: Reading period is from August 1 to March 31 (postmark and online dates). All submissions sent from April to July are returned unread. Please see page 228 for editorial and submission policies.

Back-issue, classroom-adoption, and bulk orders may be placed directly through PLOUGHSHARES. Microfilms of back issues may be obtained from University Microfilms. PLOUGHSHARES is also available as CD-ROM and full-text products from EBSCO, H.W. Wilson, ProQuest, and the Gale Group. Indexed in M.L.A. Bibliography, American Humanities Index, Index of American Periodical Verse, Book Review Index. Full publisher's index is online at pshares.org. The views and opinions expressed in this journal are solely those of the authors. All rights for individual works revert to the authors upon publication. PLOUGHSHARES receives support from the National Endowment for the Arts and the Massachusetts Cultural Council.

Retail distribution by Ingram Periodicals and Bernhard DeBoer. Printed in the U.S.A. by Edwards Brothers.

© 2007 by Emerson College   ISBN 1-933058-06-4

CONTENTS

Spring 2007

Cover art:
Untitled by
John Walker
Oil on bingo card, 7″ x 5″, 2006

Ploughshares Patrons

This nonprofit publication would not be possible without the
support of our readers and the generosity of the following
individuals and organizations.

EDWARD HIRSCH

Introduction

I want to send out this issue of *Ploughshares* in the high spirits of a Saturday morning in late March. I was alone and took a long walk by myself, but I also carried with me this surprising gathering of writers, this sudden congregation of solitaries, some from different countries, a few no longer living. It was solitude with others, some of whom scared me with their intensity, which is what one wants from art.

The day was clear, unusually clear, like a freshly wiped pane of glass, a window over the water, and blue, preternaturally blue, like the sky in a Magritte painting, and cold, vividly cold, so that you could clap your hands and remember winter, which had just left a few moments ago—if you strained you could still see it disappearing over the hills in a black parka. Spring was coming but hadn't arrived yet. I walked on the edge of the park. The wind whispered a secret to the trees, which held their breath. On the other side of the street, the skyscrapers stood on tiptoe.

I walked down to the shore to watch the launching of a passenger ship. Ice had broken up on the river, and the water rippled smoothly in blue light. A Dutch painter would have appreciated the scene. The kiosks were open. Couples moved slowly past them, arm in arm, festive. Children darted in and out of the walkways, which sprouted with vendors. Voices cut the air. Kites and balloons. Handmade signs. Voyages to unknown places. The whole day had the drama of an expectation. It stood on the threshold of a discovery.

I thought of the lyric "Song" by the Spanish poet Rafael Alberti:

> If my voice dies on land,
> take it down to the sea
> and leave it on the shore.
>
> Take it down to the sea
> and make it captain
> of a white man-of-war.

Honor it with
a sailor's medal:
over its heart an anchor,
and on the anchor a star,
and on the star the wind,
and on the wind a sail!

translated by Mark Strand

There is a deep sense of mortality in this poem, but Alberti very specifically doesn't say, "If *I* die on land." He proposes—he would sing it if he could—something stranger: "If *my voice* dies on land." He wants his voice, metonymy of the self, symbol of poetry and music, to flow past the body, its earthly home. Take it down to the sea, he presses, and let it go. Don't let it get stuck; don't bury it. Let the voice captain a ship and be honored with a medal. Let it have an anchor with a star. Let it go beyond. Let it soar and sail.

Passion is what one craves in art—and life. Precision matters. Down at the water, the queenly ship was beginning to move away from the pier. Banners fluttered. One said: *"Only mystery enables us to live. Only mystery."* The passengers clustered at the rails on deck. I stood with a group onshore and waved goodbye to the travelers. People were laughing and crying. Some were jubilant; others were brokenhearted. I have always been both. Suddenly, a great cry went up and the ship set sail for the horizon. The ship rumbled into the future, but the cry persisted. I had no idea where that ship was going, but I felt lucky to see it off and bereft when it disappeared.

Ghosts

Out on the front lawn, Melinda was weeding her father's garden with a birdlike metal claw when a car drifted up to the curb. A man with brown hair highlighted with blond streaks got out on the driver's side. He stood still for a moment, staring at the house as if he owned it and was mulling over possible improvements. In his left hand he held an apple with teeth marks in it, though the apple was still whole. Melinda had never set eyes on the guy before. Her father's house was located in an affordable but slightly rundown city neighborhood with its share of characters. They either gawked at you or wouldn't meet your gaze. Many of them were mutterers who deadwalked their way past other pedestrians in pursuit of their oddball destinations. She returned to her weeding.

"Hot day," the man said loudly, as if comments on the weather might interest her. Melinda glanced at him again. With a narrow Eric Claptonish face, and dressed in blue jeans and a plain white shirt, he was on his way to handsomeness without quite arriving there. The apple was probably an accessory for nerves, like a chewed pencil behind the ear.

The baby monitor on the ground beside her began to squawk.

"I have to go inside," Melinda said, half to herself. She dropped her metal claw, rubbed her hands to get some of the topsoil off, and hurried into the house, taking the steps two at a time. Upstairs, her nine-month-old son, Eric, lay fussing in his crib. With dirt still under her fingernails, she picked him up to kiss him and caught a whiff of wet diaper. At the changing table, she raised her son's legs with one hand and removed the diaper with the other while she observed the stranger advancing up the front walk toward the entryway. The doorbell rang, startling the baby and making his arms quiver. Melinda called over to her father, whose bedroom was across the hall, to alert him about the stranger. Her father didn't answer. Sleep often captured him these days and absented him for hours.

She pinned the clean diaper together, and with slow tenderness brought Eric to her shoulder. She smoothed his hair, the same shade of brown as her own, and at that moment the man who had been standing outside appeared in front of her in the bedroom doorway, smiling dreamily, still holding the bitten apple.

"I used to live here," the man said quietly, "when I was little. This was my room when I was small." After emphasizing the last word with a strange vehemence, he seemed to be surveying the walls and the ceilings and the floors and the windows until at last his gaze fell on Eric. The baby saw him and instead of screaming held out his arm.

"Jesus. Who are you?" Melinda said. "What the hell are you doing up here?"

"Yes, I'm sorry," the man said. "Old habits die hard." The baby was now tugging downward at Melinda's blouse buttons, one after the other, which he did whenever he was hungry. "I heard him crying," the man said. "I thought I might help. Is that your father?" He pointed toward the second bedroom, where Melinda's father dozed, his head slumped forward, a magazine in his lap.

"Yes, it is. *He* is," Melinda said. "Now please leave. I don't know you. You're a trespasser. You have serious boundary issues. You have no right to be here. Please get the fuck out. Now." The baby was staring at the man. "I've said 'please' twice, and I won't say it again."

"Quite correct," the man said, apparently thinking this over. "I really *don't* have any right to be here." He made a noise in his throat like a sheep-cough. He had the unbudging calm of a practiced intruder. "Truly I didn't mean to scare you. It's just that I used to live here. I used to *be* here." Holding the apple in his left hand, he held out his index finger to Eric, and the baby, distracted from the button project, grabbed it. The man loosened the baby's grip, turned around, and began to walk down the stairs. "If I told you everything about this house," he said as he was leaving, "and all the things in it, you wouldn't live here. I'm sorry if I frightened you."

She followed him. From the landing she watched him until he had crossed the threshold and was halfway back to his car. Then he stopped, turned around, and said in a loud voice, a half-shout, "Are you desperate? You look kind of desperate to me." He waited in the same stock-still posture she had seen on him earlier. He seemed to be in a state of absolute concentration on something that was not there. People were getting into this style nowadays; really, nothing could outdo the urban zombie affect. It was post-anxiety. It promised a kind of death you could live with. He was waiting eternally for her to answer and wouldn't move until she replied.

"Yes. No," she called through the screen door. "But that's no business of yours."

"My name's Augenblick," the man said, just before he got into his car. "Edward Augenblick. Everyone calls me 'Ted.' And I won't bother you again. I left a business card in the living room, though, if you're curious about this house." He turned one last time toward her front screen door, behind which she was now standing. "I'm not dangerous," he said, holding his apple. "And the other thing is, I *know* you."

The car started—it purred expensively, making a sound like a diesel sedan, but Melinda had never known one brand of car from another, they were all just assemblages of metal to her, and he, this semi-handsome person who said he was Edward Augenblick, whoever that was, and the car, the two of them, the human machine and the actual machine, proceeded down the block in a low chuckling putter, turned right, and disappeared.

Picking up the baby, she went out to gather up her trowel and the birdlike metallic weeder. She would leave the weeds where they were, for now. Doing another sort of chore might conceivably restore her calm.

After taking the tools back to the garage, she surveyed her father's things scattered on the garage's left-hand side, which now served mostly as a shed. You could get a car in there on the right-hand side if you were very careful. Castoff fishing poles, broken flashlights, back issues of *American Record Guide* and *Fanfare*, operas and chamber music on worn-out vinyl, and more lawn and garden implements that gave off a smell of soil and fertilizer—everything her father didn't have the heart to throw away had been dumped here into a memory pile in the space where the other car, her mother's, used to be. Melinda put her gardening implements on a tool shelf next to a can of motor oil for the lawn mower, and she bowed her head. When she did, the baby grabbed at her hair.

She wasn't desperate. The almost-handsome stranger had got that particular detail wrong. A man given to generalizations might launch into nonsense about desperation, seeing a single mom with a baby boy, the two of them living in her father's house, temporarily. Eric pulled hard at her bangs. She was trembling. Her hands shook. The visitation felt like…like what? Like a little big thing—a micro-rape.

She had grown up in this house; he hadn't. It was that simple.

As if taking an inventory to restore herself, she thought of the tasks she had to perform: her property taxes would come due very soon, and she would have to pay them on her own house across town, where she would be residing this very minute if her father weren't in recovery from his stroke. She imagined it: her arts-and-crafts home stood empty (of her and of Eric) on its beautiful wooded lot, with a decorative rose arbor in the backyard, climbing in spite of her, in her absence. She missed its orderly clean lines and its nursery and its mostly empty spaces and what it required of her.

"Desperate"—the nerve of the guy.

Over there, at her own house, she would not be susceptible to the visitations of strangers. Over there, she would be walking distance from a local college where she taught Spanish literature of the nineteenth century—her specialty being the novels of Pérez Galdós. Over there, she was on leave just now, during her father's convalescence, while she lived here, the house of her childhood.

Looking at her father's ragtag accumulations in the garage, she worried at a pile of books with her foot. The books leaned away from her, and the top three volumes (*Gatsby,* Edith Wharton, and Lloyd C. Douglas) fell over and scattered. The baby laughed.

These garage accumulations exemplified a characteristic weakness of the late middle-aged, the broken estate planning of all the doddering Lear-like fathers. Still holding Eric, she sorted the books and restacked them.

Melinda's ex-husband had been a great fan of *Gatsby.* He loved fakery. He had even owned a pair of spats and a top hat that he had purchased at an antique clothing store. He had been the catalyst for a brief trivial marriage Melinda had committed herself to during graduate school. A month or so ago at a party where, slightly drunk on the chardonnay—she shouldn't have been drinking, she knew, she was still nursing the baby—she was telling funny stories about herself, and for a few moments, she hadn't been able to remember her ex-husband's name. Anyway, he was just an ex-husband. Now that she had the baby, solitude and its difficulties no longer troubled her. Her child had put an end to selfish longings. And besides—she was gazing at her father's old *National Geographics*—she had the languages. She spoke four of them including Catalan, which no one over here in the States spoke, ever; most Americans didn't seem to have heard of it. And of course they didn't know where it was spoken. Or why.

Her languages were a charm against loneliness; they gave her a kind of imaginary community. The benevolent spirits came to her in dreams and spoke in Catalan.

During her junior year abroad she had lived in Madrid for a few months and then in Barcelona, where she had acquired a Catalan boyfriend who had taught her the language during the times when he prepared meals for her in his small apartment kitchen—standard fare, paella or fried sausage-and-onions, which in his absentminded ardor he often burned. He gave her little drills in syntax and the names of kitchen appliances. He took her around Barcelona and lectured her about its history, the Civil War, the causes for the bullet holes still visible in certain exterior walls.

He had told her that anyone could learn Spanish, but that she, a stupendously unique and beautiful American girl, must learn Catalan, so she did. What a charming liar he'd been.

Time passed, she returned to the States, got her degrees, and then eighteen months ago, when she had taken a college group to Barcelona for a week, she had met up again with him, this ex-lover, this Jordi, and they had gone out to a tapas bar where she had spoken Catalan (with her uncertain grammar, she sounded, Jordi said, like a pig farmer's wife). At least with her long legs, her sensitive face, and her Catalan, she wouldn't be taken for a typical American, recognizable for innocence and obesity. Then she and Jordi went back to his apartment, a different apartment by now, larger than the one they had spent time in as students, this one near the Gaudí cathedral. Jordi's wife was away on a business trip to Madrid. Melinda and Jordi made love in the living room so as not to defile his marriage bed. Out of the purity of their nostalgia, they came at the same time. He had used a condom, but something happened, and that had been the night when her son was conceived.

She had never told Jordi about her pregnancy. He possessed a certain hysterical formality and would have been scandalized. As the father, he would never permit a Scandia-American name like "Eric" to be affixed to his child. God, he would think, had intervened. Sperm penetrating the condom would be so much like the immaculate conception that Jordi, a Catholic, would have trouble explaining it away. And because he wept easily, he would have first wept and then talked, the talk accompanied by his endearing operatic gestures. The sanctity of life! The whatever of parenthood. He had a tendency to make pronouncements, like the Pope. Or was this Spanish in nature? A Catalan tendency? A male thing? Or just Jordi? Melinda sometimes got her stereotypes confused.

Anyway, her news about the baby would have in all likelihood destroyed his marriage, an arrangement that Melinda supposed was undoubtedly steady, in a relaxed Euro sort of way, despite Jordi's one-off infidelity that particular night, with her.

Maybe he was habitually unfaithful. What was a married man doing with a condom in the drawer of the bedside table? Hidden but in plain view? Did husbands use condoms when making love to their wives? It seemed defeatist.

It was what it was. Still, she had loved Jordi once. She would say to her Catalan friends, "Have you seen his eyes, and those eyelashes?"—the most beautiful brown eyes she had ever seen on a man. He had other qualities difficult to summarize. All the same, men, at least the ones she had known, including Jordi, were a long-term nuisance, a drain on human resources. Whenever intimacy threatened, they often seemed unexpectedly obtuse. If you were going to couple with straight men—and what choice did you have?—you often had to deal with their strange semicomic fogs afterwards. Jordi snored and after lovemaking clipped his toenails. To quote one of them, the bill always came.

Anyway, she was not desperate. Melinda roused herself from her reverie. Augenblick! The stranger had got that part wrong, about the desperation.

She went back upstairs. She put Eric into his crib. Standing there, the baby occupied himself by listening to a white-throated sparrow singing outside the window. Across the hall, her father sat staring at his dresser. It had been positioned beneath family pictures—Melinda, her brother, her mother, and her father—hung in a photo cluster where he could see them as he made his heroic post-stroke efforts to dress and to greet the morning. Behind the pictures was the ancient wallpaper with green horizontal stripes. He turned toward her, and the right side of his face smiled at her.

"Do you hear it?" he asked.

She waited. Hear what? The sparrow? He wouldn't be asking about that. "No," she said; the room was quite silent. Lately her father had been suffering from music hallucinations, what he called *ear worms,* and she wasn't sure whether to grant him his hallucinations or not. Did the pink elephant problem grow larger whenever, being affable, you agreed that there was indeed a pink elephant right outside the door, or shambling about in the street? "What is it? What do you hear?"

"Somebody far away, practicing," he told her. "A violinist. She's doing trills and double-stops. She's practicing someone-or-other's concerto in D. You really don't hear it?" Her father had not been a professional musician, but he had always had perfect pitch. If he heard music in D major, then that was the key signature, hallucination or not.

In the silent room, Melinda gazed down at her father, at his thinning gray hair, the food stains scattered on his shirt, the sleepy, half-withdrawn look in his eyes, the magazine now on the floor, the untied shoelaces, the trouser zipper imperfectly closed, the mismatched socks, the shirt with the buttons in the wrong buttonholes, the precancerous blotches on his face, the half-eaten muffin spread with margarine nearby on the side table, and she was so overcome with a lifelong affection for this calm decent man that she felt faint for a moment. Her soul left her body and then came back in an instant. "Oh, wait," she said suddenly. "Yup. I do hear it. It's very soft. From across the street. You know, it's who, that scary brilliant teenager, that Asian girl, what's her name, Maria Chang. And I know who wrote that music, too."

"You do?"

"Sure," Melinda said. "It's Glazunov. Alexander Glazunov. It's the Glazunov concerto for violin in D major." She was making it all up as she went along.

"Yes," her father said. "Glazunov. The teacher of Shostakovich. That must be right." He smiled again at her. "But that concerto is in A, baby doll." Turning his head to face her at a strange angle, he asked, "Who was that person who j-j-j-j-just came to the door? Did he come upstairs? Did he watch me? Did he come for me? Was it death? I was half asleep."

"An intruder," she said. "Somebody who said his name was Augenblick."

"Well, that's almost like death. What'd he want?"

"He said he used to live here. As a baby or something."

"Impossible. I know who I bought this house from thirty-five years ago, and it wasn't anybody by that name. Besides, that's not his real name. It's German. It means..."

"Blink of an eye," Melinda said. "An instant."

"Right. But he's lying to you. I never heard of any German person named Augenblick. It's a fiction, that name. There's no such name in German. It's total bullshit." He waved his hand dismissively. Since his stroke, her father had started to employ gutterisms in his day-to-day speech. His new degraded vocabulary was disconcerting. His mind had suffered depreciation. She didn't like obscenity from him; it didn't match his character, or what remained of it.

Her father's potted plant in the corner needed watering—its leaves were shriveling. Lately she had become a caretaker: Eric, and her father, and the lawn and garden out in front, and her father's house, and the plants in it—and if she weren't careful, that caretaking condition might become permanent, she would move into permanent stewardship, they would be her accumulations, and they would pile up and surround her. The present would dry up and disappear, except for the baby, and there would be nothing else around her except the past.

Downstairs on a side table was a business card.

> Edward Augenblick
> Investment Counselor
> "Fortune Favors the Few"
> email: eyeblink@droopingleaf.com

Anger spat up from somewhere near her stomach. "Fortune favors the few"! Damn him. And this zealotry from an intruder.

At once, the languages roused themselves, spewing out their local-color bile. First, the Catalan. ¡*Malparit. Fot el camp de casa meva ara mateix!* And then the Spanish. ¡*Me cago en tu madre, hijo de puta!* What a relief it was to have other languages available for your obscenities. They pitched in.

A day later, she and her friend Gabrielle were walking in Min-nehaha Creek, their pants rolled up, shoes in hand, Eric baby-packed on Melinda. They were searching the creek for vegetative wonders as they bird-watched and conversed. Melinda liked Gabrielle's bad temper and had befriended her for it. They had bumped into each other in a bookstore a year ago, and Gabrielle had cursed her affably. Melinda was bowled over by her comic vehemence and asked her out for coffee, an invitation that Gabrielle accepted. Gabrielle, a stockbroker, was now back from a cruise. She had planned to meet men. There hadn't been any avail-able ones, at least none, she said, you'd want to take home or to converse with. All the cruise-males were old or stupefied by alco-hol or money. She had been criminally misinformed.

"There's a blue jay," Melinda said, pointing. She splashed her feet in the water, being careful not to slip on the rocks.

"Did I tell you how all the staff spoke with an accent? Did I mention that?" Gabrielle asked. " 'Ladies and gentle, let me know eef I can help you in any how.' Their accents were worse during the winetasting session. 'Yooou like theeese vine? Have a zip.' " She walked up to Eric and kissed him on the ear. The baby giggled. " 'Hold theeese vine to the liiiight to determinate the lascivity.' "

"You should be more tolerant of foreigners," Melinda mur-mured, turning to face her.

"Why should I? I'm not like you. I'm a provincial. I put salt in my coffee." She looked at her friend. "You take that beautiful baby of yours around on your back just to flaunt him in front of me."

"No, I don't. Your leg is cut," Melinda said, pointing. "Where'd you get that mess of scabs?"

"Roses. I was staring at the clematis vine. Its growth habits were unpleasing. I held the ideal in my head so firmly that I obliterated awareness of the rest of the garden, especially the very large, known-to-be-violent rosebush between the clematis and me. I must have lunged at the vine. The rosebush grabbed at my leg, which continued to move. Seconds later I realized that the whole front of my leg had been savagely torn."

"Savagely torn? That's awful."

"'Laceration' is what the form said, when I finally got out of the ER. I looked the word up, from *lacerate, distress deeply, torn, mangled.* Then I had a drug reaction to the prophylactic antibiotic. It sent me back to the ER. I couldn't walk."

"What's that?" Melinda nodded toward something growing in the creek.

"Watercress?" Gabrielle said. Her black hair fell downward as she bent to see it, and for a moment Melinda thought of Persephone on her way back from the underworld. She had the wildly intelligent eyes of a genius. "No, it's just an unknown, anonymous weed. By the way, how close are we to the Mississippi? I have an appointment. Well, *I* think of it as an appointment. You might not."

Melinda stood up straight, feeling the baby's weight shift. He was making sucking sounds. "I had a visitor yesterday. Well, not a visitor. A man, an intruder. He looked like Eric Clapton. He walked right into the house. He said he used to live there. But he didn't. He couldn't have. His name was Augenblick."

"You call the cops?"

"No."

"I would have," Gabrielle told her. "I'd have the law scurrying right over, with the cuffs and the beaters out."

"He said Eric's nursery had once been his own room. He said he knew things about the house, bad things. He said, this stranger, that I was *desperate.* Can you imagine?"

"He got the wrong address," Gabrielle said. "He meant me."

"Damn him, anyway," said Melinda. She pointed to an opening of the creek where the Mississippi River was visible. "There it is. There's the river. We made it."

"Yeah." Gabrielle slapped at a mosquito on her forearm, leaving a little smear of blood just above her wristwatch. "Is this about your mother?" she asked. Her tone was studiously neutral. "This is about your mother, isn't it? Maybe this guy lived in the neighborhood when you were growing up. Maybe your mother was known to him."

Melinda stopped and looked at her friend. Seedpods from a cottonwood overhead drifted down onto her hair and into the water. "Oh, well," she said, as if something had been settled. Melinda's mother had been in and out of institutions. Melinda refused to come to terms with it, now or ever; a mad parent could not be rescued or reasoned with. Things were getting dark all of a sudden. "I'm, um, feeling a bit lightheaded." She felt her knees weakening, and she made her way to the side of the creek, where she sat down abruptly on the wet sands.

"You aren't going to faint on me, are you?" she heard Gabrielle say, in front, or behind of, a crow cawing. "I'd appreciate it if you didn't faint on me, with that baby strapped to your back, and my appointment coming up…" The force of her friend's irritation drifted into her consciousness, as did her voice, someone turning the volume knob back and forth, as she held her own nausea at bay, her head down between her knees. Creek water was suddenly splashed on her face, thrown by her friend, to rouse her.

At certain times, usually in the afternoons, her father would ride the buses, but Melinda had no idea where he went, and he himself could not always remember. He said that he visited the markets, but one time he came back and said that he had knocked at the Gates of Heaven. He would not elaborate. Where were these gates? He had forgotten. Perhaps downtown? Many people were going in, all at once. He felt he wasn't ready, and took the bus home.

This traveling around was a habit he had picked up from his wife, whose wandering had started right after the death of their first child, Melinda's older sister, Sarah, who had died of a blood infection at the age of two. Her mother gave birth to Melinda and then went into a very long, slow, discreetly genteel decline. One day, when Melinda was eleven, her mother, unable to keep up appearances anymore, drove away and disappeared altogether. She was spotted in Madison before she evaporated.

Back in her father's house, Melinda went straight from the phone to her computer. She typed in Augenblick's email address and then wrote a note.

hi. i don't know who you are, but you're not who you say you are, and my father

has never heard of you or your family. i shouldn't be writing to you and i
    wouldn't be except i didn't like it that you said you knew me. from where? we've never
    met. you don't know me. i hardly know myself. kidding. i mean, i've met you and i still
    haven't met you. you're a ghost, for all i know.

She deleted the last three sentences—too baroque—both for their meaning and her responsibility for writing them. The joking tone might be mistaken for friendliness. She ducked her head, hearing Eric staying quiet (she didn't want to breastfeed him again tonight, her nipples were sore—but it was odd, she also had suffered a sudden brokenhearted need for sex, for friendly nakedness), and then she continued writing.

as far as i know, the previous owners of this house were named anderson. that's who
    my mom and dad bought it from. 'augenblick' isn't even a name. it's just a german noun.
    so, my question is: who are you? where are you from? what were you doing in my
    house? —melinda everson, ph.d.

She deleted the reference to the doctoral degree, then put it back, then deleted it again, then put it back in, before touching the SEND button.

Half an hour letter, a new letter appeared in the electronic in-box, from eyeblink@droopingleaf.com.

THINK OF ME AS THE RAGE OVER THE LOST PENNY. BUT LIKE I TOLD YOU IM ACTUALLY VERY HARMLESS. W/R/T YOUR QUESTIONS, I CAN DROP BY AGAIN. INFORMATION IS ALL I WANT TO GIVE YOU. eye two LIVED THERE. HA HA. —TED

The school year would be starting soon, and she needed to prepare her classes. She needed to study Peréz Galdós's *Miau* again, for the umpteenth time, for its story of a man lost in a mazelike bureaucracy—her lecture notes were getting mazelike themselves,

Kafkaesque. And worse: bland. She would get to that. But for now she was waiting. She knew without knowing how she knew that when Augenblick came back, he would show himself at night, when both her father and her son were asleep; that he would come at the end of a week of hot, dry late-summer weather orchestrated by crickets, that he would show up as a polite intruder again, halfway-handsome, early middle-aged semi-degraded-Clapton, well-dressed, like a piano tuner, and that he would say, as soon as he was out of the driver's-side door of his unidentifiable car, perhaps hand-made, and had advanced so that he stood there on the other side of the screen door, "You look very nice tonight. I got your letter. Thanks for inviting me over."

These events occurred because she was living in her father's house.

"And I got yours," she said, from behind the screen. The screen provided scanning lines; his face was high-definition. "You're the rage over the lost penny. But I didn't invite you over. You're *not* invited. It wasn't an invitation." She hesitated. "Shit. Well, come in, anyway."

This time, once inside, he approached her and shook her hand, and in removing his hand, rubbed hers, as if this were the custom somewhere upon greeting someone whom you didn't know but with whom you wanted a relationship. It was a failed tentative caress but so bizarre that she let it happen.

"My father is upstairs," she said. "And my son, too. Maybe you could explain who you are?"

"This is the living room," he told her, as if he hadn't heard her question, "and over there we once had a baby grand piano in that corner, by the stairs." He pointed. "A Mason and Hamlin. I was never any good at playing it, but my sister was. She's the real musician in the family."

"What does she play?" she asked, testing him. "What's her specialty?"

"Scriabin etudes," he said. "Chopin and Schumann, too, and Schubert, the B-minor."

"She didn't play the violin, did she?"

"No. The piano. She still does. She's a pediatric endocrinologist now. Doctors like music, you know. It's a professional thing." He waited. "Ours was the only piano on the block." He glanced toward the dining room. "In the dining room used to have another chandelier, it was cut glass—"

"Mr. Augenblick, uh, maybe you could tell me why you're here? And why you're lying to me?" She scooped a bit of perspiration off her forehead and gazed into his game face. "Why all these stories about this locality? Scriabin, Schubert: every house has a story. The truth is, I'm not actually interested in who did what, where, here." She saw him glance down at her body, then at the baby toys scattered across the living room floor. Her breasts were swollen, and she had always been pretty. She was a bit disheveled now, though still a beauty. "I'm a mother. New life is going on here these days. My son is here, my father, too, upstairs, recuperating from a stroke. I don't have time for a personal history. For all I know, you're an intruder. A dangerous maniac."

"No," he said, "I've noticed that. No one has time for a history." Augenblick stood in the living room for a moment, apparently pondering what to say next. At last he looked up, as if struck by a sudden thought, and asked, "May I have a glass of iced tea?"

"No." She folded her arms. "If you were a guest, I would provide the iced tea. But, as I said, I didn't invite you here. I don't mean to be rude, but—"

"Actually," he said, "you *are* rude. You wrote back to me, and that was, well, an invitation. Wasn't it? At least that's how I took it, it's how any man would have taken it." He pasted onto his face a momentarily wounded look. "So all right. So there's to be no iced tea, no water, no hospitality of any kind. No stories, either, about the house. All right. You want to know why I'm here? You really want to know why I'm here? My life hasn't been going so well. I was doing a bit of that living-in-the-past thing. I was driving around, in this neighborhood, *my* former neighborhood, and I saw a really attractive woman working in her garden, weeding, and I thought: *Well, maybe she isn't married or attached, maybe I have a chance, maybe I can strike up a conversation with that woman working there in that garden.* I wasn't out on the prowl, exactly, but I *did* see you. And then I discovered that you had a baby. A beautiful boy. You know, I'm actually a nice guy, though you'd never know it. I'm a landscape architect. I have a college degree. All I wanted was to meet you."

"You said I was desperate. You said you knew me. That was unkind. No. It was wicked."

"You *are* desperate. I do know you. Desperation is knowable."

"That's a funny way of courting a woman, saying things like that."

"We have the same soul, you and I," he said. He said it awkwardly. Still, she was moved, beside or despite herself. The sovereign power of nonsensical compliments: a woman never had any defenses against them.

"I don't know," she said. "Come back in a few days and tell me about the house."

"It's just an ordinary house," he told her, glaring critically at its corners. "Anyway, you're right, I never lived here. I lived a few blocks away."

"So make it up," she said. "You were going to make it up, anyway. Do what you can with it. Impress me."

The next time Augenblick came by, he brought a bottle of wine, a kind of lubricant for his narrative, Melinda thought.

They drank half the bottle, and then he began with the medical details about the house and what had happened in its rooms. There had been a little girl with polio who lived in the house in the 1950's, encased in an iron lung, with the result that her parents had been the first on the block to buy a TV set, in those days a low-class forgetfulness machine. In those days only two stations broadcast programs, a few hours in the morning, then off-the-air during the afternoons until four p.m., when the *Howdy-Doody Show*, *Superman*, and *Beulah* came on.

He touched Melinda's hand. From somewhere he poured her another glass of wine, a glass that she had taken down from her kitchen shelf an hour or two ago, and she took it. He did an inventory of ghosts. Every house had them. He told her that the living room had once been an organizing center for Farmer-Labor party socials of the Scandinavian variety, and that they had planned their strikes there, including the truckers' strike in the 1930's.

"Any violence?" she asked, taking the wine for her second glass.

"None," he said. As a little boy, he said, he had heard that there had once been a murder in these environs, and maybe it had been in this house. He wasn't sure. The body of the murder victim, it was said, had been propped up on the freezer, sitting there, and the police had come in to investigate after the neighbors had called in with reports of screaming, and one of the cops looked directly at the body of the murdered woman, her hair down over her face, and he hadn't seen it, and the police had left.

"Who are you?" Melinda asked Augenblick after they had finished the wine and he had concluded his story. Now they sat on the back porch in discount-store foldout chairs, and through the screens they could see her father's garage with the car on one side and her father's discards, his memory pile, on the other. "Because, right here, there's quite a bit about you that's completely wrong. You tell me a story, the absolutely wrong story, about happiness and a murder, and you say you know me and you say I'm desperate, and I think you said that you and I have the same souls, and your card claimed that you were an investment counselor, and then you informed me that you were a landscape architect." Melinda put her tongue inside her wineglass and licked at the dew of wine still affixed there. "None of it adds up. Because," she said, "what I think it is, what I think you are, sitting here beside me, is a devil." She waited. "Not one of the major ones, in fact really minor, but one all the same."

Through the air pocket of dead silence the crickets chirped. Augenblick did not immediately reply. "Um, okay," he said.

" 'Okay'?"

"Yeah, okay. I used to be an investment counselor until I went broke. I couldn't part with the business cards. So then I went into planting things, landscaping. Not much income, but some. The life I have is modest. I have a kind of ability to, you know, hit the wrong note. Somebody once told me I was a borderline personality but not a success at it. And sometimes I tell stories that aren't quite true. Untruths are what I learned how to do in high school and never quite shook off."

"You should work at it," she said.

"I should work at it," he repeated.

"Was there anything, anywhere, you said that was true?"

"Yes," he said. "My name's really Augenblick. You and I have the same souls. I believe that. I still sort of believe that you're desperate. I used to live in this neighborhood. You had a mother once. I remember her. And actually, from the first moment I saw you, weeding out there in the garden, I haven't been able to stop thinking about you."

She waited. "Could we go back to the topic sentence?"

He leaned sideways in her direction. She could smell the wine on his breath. "About devils, you mean?"

"Yeah, that part."

"There are no devils anymore," he said. "There are only people who are messed up and have to spread it around. And they're everywhere. See, what you have to do is, if you're going to get it, you have to imagine a devil who is also maybe a nice guy." And he leaned over further, so that he almost lost his balance in his chair, and he gave her a peck on each cheek, a devil's kiss.

Making love to him (which she would never, ever do) would be like taking a long journey to a foreign locale you didn't exactly want to visit, like Tangier, a place built on the slopes of a chalky lime-stone hill. The sun's intensity would be unpleasant, and the general poverty would get in the way of everything. He would make love like a man who didn't quite know what he was doing and who would press that ignorance, hard, on someone else, specifically on her, on her flesh. Still, he would be careful with her, as if he remembered that she was still nursing a child. In the middle of the bed, she would suddenly recall that when she had first seen him, she had thought that there was nothing to him, and she would wonder if there was still nothing to him now. Whether he was actually named Augenblick, despite his claims, whether he did anything actual for a living, whether he would ever hurt her, whether he really might be a devil, though devils didn't exist. Because if they did, times would change and the devils would take new forms. If the name of God is changing in our time, then so are the other names. Then she would come, rapidly, and would forgot her questions the way you forget dreams. But it would never happen, not that way.

"You made love to him?" Gabrielle was outraged. The cell-phone itself seemed to be outraged with her anger; even the plastic seemed annoyed. Melinda had called her friend in the middle of the night to consult.

"No, I didn't," Melinda said. "No. No love. But I did fuck him. I was lonely. I wanted to get naked."

"How was it?"

"Okay."

"Well, as the great Albert Einstein once said, 'Don't do that again.'"

She wondered if he would disappear. Everything about him suggested a vanishing act. He would not invite her to his house, wherever that was, nor would he ever give her an address. Like everyone else, though, he did have a cellphone, and he gave her the number to that. One night when he told her (she was lying in her bed, and he was lying in his bed, across town, and the phone call had gone on for over an hour), "I lived in your soul before you owned it," she decided that he was one of those crazy people who gets by from day to day, but just barely—he was what he said he was, a failed borderline personality. She resolved to tell him that she would not see him anymore, under any circumstances, but then he invited her to dinner at a pricey downtown restaurant, so she located a babysitter both for the baby and for her father, and when Edward Augenblick arrived to pick her up, she felt ready for whatever was going to happen, accessorized for it, with a bracelet of beautiful tiny gold spikes.

But in the restaurant, he played the gentleman: he talked about landscape architecture, landscaping generally, so that the conversation took a lackadaisical turn toward the work of Frederick Law Olmsted, and she talked about her work and her scholarship, about Pérez Galdós, the polite chitchat of two people who possibly want to get to know each other, post-sex, and she wondered whether they would ever talk about anything that mattered to them, and whether all his talk about souls was just a bluff, a conversational shell game. She was about to ask him where he had grown up, where he had been educated, what his parents had been like, when he said, "Let's take a walk. Let's go down to the river." The bill for the dinner came, a considerable sum, and he paid in cash, drawing out a mass of twenty-dollar bills from his wallet, a monotonous and mountainous pile of twenties, all the cash looking like novelty items, and Melinda thought, *This man has no usable credit.*

Across the Mississippi River near St. Anthony Falls stands the Stone Arch Bridge, built of limestone in the nineteenth century for the railroad traffic of lumber and grain and coal in and out of Minneapolis. After the railroad traffic ceased, the bridge had been converted to a tourist pedestrian walkway, and he took her hand in his as they strolled over the Mississippi River, looking at the abandoned mills on either side, and the rapids and the locks directly below.

"They don't manufacture anything here anymore, you know," he said to her, close to a whisper.

"The buildings are still here."

"Yes," he said, "but they're ghosts. They're all ghosts. They're shells."

"But look at the lights," she said. "Lofts and condos."

"They don't make anything in there anymore," he said. "Except babies, sometimes, the thirty-somethings. Otherwise, it's all a museum. American cities are all becoming museums." He said this with a wild, incongruous cheer, as a devil would. "Okay," he said. "I'll tell you one true thing. Listen up."

"What's that?"

"When I was a little boy, I lived three or four blocks down from where you lived. I've told you this. You don't remember me. That's all. You don't remember. I remember you, but you don't remember me. No one ever remembers me. One night I was playing in the living room, with my toy armies, and your mother came to our door. I think she was drunk. But I didn't know that. She rang the bell and she entered our house. My parents were upstairs, or somewhere. Your mother came into the house and looked at me playing with my soldiers, and she looked and looked and looked. She smiled and nodded. And then she asked me if I would like to go away with her, that she had always wanted to take a boy like me with her on her travels."

"How did you know it was my mother?" Melinda asked, between shivers.

"I was eight years old. Maybe nine. Everyone knew about your mother. Everyone. I had been warned. You knew that. Everyone knew that. But she had a nice face."

"Where did she say she wanted to take you away to?"

"She had this look in her eyes, I still remember it," Augenblick said. "You have it, too. She wanted to disappear and to take someone along with her. That night, it was going to be me. Your mother was famous in this neighborhood. But everybody thought she was harmless."

"Well, she was a success," Melinda said, the shivers taking her over, so that she had to clutch onto a guardrail. "In disappearing." She leaned toward him and kissed him on the cheek, a show of bravery. "Death is such a cliché," she said. "She disappeared into a cliché."

"Is it?" He wasn't looking at her. "That's news to me. She grabbed me by the hand and she took me for a walk and then she tried to get me into the car, but I broke her hold on me and I ran back to my house."

"Yeah," she said, dreamily. "Death. It's so retro. It's for kids and old people. It's an adolescent thing. You can do better than dying. *You're tired. But everyone's tired. But no one is tired enough,*" she quoted from somewhere. "Anyway, she disappeared, and so what?" It occurred to her at that moment that Augenblick might have leapt off the bridge to his death but that he had, just then, changed his mind, because she had said that death was a cliché. That was it: he looked like a failed suicide. He was one of those.

"She gave me the scare of my life," he said. "Your harmless mother. She scared everybody until she was gone. Shall we go back now?" he asked. "Should we go somewhere?"

"No," she said. "Not again. Not this time." She waited. "We're going to stay right here for a while."

He eventually dropped her off at the front door of her father's house, thanked her, and drove off in his car, which, he had explained, was a Sterling, a nonsense car. She guessed that the license plates on the car had been stolen so that he could not be traced. Whoever he was—Augenblick! what a name!—he would not return. She wondered for a moment or two what his name actually had been, where he had worked, and whether any of it, that is, the actual, mattered, now or ever.

She paid the babysitter and then went upstairs to check on Eric.

The ghosts of the house were gathered around her son. The couples who had lived here from one generation to the next, the solitaries, the happy and unhappy, the gay and the straight and the young and the old: she felt them grouped behind her as a community corralled in the room, touching her questioningly as she bent over the crib and watched her boy, her perfection, breathe in and out, his Catalan-American breaths.

She tiptoed into her father's room. He was still sitting up, carefully studying the wallpaper.

"Hey, Daddy," she said.

"Hey, Sugar," he replied, tilting his head in his characteristically odd way. "How did it go? Your date with this Augenblick?"

"Oh, fine," she said, shunning the narrative of what had happened, how she had fought off his information with a little kiss. Her father wouldn't be interested—especially about her mother.

"I didn't like him. I was hoping you wouldn't have sex with him again. I didn't want to listen. He wasn't out of the top drawer."

"More like the middle drawer. But that's all right," Melinda said. "I won't see him again."

"Good," her father said. "I thought he was a fortune-hunter, after your millions." He laughed hoarsely. "Heh heh. He looked very unsuccessful, I must say, with that dyed hair." He tilted his head the other way. "I went to the Gates of Heaven today," he said, "on the bus. The number eight bus."

"How did it look?" she asked. "The gates?"

"Tarnished," he said. "They could use a shine. No one ever seems to do maintenance anymore. The bus was empty. Even though I was the thing riding on it." He tilted his head the other way. "Completely empty, with me at a window seat. That's how I knew I was almost gone. Honey, you should have more friends, better friends. Someone who doesn't make you groan during sex."

It didn't shock her somehow, that he had heard them. "I have friends. Just not here. I'm moving back home," she said. "To my house. Where I live. I can't stay here anymore, Daddy. I can't take care of you anymore. I love you, Daddy, but I can't do it. I'll arrange for somebody to watch you and to cook." She leaned down to kiss the top of his head.

"I know," he said. "Oh, I know, honey. Staying here makes you a child, doesn't it?"

"Yes." She could feel the goddamn tears flooding over her. And she could feel the ghosts of the house gathering around *him*, now, easing his way into the next world that awaited him. And somewhere on the planet, her mother, too, drove toward the horizon, forever. "I'll watch out for you, though. I'll drop in. I'll check on you."

"No, you probably won't," he said. "No one does. But that's all right. That's how it happens. By the way, do you hear that violin? That girl is practicing as if her life depended on it."

Melinda bent her ear to the silence. "Yes," she agreed. "I do hear it. All the time. Morning and night. It never stops."

MARJORIE AGOSIN

Essaouira

translated by Laura Rocha Nakazawa

That night,
the wind was a lament,
a daring wound above the voice of the sea.
That night, someone called me
amid deep darkness
to take me to the Melah,
the Jewish quarter.

Inebriated, I walked,
covered in white tulles to protect me
from the fine and savage sand.
Alone, I walked among the dead,
they, perhaps, next to me.

And the houses with their blue doors
opened up,
and the houses with their sad Stars of David
moved alone,
like a single lament.
And in that emaciated night,
I sat down to pray for the Jews of Essaouira.
Nothing remained of them,
only blue doors,
only the screeching sound of a blue door,
only myself invoking them,
and the dead next to me,
keeping me company in this night of Essaouira
when a hand took me to see the Jews
who fled
leaving steps in the salt,
melodies of sea and darkness,

blue doors swinging among
the dead.

In the distance,
the wounded, absent sea.

The Deer

are tentative. Of course. To be an animal
is to watch. Is to think
about eating all the time. I watch them
be so watchful. My window
takes them one by one through trees
winter strips down
to a few species.
                        When I saw the deer,
I was beginning to type, not
it came to me, full of: I made this.
But two or three were smaller than the others.
And all so thin,
each forgetting for a moment, a head turned
or down to the ground. Then the rush
to catch up. Maybe
a mother among them.
I'm hopeless about kinship, which cousin, which way
the bloodline hollows out a life
and connects us back
to a pin dropped once in a field
or in woods like these.
                        The poem to be typed—
I forgot the window's job
is to disappear. The deer,
just there, drawn
by a leaf or two left to the weather, a bud in its
vague dream of some future—
                        mid-sentence. Stop.
They're gone. Because beauty's
not generous, isn't anything
but its passage.

DAVID BOTTOMS

My Poetry Professor's Ashes

remembering Lem Norrell

All those rhetorical contraptions of the metaphysicals
prying us loose from the world!
                    And those licentious exhortations to squeeze the day!
Something about the Anglican burial
brought those back, and with them your voice rousing those
    metaphors off the page.

It's not like I didn't get a heads-up, right?

But I'd never seen a man's ashes, the human dust, fine, gray,
and when the priest upended the urn
and shook yours into the grass, I thought how much they looked
    like chalk dust,
like a lifetime of notes erased from a blackboard,
which seemed right enough
                    given what we are and what words come to.

Learning to Become Nothing

for Carl Hays

Drizzle this morning,
but a cool glare in the brain, and I'm staggering again down
    Cherry Street
toward that cratered-out joint on Broadway
where one happy night, eons ago, I cut a rug with a hopped-up
    redhead.

Nothing came of that, Carl, except a few short hours of
    inexplicable joy,
so that each bad tooth in her gorgeous smile
                        hardened into a little gem of memory.

Gems, Carl, gems. And this whole street paved with them—
    Otis Redding
strutting into your jewelry store, a sunburst off
the cracked face of his watch,
                    or that saintly Pearly Brown, blind as the future,
pounding the sidewalk, slashing out a sermon on his
    National Steel.
God love a cheerful giver, Carl.

Yes, sir. His sign caught the whole shebang—
and now that we're learning to become nothing, we have to learn
to give it all away—every radiance,
every gem—
            cheerful, as you say, being the enigma.

In the Center of Water

translated by Maria Koundoura and the author

In its center all is water
you were saying that night, if you remember
as the fire was dimming the light
on the moist fingernails slowly peeling
the dry skin from the orange
before sinking into its yellow succulence

A woman, the boy, fruit
in this world is made of water
simmering indifferent or silent within them
languidly sometime breaking out in sweat
to quench the thirst of its creatures
before evaporating upward again

The surface of water is called earth
and its homeland the clouds
in the impenetrable center of air
while fire is extinguished at its shudder
batting eyelashes, I think you were saying
with the end's fiery gaze

I am afraid, I had said, before you spoke
of inflicting evil on you with all I carry
with hands that do not resist the cold
when my thought freezes as
the wind burns the face behind it
deserting dust carved in relief

You rose then not to stoke the fire
but to bring me some water
without my asking for it yet
letting it run for a while

closer to the heart of the liquid deposit
that shines precious drops on the glass

I have tried many times to remember
exactly what you said that night
and why your words, unforgotten
though not remembered
comforted me in a translucent way
softening on me wherever they flowed

I know that when I come home burdened
I peel the dry garments off now
let the water run naked on the body
and have the sense of bathing with light
in the dark bathroom, but even if light enters
I close my eyes

Don't be afraid, you said, if this love is not
as you think, something solid, of earth
—a sandcastle sinking
from a boat traversing the deep
mailing waves to shore
sprinkling babies with salt

A being is fluid
so it can flow on the body's slopes
and fit in the vessels of the soul
before it returns water to water
before it discovers its ends at the center
before it becomes centered

Nothing can hide in water

As upon it falls the grain imprinting
the universe and before it dissolves
it rocks its hard surface
reconstructing reflections
in water's memory—remember?
forgetting impressions of moments

Cleanse your own words if not mine
at the sound of the tap or the waterfall
which bring water from the center of water
being within us so deep at the origin
until that moment arrives
when it has finally circled us all

No need to remember my exact words
Let go, though
Don't let me go

14 *rue Serpentine*

1.

In the yard of the children's prison
the fruit on the solitary tree is blue
shriveled beyond recognition
At the turn of the last century
the inmates (aged 7 to 13)
pickpockets petty thieves & vandals
ate gruel from wooden bowls
and slept on iron cots
gazing down from their cells
at that tree when it blossomed in April
and in September bore fruit
which the guards pocketed rocking
on their heels into the long afternoons
It was an apple tree

2.

Dip your rotting oars
into the brown waters of the lake
and row toward the floating temple
Splinters of light escape its shuttered windows
a red lantern sways on the dock
a candle flutters by the door
You can hear the faintest sound:
fruit falling in the orchard
a snake shedding its skin in the reeds
Your breathing too is shallow
your hands are one with the darkness
and you know when you reach the temple
your oars will be gone

3.

Beside the sundial in the triangular park
the war veteran with medals pinned
to his coat plays an accordion
for a poodle that dances on its hind legs
Children line up to buy ices
persimmon apricot grenadine
from an old woman with a parrot on her shoulder
that asks their names one after the other
until sunset when the old woman
closes up her cart and rewards the parrot
with grapes and on the way home
he repeats the names one after the other
Theresa Roberto Clarissa Victor Marie...

4.

In a basement on the rue Quincompoix
a woman in a top hat and gloves
will demonstrate that even in a universe
in which polar absolutes (matter&spirit
good&evil) are thought to be the norm
things can jump the divide and become their opposites
She raises her wand and turns a white
rat black and a black rat white
while her assistant the dwarf his domino askew
plays a drumroll and with a laugh turns up
the lights and reveals both rats to be gray
not just interchangeable but identical
slipping into separate cages to await the next show

5.

A city in Central Asia
a square walled in by four granite buildings
bits of paper rising twenty stories on the wind

the two walkways an X
choked with weeds
at its center a cement Buddha
with a forehead cracked by the cold
From one of the rooftops
a woman in a green dress
calls to a child whose name
you would like to tell her is scrawled
in crayon beneath a face—
eyes closed and a downturned mouth—
on a door you're about to open

6.

With the sun glancing off your lips
you quarter an orange on the blue table
and watch the lizards watching
you from the grape trellis
and the woman fresh from a shower
who leans out a window combing her fox-colored hair
and the cloud shaped like Antarctica
inching across the sky
In your heart the chambers are filling with light
awaiting that elusive moment
when they might spill over and allow you to see
the world as you've always imagined it could be
silent and still and—just this once—whole

Prayer

I live in the USA, where we take
Our right to pray / not to pray
As fundamental, as unalienable.

My friend prays what he calls fake prayers
And wonders if these prayers are doomed
To fall on deaf ears because they are full

Of fake, prayers of one who *will* not be sincere.
My husband prays with the guileless faith
His mother and father and those well-meaning

Sisters and Brothers took away from him,
When he was a boy. He knows it is naïve,
But he doesn't care. He finds comfort there.

He finds he really can come to God
This way, and to the Virgin Mother, too.
My grandson prays, *Jesus keep me safe*

While I sleep. Amen. God is good, all the time.
All the time, God is good. And some nights
Adds: *And keep all those bad dreams away.*

Many pray to Allah, many times a day.
Others pray to Jesus, to Buddha,
To Quetzalcoatl, or to Yahweh.

There are those whose very lives seem to be
Prayers as they every day live them, and among
Those are those who don't believe in any god,

Who never pray, say, a formal prayer, who,
By god, decide that *will* will not make
The thing so. And among those some

Choose bitter angry lives. Others choose
The way of Lao Tzu: *From wonder into*
Wonder existence opens. My father, when

He was alive, used to lead the congregation,
Singing: *Praise God from whom all blessings*
Flow. Praise Him all creatures here below.

Praise Him above ye heavenly hosts. Praise
Father, Son, and Holy Ghost. Amen:
Which, when I was my daddy's girl,

Seemed a perfect sentiment to me. All
That holding up, all that praising
Seemed right, seemed sincere.

MICHAEL COLLIER

To a Horseshoe Crab

Strange arachnid, distant cousin
of deer ticks and potato bugs,
those armored pellets
that live between bark and wood,
stone and dirt.
Unlike them you wash up
hapless on beaches
more a bowl than a shoe.

You come in squads
after mating in the waters
of your birth, dragging the useless scabbard
of your tail.

Often you die
still attached, fucked
but not fucking, though once
I watched the loved one
drag her expired lover in a circle
before she died, too.

And sometimes
in your death throes
you capsize on the sand, which means
you turn up not down
and your legs row at nothing
so for a while you keep the flies away
but not the merciless fleas.

for José Emilio Pacheco

In the Darkness

In the darkness I can see every line
of your face. As if you are in my womb.
Your fingers feel for its entrance and I
am your mother, imagining what you
will look like when you are born. When I climb
after you into the freshly laundered
white duvet, and look at your face as you
sink into an involuntary slumber,
tender are my feelings for you, as though
you were my child. I ask if you want
me to turn out the light, which I do, and
so we nestle into each other, my
back to your front, and suddenly you are
a grown man, and I experience all
the pathos of the intervening years
and attempt to quench your searching mouth by
placing on it my own though I must trust
and contort my body to reach it and
you are back inside me now and you are
feeling with your fingers the ripeness of
my nipples which you cannot reach with your
mouth yet as your body ripples inside
me and the filaments of your face take
shape and glow in that invisible space
and dizzyingly fill the space with light.

You

At the moment when you stop mid-step
and look into my eyes, as if at a ship
on the horizon, blue sea and sun, and light
drains out of the sky and your face is lit
by its own sun in the far-off land we will sail
to in the boat whose mooring line you are unwinding
slowly with your hand, free of all
its many twists and knots, untwining
till, untethered and tacking in stays,
the boat will float free off fenders, but for now
your hands caress the rope, and rays
of light in the harbor point to you and the shadow
of the watcher disappears and floods
the waxing moon in red Mars light behind the soft, deep clouds.

Pan

Old man, why
shake a wrinkled prick
at the young girls?

They scream in harmony,
scramble off, and then
in mottled light, our eyes

meet: you, unbalanced
on the hoof
of an orthopedic shoe,

leaning on a stick,
gumming your sly grin
back into stubble

as with a palsy-
humbled hand you try
to zip your fly.

2

Later on, I hear them
along a lovers' lane—
five breastless girls
giggling as they spy

upon a couple
who've thrown down a coat
and lie pressed
together on the grass:

a sailor and a punked-
out cosmetologist
beneath the cosmos
of a lilac bush,

fragrant stars
confettied in their
hair, her mouth
a lipsticked *oh!*

nails to match
today's terror code
alert, pinioning
his pimpled ass,

and the girls you flashed,
a chorus now,
moaning in harmony
with every thrust.

3

Old man, your funky
gross-out that's exposed
the secret

decrepitude of lust
has only made them bolder,
disabused of mystery

if not of cheap romance;
another toppled god,
another fraud, another

sacred trust between
the supplicants and See
of Perverted Deity

broken, another parasite
feeding off the fever
of the delirious young.

4

Lithe city nymphs,
all laughter, leg, and shoulder,
they scatter,
elongating echoes

down an underpass
of willows
that shroud a pond
whose swan has fled,

a shore where shadow-
scuttled rowboats rot
before a boathouse said
to be haunted

by a girl who drowned
while anonymous heroes
looked on dumbly
as she sank

into the eternal
without the benefit
of the permanence
of marble.

5

Past raunchy pigeons
tidying the shuttered
popcorn stand,

and the goat-footed
balloon man
who has floated up to god-

knows-where, joined
there by the missing sword-
swallower, juggler, mime,

and organ grinder
with his monkey, cup,
and sign: SUPPORT

UNINTELLIGIBLE DESIGN,
past all the myths and
archetypes that fade

into the unofficial curfew
of another vicious
American night.

Only the homeless,
bedding down
in headlines of the new

preemptive strike,
are left to bow
as the last cloaked lord

who's not a joke
unleashes his dog
on their evening walk.

The Man at the End of My Name

My mother, given one name, exchanged it
for another—*Cohen* for *Carlan*, less "Jewish"—
and then for my father's, whose Edelman had lost its *E*
during the war for "business reasons."
What's in a name? A Rosenblum without the *blum*
would still a Rosen be. And what about me—
Girl who met Goy, and gave away
the last remaining part of her family? Like Adam
wearing the stunned look of an amputee,
the man at the end of my name is no longer there.
Bare bulb forcing her roots into water: it was Eve
who left the garden willingly. On the way out,
did he ask for his rib back, or just a few letters
with which to sign his plea?

GARY FINCKE

The Dead Girls

1

The girl who martyred her dolls, sending them
To heaven to wait for her arrival,
Sentenced them to stones or fire or the force
Of her hands to tear them, methods she'd learned
From the serious, dark nuns who taught her.

She would press a pillow over my face
To encourage sainthood. "Now," she would say,
Leaning down, and I'd let myself go limp
And lie quietly for her arrangements.

Her hands clasped like Mary's in the painting
Over her bed, she prayed for my body.
Sparingly, she sprinkled me with lotion.
Always, because she'd taught the proper way
To stare, my eyes were open when I died.

That summer, in the months before fourth grade,
Her uniforms waited in the closet
For September, her white communion dress
Beside them, declaring to St. Agnes,
Who watched from the sunlit, opposite wall.

In August, her mother ran a vacuum
Through the house, moving from the living room
Of St. Francis to the narrow hallway
Of Our Lady of Lourdes, and I stayed dead

Until the sound reached that girl's room, rising
To her mother's clenched roar of cleanliness,
Both of us keeping our feet off the floor,
Giving her a swipe of room to work, clearing
The way for temporary perfection.

2

The girl who loved to be touched in cemeteries,
Who said the dead reminded her to ecstasy,
Offered her body to my hands while I agreed,
Thanking the lost for their shadowed grove of headstones.

Always it was dark or nearly so, that girl shy
About her disrespect or nakedness, until,
At last, approaching cemeteries in weak light
Made me want to fuck above a thousand strangers.

One night, accidentally, the death of someone
Both of us knew, someone our age, meaning nineteen.
The violence of loss a lump underneath us
No matter which well-tended garden we entered.

Though frankly, we were exhausted by then, tired
Of each other's needs, and the dead could do nothing
Except talk among themselves about our absence,
Using the inaudible language of the earth.

3

The girl who died the following day
Is still talking in my car. She sits
Beside me, knees drawn up to her chin
Like a pouting child. Expectation
Is the only thing that will happen
Between us, the car's radio full
Of the British Invasion until
I follow her under the driveway's
Double floodlights to the house I will
Never be inside. "Next week," she says,
Before I drive past where she will die
In another boy's new car, the sight
So often seen I notice nothing
But oncoming headlights, the bright ones
Under the influence of midnight,
The day she will die just now begun,
The radio switched to Marvin Gaye

And James Brown, the road so familiar
I can be careless with attention
As I speed toward the unexpected,
What weekends are for, story makers.

CHRIS FORHAN

Love, or Something

The way, at last, a sloop goes sailorless and bobs at the dock,
    swathed in darkness,
the way waves swell and, swelling, slay themselves—
water, whatever you want, I want to want that.

A nickel's in the till, then it's not, it's in a pocket, forgotten,
and the pocket's in a laundry shoot. A puddle's in the parking
    lot, drying
to a ring of rust, asphalt buckling from something under it.

Conspiracy of earth and air in me, slip me your secret,
    I won't fret,
you want me stoneground, I want to want that. I want
the fire to find me ready. Let it be not scorn or pluck

I summon as I'm swallowed—I'm sick of pluck. Let it be love,
or something like it, assuming love is to the purpose, assuming
I'm not being maudlin, merely human, to bring love up.

JUDITH HALL

The Morning After the Afternoon of a Faun

If memory were easy, I wouldn't care for it:
Not the poorest truth, the hard-won winter
Darling, without a single trick of light or
Cloud light-burred and blurred for light green
Air to play on. Worse the flirty silliness:
The soft, lost summer lies. The hedonist
Inheritance: Pressed like a nymph to faun
On flesh ephemera: Green-gray flux: A phallus

Flares, frank and frankly spoiled. Demanding
Faun, who whines if I throw the scarf too slowly,
Whines a dank stink, abject when most dependent.
If I chose the dance and love the dream: So?
Why make the usual adieux, the scenes
Difficult among conventional apothecary weeds?

PATRICK HICKS

Not Springing Forward in Barcelona

In a time zone all our own,
we were a bubble of the past,
a cleanser upon the last sentence of history.
Lazing through tangled medieval lanes
we offered everyone a do-over, a mulligan,
and as time flowed backwards to greet us
we imagined the world transformed—

gashes were healed by knives,
seatbelts were remembered,
nets of salmon effervesced the ocean,
bombs rebuilt cities, swallowed firestorms.
M16's sucked bullets from the resurrected,
disease brought health, everyone got younger,
showers lifted poison from innocent lungs,
refugees returned home to their flats,
their huts, their wigwams, and
here, in the port of Barcelona,
galleons ballasted with gold
set a course for the Aztecs.
They returned with unused blankets.
In our little mythology,
history was not to be feared.
We listened to the metronome
of the Mediterranean, waved to Odysseus,
the clockwork of a spoon in coffee
held the timing of a galaxy.
Long before the moon cut a calendar
or the sun shadowed the rhythms of sleep,
we watched an apple fall up, into a tree—
two famous lovers strolled along,
their wrists as naked as ours.

Closely Held

Molly's father was a physicist, and not the garden-variety kind. He had been in one of Orion's college textbooks as the Eisenstat Principle of something or other. Matter? Motion? Orion didn't remember, although it was assumed he knew which. The Eisenstats assumed many things. "I take it the two of you are planning to get married," Carl Eisenstat told Orion once with scientific bluntness. Orion had started back, offended that Carl would touch on a matter so private and confusing, but Molly's father pressed on, implacably, "and I make that assumption because you've been seeing each other for so long."

Not counting their time at Harvard, Orion and Molly had been together for almost five years. After graduation in 1995, the college sweethearts had never left Cambridge, and whenever they saw their classmates and heard about their friends' adventures in South Africa and Russia and Wall Street, Orion and Molly felt both old and childish. They lived off Putnam Avenue in a third-floor warren with a ramshackle but surprisingly large roof deck. They kept a hibachi there, aluminum lawn chairs, and a camping table they'd found on the street. On summer nights, when people came up for drinks, they passed around a pair of tweezers for the splinters that split off the sun-warped railings.

They had talked about getting engaged, of course. Molly's plan was to get married when Orion finished grad school, and he had always liked this idea—keeping marriage at an indeterminate distance along with his dissertation. Then Orion took a leave from school to help start a little Internet security company called ISIS. VC money came flooding in, businesses stampeded to sign on for ISIS's cryptographic service LockBox, and the premium data protection package ChainLinx. Future earnings were shooting through the roof, and Orion's professional and financial prospects, once pleasantly vague, were now unavoidably bright. This was not lost on Molly's father. Nothing was. Carl and Deborah drove up from Princeton often, and made Orion squirm with their approval.

One chilly April afternoon, the Eisenstats took Orion and Molly to Sunday brunch at Henrietta's Table. Lanky, white-haired Carl forged the way at the buffet, loading his plate with lox and whitefish, eggs and sausages. Orion and Molly hurried to the carving board where a chef stood slicing slabs of meat, and Molly's mother, Deborah, brought up the rear, pausing wistfully at the waffle station, but settling on yogurt, fruit salad, and a tiny dish of Irish cut oatmeal. The resemblance between Deborah and Molly was striking: dark eyes, a heart-shaped face, lovely from the front, less so in profile. Molly had her mother's slight bump in the nose and tiny chin. They were both petite, but Deborah was also zaftig, a short, wide gerontologist who wore tunic-length sweaters and long necklaces, silk cords hung with unusual pendants: a woven bag or many-hinged locket, a miniature kaleidoscope bouncing like a buoy on her vast bosom.

"Well, this is nice," said Deborah when they reconvened at the table.

Molly and Orion, who had already started eating, nodded and kept at it.

"How's ISIS?" Deborah inquired warmly, as if Orion's company was a person.

"Fine," Orion said.

"More than fine," corrected Carl Eisenstat. "You've been getting a lot of press," he informed Orion, who ducked his head, something between a nod and a shrug. The four ISIS founders had just appeared in the March 2000 issue of *Fortune* magazine under the heading "Tycoons in Training."

"I hear you're talking about going public," said Carl.

"No, no, not yet," Orion demurred, although that was all anyone at ISIS did talk about. At the computers, at the vending machines, in the elevators, Orion heard the programmers discussing what they'd do after the company's IPO.

"I'd get a boat."

"Motorboat!"

"Speedboat!"

"Nah, boats suck! Get a Harley."

"Yeah!"

"A Ferrari!"

"Sweet!"

Some of the guys—they were almost all young men—were still un-
dergraduates, working at ISIS in between classes. When they talked
money, they sounded like teenagers boasting what they'd do to girls.

Now, at brunch, even Carl Eisenstat had a gleam in his eye. He
actually whipped out that morning's *Boston Globe* and began to
read: "*The closely held company does not*... wait... it's down here:
*Asked about his heroes, company co-founder Orion Klingenstein
cites computer pioneer Donald Knuth, and maverick Free Software
activist Richard Stallman*... Did you see this?" Carl asked.

How different Molly's father seemed from the man Orion had
first met, almost eight years before. The Eisenstats had driven up
to see their daughter, and she'd brought her new boyfriend to
breakfast. On that occasion, he and Molly had shared one side of
a booth like brother and sister facing their parents. Orion wore
jeans and a T-shirt, and his wet blond hair fell in his eyes. Molly
was dressed more formally in jeans and a button-down plaid
shirt; her short curls were damp, her eyes magnified by round
wire-rimmed glasses. He and Molly looked a little too clean to be
entirely innocent, having just come from Mather House, where
they'd shared a shower, but they sat straight with the seam of the
upholstered booth running up between them. Molly's mother
had tried to make conversation, but Professor Eisenstat kept his
eyes on Orion at all times. Under Carl's gaze, Orion had tried not
to eat so fast or gulp his juice, although he was famished and
thirsty. He had tried not to think of the night before, lest some
memory of warmth and dark nakedness flash across his face.
Concentrating on his omelet, he'd attempted to seem thoughtful
and interesting and utterly unlustful. Still, Carl gazed at him with
a grim, penetrating look, as Deborah chatted about where Orion
was from: Middlebury. Where he'd gone to high school: Putney.

"Are there astronomers in your family?" Deborah had asked.

"Nope," said Orion. "My mom just liked the name."

"Do you have siblings?"

"No." Orion tried a little humor. "Were you thinking they'd be
called Sagittarius?"

"I have a question for you," Carl broke in. His voice was taut
and slightly amused, as though he were sharpening cruel ironic
skewers and looking forward to running Orion through. "How is
it, majoring in an auxiliary field?"

Orion looked up in surprise. "Auxiliary? You mean computer science?" He had been so busy guarding against attacks on his character, that at first he didn't recognize Carl's scientific gambit as such.

"Right. Auxiliary in that computer science is not a true science in itself, but a handmaid to physics, math, biology..."

"Oh, don't be such a snob," Molly the premed scolded her father. "Just because we aren't all unlocking secrets of the universe..."

"I like CS," Orion said stoutly.

"But that's my question," Carl pressed. "What exactly do you like about it?"

Orion paused. "Programming," he said.

"Hmm." Carl sipped his coffee.

"I don't mind being a handmaid. I think I'd like to..." Orion's voice trailed off.

There he'd been, squirming, twenty years old and utterly ridiculous. He'd gazed across the table at Molly's father with a mixture of resentment and misery. How had Carl known that Orion had come to Harvard intending to study astronomy? Did it show that as a child Orion stayed out late stargazing with his birthday telescope?

Orion had once dreamed of peering into space to glimpse the oldest stars. He had imagined studying the origins of the universe, but he wasn't good enough at physics to pursue the idea properly. Where he excelled was in building little computer systems piece by piece. Orion loved to tinker. He was a puzzle solver, no deep-thinking puzzle maker. He did well in his CS courses: programming, distributed systems, hardware, algorithms, graphics, where he rendered a faceted crystal vase filled with water and a single red rose which cast an accurate shadow on a wood-grain tabletop. Were these exercises at all important? In Carl's presence he'd felt acutely that computer science lacked a certain—he would never say the word aloud—but yes, the field lacked a certain majesty.

These days, Molly's famous father seemed thrilled with Orion's programming habit. When he spoke of ISIS, Carl sounded eager, almost boyish. He found the whole business absolutely delightful, and looked upon his daughter's future fiancé with such benevolent pride that Orion almost missed the Carl of old, the fire-breathing academician. What a strange effect money, or even the idea of money, had on people.

Orion hadn't set out to be wealthy; he hadn't begun his research project on Internet security to make serious money, although he had ended it that way—incorporating with Jonathan, Aldwin, and Jake. Truly, his goal a year ago was to put together some code for fun, and make a pile of money along the way—but only money in the lighthearted sense, not funds involving lawyers and trusts and lockups and talk of writing wills. There was a big difference between money and being rich. Money meant freedom—endless quarters for the laundromat and no worries about rent or going out to dinner or the movies. Money was spontaneous: flying last minute to Paris, buying all the comic books and games you wanted, laying down cash at Pandemonium for the latest Neal Stephenson in hardback. Being rich, however, was all about paperwork and contingencies. Money was pleasure. Richness was just sick. He hadn't realized before ISIS that the two went together; sometimes he forgot. At other times—at the table now—he quailed at the way one followed the other. Money was a joy ride, and afterward you got rich all over.

He was going to be wealthy. He couldn't avoid it. No more long vague years of graduate school. No obstacles to marrying. How could he put off shopping for a ring? In a year, he could afford any ring or bracelet or necklace; he could afford anything. Orion looked at Carl's smooth close-shaven cheeks and his hawkish gray eyes, and he saw what wealth would mean: not just traveling the world and buying toys, but paying huge complicated taxes and living in a house with Molly forever—not forever in the romantic sense—forever like her parents, with a loud dog and yellowing houseplants. Molly would gain a hundred pounds, and Orion would have to start collecting humongous ugly paintings. They'd have a three-car garage and seven bathrooms, and they would sit around at night and debate whether it was better to timeshare or buy planes.

"How many employees are you up to now?" Carl asked.

"I think we're at..." Orion hesitated, distracted by the cellphone in his pocket, buzzing against his leg. "Eighty-three?" he ventured, checking the caller ID. "Ninety-three?" It was Jonathan, but Orion ignored the call. He and Jonathan were close friends, and ISIS co-founders and all that, but lately they hadn't been getting along. "Maybe a hundred in Cambridge," said Orion.

Deborah focused on Orion with a look of quiet pride. Carl

leaned forward, keen and curious. Only their daughter paid no attention. Orion realized with annoyance that Molly, who was now an intern and post-call, had closed her eyes and left him to entertain her parents' expectations on his own. She was still sitting upright in her chair, but she had fallen fast asleep.

All the way home in the back of the Eisenstats' car, Orion had to talk to Carl and Deborah. Their daughter's eyes fluttered, but Orion had to answer. Molly had been working at the hospital, saving lives for so long, that she just could not stay awake. He tried to remember their last real conversation. He thought it was about getting a cat. Or maybe not. Maybe it was last summer before her internship began. The power was out on their street, and they'd walked to Toscanini's for ice cream and air conditioning. They'd been discussing the khulfee flavor—a mixture of pistachio and cardamom. "No, I'm not getting that," Orion told Molly as they stood in line.

"Oh, come on. Just a taste! You never try anything new," she'd accused him. "You hate new things."

"Not true," he protested.

"You won't move," she pointed out. "You won't take Dad's Volvo. You don't want to—"

"We don't need to move," he reasoned. "We don't need a car."

"Try it. You'll like it," she teased him, whispering in his ear.

He looked at Molly now, slumped over in the car, and he hated her for being away all the time. She was always gone—even now, when she sat at his side.

"So you'll be coming down for Memorial Day weekend?" Deborah asked from the front seat.

"I don't know," Orion muttered.

"You don't have plans already!" Deborah exclaimed.

"Molly's brother will be home," Carl said in a voice that decided the matter.

"We can't make plans till we know Molly's call schedule," Orion countered, undeciding the matter as best he could.

"Molly—what's your schedule in May?" Deborah asked, looking searchingly at her daughter slumped in the back seat.

"I'm sure she could get someone to cover for her," Carl said.

Orion stared out the window at the budding trees and Victorian houses of Cambridgeport. He gazed at his neighbors' cars rusting quietly in their driveways, and the flaming tulips opening in side gardens.

"Well, she could get someone if she arranged it early," Deborah speculated.

"What?" Molly roused herself.

"I said if you arranged it with someone early you could get a friend to cover you for..."

"Your brother will be home," Carl reiterated.

Orion wished briefly for the rented car to hit a pothole and flip over. He wished for an accident. Nothing serious—just enough to shake everybody upside down.

Orion helped Molly up the stairs and unlocked the door of their apartment. She dropped her bag just inside the door and bolted for the bedroom. "Wait," he said. "Molly?"

Gone again. Fully clothed, she lunged for the bed, seized her pillow, and smiling blissfully she closed her eyes.

"Aren't you going to take off your shoes?" Orion tugged at one shoe and then the other. Her legs were dead weights in his hands. He reached around her waist, unbuckled her belt, and unzipped her pants. "Ouch," he murmured. Her belt had cut into her soft stomach and left red marks. He tried to turn her over all the way to unbutton her blouse, but she clung to her pillow, and he couldn't get it off. "I give up," he said. He waited a moment to see if she would answer.

There was a reason he and Molly avoided inviting her parents up to the apartment. The floor was covered with dirty clothes, the table strewn with bills and mail, bank statements from Fleet. Orion didn't bother looking at them. Despite his huge equity in ISIS, he had, of course, no money to speak of in his account. The kitchen counters were stacked with dishes, the television coated with dust. The answering machine was blinking, as usual. He opened his notebook computer, scanned his seven hundred new emails—two from Jonathan, subject: URGENT, message: "get your butt over here NOW." He snapped the computer shut again. He thought briefly about taking some laundry downstairs. Then he stuffed his computer into his backpack and put on his fisherman sweater, stretched out and worn to threads at the elbows. He strode into the bedroom. "Okay, Molly, I'm going," he said. He bent down over her curly head. "Bye."

She stirred and turned. Her face was tender with sleep. She reached out and wrapped her arms around him. She drew him close, and she was warm, her skin smoother than the silky blouse she was wrinkling. Her eyes opened. Her lips parted, and he was about to kiss her, when suddenly she spoke. "Get milk," she said.

At the bottom of the stairwell, he couldn't find the bicycle pump. He'd had a slow leak for a while, and now his front tire was too mushy to get far. He thought about walking his bike to Broadway Bicycle School. Then, remembering that they were closed Sunday, he shouldered his backpack and set out on foot for ISIS. It was almost four in the afternoon by the time he made it to the offices in Kendall Square.

"Where the hell have you been?" demanded Jonathan as soon as he got off the elevator. It was uncanny, as if Jonathan had been there standing all the time, waiting for the elevator doors to open.

"Having brunch," Orion said.

"Brunch?" Jonathan echoed in disbelief, as if he'd never heard the word before.

They were walking through what had recently been a great open space, the top-floor wilderness of the company. At one time Jonathan and Orion had played a form of indoor badminton here, but new cubicles were now installed, and programmers packed in together. There were private offices as well for Dave, the company CEO, Aldwin, the CFO, and Jonathan, the CTO. Jake was the chief programmer, or something like that. CPO? No, that wasn't right. Only Orion wasn't chief of anything. That had been his choice. They'd offered him some sort of vice presidency, but at the time, the whole thing had sounded too ridiculous, like one of those old movies about tiny pretend countries, as if ISIS were Ruritania or he was going to be Communications Minister of the Duchy of Grand Fenwick. Of course, Orion had been wrong about this. The titles meant membership on the executive board. The CFO and CTO were, in fact, piloting the company, and ISIS was a cash-rich powerhouse, no fictional grand duchy. But Orion told himself he'd stick to writing code. He knew far more about the inner workings of the ISIS system than Dave ever would with all his business experience and his "Statement of Values"—his credos posted everywhere like something out of Orwell's Ministry of Love: "We are a community. We value excellence. We honor truthfulness. We believe in the capacity of each individual to make a difference."

"We need to talk to you. Now," said Jonathan.

"Why?" asked Orion as he picked his way through the maze of cubicles.

"Get in the conference room." Jonathan had the broad shoulders, thick neck, and small blue eyes of a former wrestler. He came from Nebraska, and he and his sisters had gone to a one-room school where they were half the students. As a teenager he'd spent summers working on ranches and reading Ayn Rand. His ambitions had been to become president, go to Harvard, play professional football, and make a gazillion dollars—not necessarily in that order. While he hadn't gotten into Harvard, and had stopped playing football after high school, he hadn't yet ruled out the presidency. The gazillion dollars went without saying.

Jonathan had been a lot of fun in grad school. His first days in Cambridge he ran around with a camera photographing everything in sight. "What are you doing?" Orion had asked him. "Taking pictures of the ivy," Jonathan explained. When they'd entered the university's business competition with their plan for ISIS, Jonathan and Orion had taken the T downtown and bought suits for their presentation. Horrible navy suits from Filene's Basement—too short in the arms for Orion, too narrow in the chest for Jonathan. They chose ties as well, the loudest ones they could find. Orion picked swirly purple, and Jonathan bought a nasty green one with a scaly design like iguana skin. Now that he was CTO, however, and working around the clock at ISIS, Jonathan's sense of humor was sadly diminished. He reminded Orion of Molly when she came home post-call with a headache and looked at the apartment and screamed that Orion never took care of the simplest things.

Jonathan marched into the conference room, and Orion took his time following. He glanced at the programmers, leaned in, and scanned their screens. He saw Clarence typing away, and Umesh, and Nadav, but the one he looked for was the new girl who'd just started on the LockBox team. He was always conscious of her, working among the guys. Her name was Sorel, like the plant. She was waiflike and English, a master's student of some kind. Her skin was fair, her blond hair straight and fine. She wore odd black clothes and had the palest eyes he'd ever seen; he wasn't sure of the color—they were like water. She had a wonderful accent. Sometimes he talked to her, just to get her to say things like "corollary," which she pronounced with the stress in the middle, a little bump and then a rush of speed at the end, "corollery," like a model train chugging up and then shooting around a tiny mountain. She glanced at him quizzically as he passed by.

"I'm going to the principal's office," he told her.

"Oh," Sorel said, suppressing laughter as she turned back to her computer. "I won't be seen talking to you, then."

He knew everyone would see him and Jonathan, however. The conference room cut right into the open plan programmers' space, and the walls were glass, another of Dave's brilliant ideas.

Jonathan and Aldwin perched atop the oval table with the *Globe* strewn before them.

"I've been getting emails all morning from investors," Jonathan accused him.

"About what?" asked Orion.

"About what? About this!" Jonathan shook the newspaper at Orion.

"You cite Richard Stallman as your hero," Aldwin said.

"Well, what's wrong with that? I happen to admire Stallman's ideas about information sharing."

Aldwin folded his hands paternally on his knee. With his baby face and mild manners, his well-groomed curly hair, clean clothes, and matching socks, he seemed, literally, best suited of the founding four for corporate life. He was Dave's favorite. Everyone knew that. Of course the very idea of Dave picking one of the founders as his favorite was strange to say the least. After all, the four of them had hired Dave. At the time, Jonathan had privately conceded Orion's contention that Dave wasn't particularly bright. They'd picked their CEO from the lineup for looks and experience, since he was old, and the established companies had heard of him. "You do see that we are in business?" Aldwin asked Orion now.

"ISIS is not the local branch of the Free Software Foundation," Jonathan snapped.

"You do see that our investors are hoping to make money here?" Aldwin continued.

"Free Software is free as in freedom," Orion insisted. "Not free as in free lunches. I never said I didn't want to make money."

"What the hell is wrong with you?" Jonathan exploded. "We are selling a proprietary security system. You are going to reporters, scaring our investors, talking about giving stuff away."

"I never said anything about giving stuff away. I mentioned Richard Stallman's *name*."

"He's a crazy anarchist."

"Not true," said Orion. "He happens to be a visionary—and I personally find his questions very interesting. Like, when you think about it, the whole notion of intellectual property is an oxymoron. How can you own something intangible? It's like, you can't own souls, can you?"

"Are you trying to make me angry?" Jonathan asked.

"Maybe you should take your name off our patents," Aldwin suggested.

"I said I admired him. I never said I wanted to be him. Jesus."

"We are in the process of filing for our IPO," Aldwin said. "This is a particularly sensitive time."

"We have one shot," said Jonathan.

"Why?" asked Orion. "Why do we have one shot? LockBox has issues. ChainLinx is still buggy—you're selling this stuff before its time."

"No, you don't understand," Aldwin said. "This is the time. This is our window of opportunity."

"Have you studied the marketplace?" Jonathan demanded.

"I've studied our code. I don't give a shit about the marketplace."

"And this is exactly the kind of statement I'm talking about," Jonathan broke in. "Do not talk to reporters again." Jonathan pointed his index finger directly at Orion's chest, but Orion didn't flinch. He had been an athlete, too, although his sport was skiing and involved no contact—only swift descents. "Do not talk to anyone," Jonathan said. "When you get phone calls, refer them to Amanda. That's her job."

"I think you're overreacting," Orion said.

Jonathan glared at him. "We're trying to build something here. We have created an entity here from nothing. You, on the other hand, spend your time whining, or shooting off your mouth, or breaking stuff—"

"Exposing problems," Orion countered.

"Aldwin and I have been in Mountain View all week," Jonathan said. "Jake is still in Singapore. We are taking care of customers and signing partners. The three of us have not been home. We have not had brunch. And we do not want to come in here and find that you—with your five million shares—have been bullshitting reporters again about free software."

Orion turned away slightly from the CTO and CFO, once his buddies, his closest friends. He gazed through the glass wall at the programmers in their cubicles. Several guys were crowded around Sorel's desk. Had she got the new high score in Quake III? She was keeping her head down, her thin shoulders hunched. "I happen to have ideas," Orion murmured. "I have my own opinions."

"Your ideas are—occasionally—great," Jonathan told him. "Your opinions suck."

"So let's review," said Aldwin. "I'm a reporter. Hello. Orion Klingenstein? I'd like to speak to you about the Free Software Movement."

They were turning on Sorel. Orion could see the guys spinning her swivel chair around, forcing her to look at them.

"Now," said Aldwin. "You say…"

"Go to hell," Orion snapped, and left the conference room.

Aldwin's voice floated after him. "And actually, that answer would be preferable to…"

"What's going on?" Orion asked Clarence. There were three of them standing over Sorel.

"She crashed the system," Clarence said.

"Really?" Orion asked Sorel.

"I did not," she countered reflexively.

"You're lying," Clarence told her.

"She checked in code that crashed the system," Umesh said.

"And so," said Nadav, "she gets the rubber chicken." Menacingly, he swung the rubber chicken in Sorel's face. It was the sort of plucked rubber chicken you got in joke shops. Its limp body was yellow and gelatinous, its neck long and scrawny.

"No," Sorel said, attempting irony, and sounding pathetic, "anything but that."

But the programmers had their rituals. "You crash the system," said Clarence, "you get the chicken."

Nadav pitched the rubber bird directly into Sorel's lap.

"Give it back to him," Orion told Sorel.

She picked up the bird and held it out to Clarence.

"She crashed the system," Clarence insisted.

"You said that already," said Orion. "Now put the chicken nicely on her desk."

Clarence glared at Orion. Orion acted like one of the guys, and now, suddenly, he pulled rank on them. Sullenly, Clarence threw the chicken down on Sorel's desk.

"Get back to work," Orion said.

"System's down," Clarence reminded him.

"We are a community," said Orion, quoting Dave's "Statement of Values."

"She's got to get the bug out," Umesh said.

And Nadav quoted Dave snarkily, "We value the contribution of each individual."

The little crowd dispersed, and Orion pulled up a chair next to Sorel. Her face was white, her hands tiny on the keyboard as she scrolled through code on the screen. She wouldn't look at him. She just stared straight in front of her.

"It's okay," he whispered.

"Go away, please," she said.

"I break stuff all the time," he told her.

"Yeah, I'm sure you...don't," she retorted.

"In college—in the summers—when I was at Microsoft," he said, "you got Tootsie Pops when you screwed up."

She kept her eyes on the screen. Then, after a moment, she asked, "Why?"

"Because you were a sucker."

"At least you could eat them," she said.

"Let's fix your code."

"I thought you only did new projects, and, sort of, meta-programming. Aren't you terribly busy?"

He thought of Jonathan and Aldwin and Jake flying around; he thought of Molly working her thirty-hour shifts. "Yeah, I guess I'm supposed to be busy," he said, "but I'm really not. Move over." She edged her swivel chair to one side so he could squeeze his in.

Slowly, they checked the LockBox system. They combed the program line by line. First they used her machine, and then he took the workstation next to hers, and they worked in parallel on separate computers. As they searched, they turned up little items and oddities they hadn't expected, missing comments, obscure bugs, strange bits of circuitous reasoning, the dust bunnies in the code. Hours passed. They didn't speak, but mumbled to themselves. "What happens when this line executes?"

"And what happens here?"

"What's the value of the variable now?"

"Now stop and try to run..."

They kept working until numbers seemed to imprint themselves on Orion's eyes, so that whenever he turned from the computer screen he saw those digits everywhere. The chambers of the program drew Orion and Sorel deeper and deeper into the software's formal logic. They counted their steps as they descended into dark passageways. The voices all around them grew muffled, the ambient light on the floor began to dim. Orion's phone rang, but he didn't even glance at it.

Night came. Programmers went home, and others took their place. Jonathan and Aldwin were long gone. Still, Orion and Sorel kept hunting underground, watching for errors, listening for rushing water, tapping walls.

"Why are you smiling?" Sorel asked at one point.

"I'm just concentrating," he murmured, half to himself. Then he confessed, "Actually I love doing small repetitive things."

"I don't," she admitted.

"You can go," he said. "I'll finish."

"I don't want to go," she said. "I just need a bit of fresh air."

"Okay," he told her, and kept on working. She pulled on a black coat much too big for her. She was heading for the elevators when he realized she would be going down alone into the dark.

"Wait," he called, and she held open the door. "I'll come down with you."

"No, don't come."

He slipped inside, anyway. The doors closed, and the elevator carried them down to the lobby of the building.

"I just wanted to smoke," she confessed, as she pushed the glass doors of the lobby open and stepped outside. She took a pack of cigarettes from her pocket. "You don't mind, do you?"

"No," he said, even though he hated smokers.

"Sorry." She fussed with her lighter. "It's a habit from when I was younger. I grew up sort of running away from a very—religious family."

"In England?"

"In Goulder's Green. Why are you laughing?"

He stopped and then confessed, "It's just the name Goulder's Green together with your name, Sorel, like the plant."

She shot him a look, earnest and slightly disgruntled. "It's not Sorel like the plant, it's Sorel like the Yiddish version of Sarah. My father is a rabbi, and he's terribly religious. Both my parents are. I went to a girls' yeshiva where we didn't learn anything. I wasn't supposed to go to college."

"What were you supposed to do?" He stepped back as she exhaled. It was all he could do not to fan the smoke away with his hand.

"What kind of question is that? I was supposed to get married. I'm already twenty-four, and I'm an old maid! I'm not supposed to be in America or working, or anything like that. I was a bad girl when I was younger. I snuck out after school and got a job at a pharmacy. I was earning extra money my parents didn't know about. I had a secret life, and I didn't even believe in God, but I won all the prizes for praying at school."

"How could they have prizes for praying?" Orion asked.

"You had to pray with the most spirit, and they gave you a prize. Whenever we had silent prayers I mumbled each word under my breath so it looked like I was praying extra hard, and then I got awards. I lied a lot," she added matter-of-factly.

"You're very strange," Orion said.

"I'm very hungry," she countered. "I think we've missed dinner."

They took the elevator back up and raided the company kitchen. "What do we have here? Chips. Salt and vinegar. Barbeque." He tossed her two bags. "Granola bars. Jelly Bellies. These are good."

"I wish there were more black ones," she said, picking through her bag of jellybeans.

"Oh, black cherry soda," he told her, taking four cans from the fridge. "This is good stuff. Let's go."

"You actually like working all night," she said as they settled back in front of her workstation.

"I'm good at it," Orion told her. He was showing off a little, but he was also telling the truth. He was good at staying up until a job was done. He was no scientist or businessman, but he had an eye for detail, an understanding of the small picture, the obsessive game-playing mind of a superb hacker. "I can finish," he said. "You don't need to stay."

"Yes I do," she said. "I got the chicken."

"Doesn't matter."

"No, I'm not going. It wouldn't be right."

They shared her computer now, and the monitor glowed before them. They sipped their drinks and traded jellybeans, and slowly found their way back inside the code. They read the lines aloud, mumbling statements to themselves. They made their way without a map; the program was their map, spreading in rivulets before them, diagramming underground rivers and branching tributaries. Their hands hovered over the keyboard and overlapped; his hand covered hers as they divined for the source of her mistake. And then she found it. Sorel found the bug. "Stupid, stupid," she groaned. "Over there. I forgot the array bounds check."

"Aha!" cried Orion. She'd neglected to specify enough computer memory for the number of items in her piece of the Lockbox system.

"It's not even an interesting mistake," she griped as she typed in proper array bounds. "Wait. Why isn't it working now?"

"Be patient," he said. "Let me."

By the time he had the system up and running again, Sorel was resting her head on the laminate desktop.

"Got it," Orion said, basking for a moment in accomplishment. "We got it back up," he announced to the nearly empty room.

"Cool," somebody said politely from across the way.

"Look," Orion called to Sorel as he danced toward the windows. "Sunrise."

"Lovely," she said, without moving.

"Come on." He dragged her over to the windows and made her look at the rosy rooftops of East Cambridge. "I love a sunrise," he said, "as long as I don't have to wake up for it." He felt joyous, masterful after the all-nighter. "I knew I'd get to the bottom of this."

"I was the one who found the bug," she reminded him.

They drifted back to her desk. He took the rubber chicken off and held it for a moment. Then he said, "Let's go up to the roof and throw this."

"You can't go up there," she said. "It's locked."

Still, he ran upstairs, and gamely she followed him. Orion pushed hard, and the door should have opened. That would have been dramatic, poetic justice to take the rubber chicken and throw it off, but as Sorel predicted, the door was locked, and so they trudged back down again to her cubicle.

He contemplated the chicken as he swung and spun it from its rubber neck. Then he knew what to do. "Let's go down to the river and drown it."

She laughed at that and hunted under her desk and pulled out the black heap that was her coat. Sleepily, she turned the coat here and there, trying to figure out which end was up. A couple of quarters and her pack of cigarettes fell out of the pockets.

"Here," he said, and held the coat for her the right way. He stuck the cigarettes far back on her desk behind the computer monitor. She didn't notice.

"Don't you have a jacket?" she asked.

"It's not bad out," he insisted. He felt warm and talkative as they took the elevator down and began walking between the half-built laboratories and biotech offices of Kendall Square. "Did you see all that ugly code?" he asked her. "Disgusting, wasn't it? Sloppy. We need standards. Somebody should be doing what we did every night. I'm going to—"

"Are you always quite so cheerful?" Squinting into the sun, Sorel shaded her eyes as she looked up at him.

"I like working," he said.

"I suppose soon you won't have to," she said.

He frowned. "We'll see."

"Don't you want to be rich?" she asked. "I would."

"I think I'd like to buy my dad a house," he told her. "He probably wouldn't stay in it, but I'd buy him one just to have."

"Why wouldn't he stay in it?"

"He's a little bit... He's an emeritus professor," he said. "He's old, and he sort of sleeps in his office a lot of the time."

"What did he teach?" Sorel asked.

"Poetry," he said. "He's a pretty well-known poet among some people. My mother was his student. He wrote a whole book of poems about her."

"How lovely."

"And about their divorce."

"Hmm. Did he write any for you?"

"I guess so. Yeah."

"Do you know any?" she asked in a very proper voice.

"No, of course not." He was embarrassed by the question, although he couldn't have explained why. "Sometimes he falls asleep on park benches on campus," Orion confided. "It's no big deal. The guards all know him. The only thing is, since he doesn't dress that well, sometimes he looks kind of—homeless. Once he fell asleep on a bench, and when he woke up, he found two dollars in his hat."

"Oh no!" She laughed, and as she looked at him, sidelong, the light caught in her eyes.

"Wait, stop a minute," Orion said. They stopped walking, and right there on the sidewalk, he looked into her eyes. "Green."

"Yes, thanks, I knew that." She shook her head a little, and hurried on. Her pale skin was pink in the fresh air, her hair spilled over the top of her coat. Her hand was so small, he scarcely noticed taking it in his.

The river was still and misty. Park benches were spaced evenly on the muddy bank, facing the water. Sorel took the rubber chicken from her coat pocket and then fumbled some more. Orion sat on a bench and watched her search for her cigarettes.

"Don't you want to throw it?" he asked her.

"I suppose." She was a little distracted, irritated she hadn't found what she was looking for. They walked right up to the edge of the riverbank, and she balanced on a wobbly rock. "You throw it," she said.

"No, you can do the honors," he told her.

She lifted the rubber chicken like a football and then stopped. "It's not littering, is it?"

"Oh, it probably is, but so what?" Orion asked.

"I just don't want to get arrested," she explained, "because I'm on a student visa."

"Throw the damn chicken!" he burst out. "I'll search." He

looked up and down. "Okay, I see geese. I see a guy in a sleeping bag. I see the bridge. No cops. Now throw."

She hurled the rubber chicken into the air with all her strength. It sailed briefly above the water and then splashed down and floated sickly yellow on the surface.

"It looks terrible," she said. "It's not biodegradable. That was a dreadful idea."

"You worry too much," he said. They were standing a little closer than absolutely necessary, but it was cold.

"Don't you worry?" she asked him.

"No," he said. "Not now," he added, more truthfully. The water glowed, and the night chill was burning off; the whole riverbank was damp and greening.

"Why not now?" she pressed. She was wondering about him, waiting for him to explain exactly what he meant standing there with her.

He looked into her questioning eyes. For a moment he saw the possibilities in front of him, each spreading outward, the branches of a decision tree. He could keep quiet. Or he could turn the question back on her. "What do you mean?" He could lie to her. He could say something, anything. He could make some excuse to leave. He could kiss her. He imagined kissing her, breaking the stillness, flustering her like that.

He pushed the hair off her face, bent down, and told her his secret instead. "I don't want to grow up," he whispered in her ear.

She laughed. "Are you already having your midlife crisis?" she asked. "Since you're about to be so rich? It's not very original."

"I don't want to be rich," he retorted.

"Poor you!" she said. "When the time comes, you'll just have to find the strength."

"You think it's funny?" he demanded.

"Yes, of course."

He pulled her toward him so she almost lost her balance there at the water's edge.

"Stop!" she cried out. "I won't tease you anymore, promise. Even if you do deserve it."

Laughing, he wrapped his arm around her shoulders, and she leaned against him. Her cheek brushed his sweater. He'd helped her fix her code; together they'd vanquished all the other programmers, and she was grateful. He felt a wave of sleepiness, or possibly just contentment, holding her. She was so small, and he felt chivalrous. He knew she'd found the bug herself. Still, he loved the idea of protecting someone. Maybe there was a hacker's form of chivalry, no order of temperance or holiness—just good solid code.

"Do you like geese?" he asked her as they watched the black geese waddle down the riverbank.

"No," she said. "They're nasty. They're like big pigeons."

"Do you like ISIS?" He spoke quietly, almost dreamily, thinking aloud.

"I can't tell you that," she said. "You'd have to fire me."

"Nah, I don't fire anybody," he said. "There's a whole department for that."

"Do you like ISIS?" she asked him.

"Not as much as I ..."

"Just because you were fighting with Jonathan?"

He didn't answer.

"I saw you through the window," she said.

"I liked the company in theory," he confessed, "but not in practice."

"You can afford not to," she pointed out. "I have to worry about funding."

"Are you trying to get a research fellowship?"

"I'm applying to Ph.D. programs in physics," she said.

"Oh, physics. Molly's father would like you, then," he mused.

"Who's Molly's father?"

"Carl Eisenstat," he said.

She gasped and stepped back, breaking his embrace. "You know Carl Eisenstat?" she asked reverentially.

And there was Molly's father again with Orion in his clutches. There was Carl, back on the scene, sometimes disdainful, sometimes delighted, always examining Orion with his quick hawk's eye.

"The Eisenstat Principle of Viscosity," said Sorel.

"Oh, that's what it's a principle of," Orion said.

"You didn't know that?" she asked him. And then, "Who's Molly?"

"My girlfriend," he said, darting a look at her. He hesitated.

Subtly, almost imperceptibly, the space between them had grown. "I probably should have mentioned her earlier."

"But she didn't come up," Sorel said.

"No."

She smiled and thrust her hands into her pockets. "Right. I should get breakfast."

"I'll come with you," he told her.

"No, don't come," she said. "I'm in a rush. I have to be somewhere this morning. I have an appointment at the dentist's at nine o'clock."

"That's in three hours," he pointed out.

"But I should get home first," she said, and added formally, "Thanks for all your help. Goodbye, good morning, and all that."

"Don't smoke," he told her.

"Why are you telling me not to smoke?" she asked. Her voice was more puzzled than angry. "You hardly know me."

"It's not good for you," he said idiotically.

"You'll have to explain about the rubber chicken," she said as she climbed up the riverbank.

"Just say it came to a bad end," Orion told her.

"It was your idea to drown it." She turned back toward him with her funny reproachful look. "Really, you should be the one to tell them."

"Okay," he called after her as she hurried away, "I'll send mail I donated the LockBox chicken to the Free Software Foundation. Everyone will understand."

When she was gone, Orion stood at the water's edge and gazed out to where Sorel had thrown the rubber chicken. He imagined the bird falling through the water, drifting until it lodged in slimy plants where fish nosed its orange feet. He wished he could swim underwater with Sorel; he wished he could disappear with her again, if only to learn the bird's fate.

On the surface, a lone rower dimpled the river with his oars. Motorboat! Speedboat! Sweet! the programmers chorused in his mind.

The full sun warmed his shoulders as he trudged up to the street. His stomach rumbled, and cars zipped by as he waited to cross Memorial Drive. He walked to Central Square and ducked into the Store 24 near the bus stop. He bought coffee there and two doughnuts, and a huge tuna sub in plastic wrap. The only other person in the store was the cashier, a young Muslim woman who wore a headscarf. The scarf was pinned to her hair with bobby pins decorated with tiny rhinestone diamonds, and she was talking on the phone. She paused for a moment and turned to Orion. "Anything else?"

"No thanks," Orion said. Even as he spoke, Orion glanced around the store at the bags of chips and pretzels, the candy bars. He saw the dairy section behind glass, the shelves of butter and yogurt and American cheese, but he forgot the one thing Molly wanted.

XIAOLU GUO

Winter Worm, Summer Weed

translated by Rebecca Morris and Pamela Casey

A young Tibetan sits in the sand by Zha Ling Lake. He is skinny and about eighteen. The throbbing sun scorches his thick dark hair. The lake is silent before him, a steely blue. The Kunlun Mountains reach up beyond the lake, iced snow coating the tops, peak after high peak.

The boy is from Maduo County in Qing Hai province. His name is Guo Luo. Every summer Guo Luo climbs the mountains to harvest the famous herb known as Winter Worm Summer Weed. He is a professional Winter Worm Summer Weed gatherer. Well-known for its nourishing, beneficial properties, the herb actually comes from an insect. In winter, it is a caterpillar, a Winter Worm. Come summer, the caterpillar dies and is absorbed by the ground. There it looks like a strange weed, a worm-like herb. The Winter Worm Summer Weed is ground up and used in medicinal soups and tonics. Even those who avoid traditional Chinese medicines will have it in their Sichuan hot pot or boiling in a spicy chili soup. Its exact merits are unclear, but it is thought to improve the flow of one's chi, the balance between yin and yang, between the cold and the fire in the body.

At the end of the summers, snow comes quickly to the mountains and Guo Luo can no longer gather the herb. Instead he travels the county's vast sand fields and catches rats. People eat rats in Maduo County. Guo Luo can make the money he needs to live by selling a summer's worth of herbs and a winter's worth of rats.

Other young men like Guo Luo, weathered and thinned by the sun, squat by the edge of the lake. The men's fingers gently fondle the herbs they've collected. They watch old fishermen hauling their catch on the decks of the boats. At the edges of the lake are notices on wooden boards. Big red characters warn: "Lake is government property. Fishing is illegal."

But the fishermen pretend they can't read. And maybe they can't, who knows? There is always someone fishing, even in broad daylight. They don't hide it. Every day there are men on the lake, concentrating on their fishing. It is illegal, but the local officials don't bother them. If you live on the mountain, you eat from the mountain. If you live by the water, you eat from the water. How else can one live?

The people living in Maduo County were originally nomads. When they first came to this place, the lands by the mountains and the lake were vast grasslands. Their herds grazed so much that now, there is no grass, only sand. The land has become a desert, a rat-infested desert. Rodent holes appear every three steps, and whole colonies every five. The rats burrow underground and feed on the remaining roots of grass. The locals complain about the rats. "The rats have destroyed the plateaus." Guo Luo and the other herb gatherers kill the rats. It can even be fun. Guo Luo doesn't have a professional weapon, he'll use any stick to kill the rats. Locals use rat skin to make bags and cases. In restaurants, chefs have four ways of cooking rat: braised in soy sauce, deep-fried, steamed, or stir-fried in a smoking wok with red chilies and spicy salts. A mouthful of rat can be as tender as the best beef fillet.

Tibetan is Guo Luo's native tongue. He has learned Mandarin and even picked up some English from tourists who travel to the lake, famous for its beautiful mountain landscape. His features are delicate, his face almost feminine despite his sunburnt skin. His eyes are bright. He moves like a little prince of the mountains. When he climbs the mountains with the others, it is always Guo Luo who returns with the most herbs. It is as though the weeds offer themselves up to him. His reputation means that when Guo Luo descends the mountain, buyers will be waiting on the sand by the lake to ask his prices. They buy the herbs in bundles and hurry back to Xi Ning, the nearest big city. There these men sell the herbs at a profit to pharmaceutical companies.

In his hands are three bunches of herbs. Guo Luo's eyes are on the faraway mountaintops, covered with the eternal solid snow. He feels as though it has never melted in the eighteen years of his life. He can picture the snow line where the white winter lotus used to grow. The white plant was hard to see against the snow. He used to ride his horse up the mountain to pick it and then sell the flowers to the government pharmacy in the town. Now the lotus has almost disappeared, picked to extinction. No point riding up to the snow line now.

He stands still, empty and drifting in the afternoon. Every afternoon is like this—the same clouds, same lake, same mountains. He pulls his eyes back from the mountain to the road below. He can make out rows of white hats, a green flag flapping at the lead. A tour group is coming.

At the head of the group is the female tour guide from Maduo Tourism Bureau. She is already thirty but wears her hair as if she were younger, in a girlish ponytail. Her plump curves stretch a tight pink sweater, her body like an overripe pear tree, heavy with blossoms. She knows Guo Luo and likes to tease him. But she is always good to him. Each time she lets him know what to expect from her tourists at the lake. "There is business here, Guo Luo. These ones are crazy for the herbs." The last group was Japanese. This time the group is from Southeast Asia. She tells him to raise his prices. "They're superstitious, and they know this county has the best Winter Worm Summer Weed herbs."

Guo Luo watches her usher the white hats toward him. The three bunches feel warm in his hand. He tilts his chin up to the sky and whistles. A scurry ensues, like a pack of rats descending, as his herb-picking companions flock from every direction. The tourists are middle-aged women with money. The typically nervous kind, carrying their money in cheap leather wallets around their necks, silver and gold chains shining. On this occasion, Guo Luo and the boys do very well.

The tourists stop coming at the end of the summer. The snow soon covers the mountains. There is no autumn here. The herbs are deep under the snow, but Guo Luo has no energy for rat work. He wanders the fields. Nothing but sand and rats and occasional clumps of ugly flowers shaped like steam buns. The rats move like Guo Luo, slowly, from one hole to another. He hits them sometimes. He doesn't know what to do with the coming winter.

One day the female guide appears, though this is nowhere near tourist season. She is excited, her cheeks are rosy.

"Guo Luo! I have good news! I'm being transferred to the Tourism Bureau in the city, and the Bureau said I could have an assistant. Do you want to come and be my assistant?"

Guo Luo is slow to react. He tightens his hat, as if to help him gather his thoughts.

"So I guess we won't see you much around here anymore."

The guide stands on the parched and shriveled former grasslands, her heart full of expectation, like a lone thin cloud hoping for rain.

"Guo Luo, don't you want to live in the city?"

"The city of Xi Qing?"

"Yes. You could work as a guide in the Tourism Bureau there. You could drive the minibus for us."

Guo Luo says nothing. He cannot even imagine what she describes.

The female guide watches him.

"What are you thinking? What do you think about all day? Do you think about girls?"

Guo Luo doesn't answer. He takes a peek at her two round breasts, as though hoping he might find some Winter Worm Summer Weed hiding there.

"If it's girls, I could introduce you to one or two."

"It would have to be a city girl," Guo Luo finally says.

"Why?"

"City girls can pay the right price for my herbs."

The female guide keeps still, but is suddenly like a bloom that's lost its freshness. Her eyes reflect the land around them, the grassland without any grass.

Guo Luo looks back at the mountain, its sides already closed in by the snow. He wishes he could be on the mountain right now, gathering his herbs.

The female guide moves away, disappearing into the sandy landscape. Guo Luo watches her go. Cities, girls, what does it matter? he mutters to himself and turns back to the mountain. The Winter Worm Summer Weed lives on these mountains. Winter Worm feeds the mountainside, and the mountain feeds us. We live from the mountain, live from the Winter Worm Summer Weed. We are Winter Worm Summer Weed people, that is all.

BOB HICOK

Modern Prototype

We melt the old thing into the new thing.
Tongs, a ladle the size of a man's head
I fill with thoughts of molten steel.
Fire below the cauldron, in our cigarettes,
in the right hand of the man coming back
from the bathroom with his skin mag.
He'd tell me, were I to ask, which stapled woman
ignites him. The night goes on without us.
On break, I read Asimov in my getaway: a bus
day shift's building that pivots in the center
to make cornering easier. I close my eyes
and think of myself as joined pieces, I'm nineteen
and the money's good and I still want
to be everything. First night, by way of hello,
a guy told me he fucked his wife
on gravel, she on her knees and he
pulling her head back to devour
her grimace. As if I asked
about sex and pain, nine hundred degrees
and how did I get here? What we create
in the foundry returns to be erased,
this bumper-shape must now become a door-shape,
I'm being taught what a borrowed force
I am, parts lion, pimp. With the overhead crane,
I float tons of cooling metal away, it takes a thumb
on a red button to be God. We're out of beer,
the foreman tells me, sending me out
under stars to fix our blood, I'm nineteen,
I'm forty-six, still trying to sing the song
of making, how on the edge of the unlit lot,

the demented pit bull growls with teeth
that it sees me, and I growl with pipe
that I see it back, and we join in attacking
the indifference.

Poem for My Mother's Hysterectomy

The bell in you out of which I was rung
long ago removed, I cannot go home.

What did they do with your uterus?

I think of it as a hat or a bird,
resting on a head or flying away, over those mountains,
on the other side of which I have never been.

Maybe that's where the navel of the Earth is,
and these womb birds go there out of memory.

I am that of you: a six-foot-tall memory, graft
that took and learned to drive, pick locks, lick
on other women the door you opened for me.

Why did they call you hysterical
when rage is essential for a pulse, to beat the drum
of being alive?

I know this dream; my face in a jar, saying
I can be anything I want, just not
me.

For you, who had seven children
and wanted more, it must have been
like having your face removed,
the Catholic mirror asking, What has your emptiness
to give?

I miss you as the only water I breathed, as a way of living
at the center of things.

You gave me nine round months, time since
is straight as a knife.

I've never asked, What was I in you; a tickle fish, thorn
in your side, a goat
kicking the night?

If I left graffiti in there, a sign or mark,
and was the monster you worried I'd be as sharp-toothed
as the one I am?

Cane Fire

At the bend of the highway just past the beachside melon and
   papaya stands
Past the gated entrance to the Kuilima Hotel on the point where
   Kubota once loved to fish,
The canefields suddenly begin—a soft green ocean of tall grasses
And waves of wind rolling through them all the way to the
   Koʻolau,
a velvet-green curtain of basalt cliffs covered in mosses.
Tanaka Store comes up then, *makai* side of the highway, *towards
   the sea,*
And, whatever it looks like now—curio conchs dangling from its
   porch rafters
Festooned with birdcages of painted bamboo, wooden wafers of
   old shave-ice cones and prices—
I think of stories and photos from nearly a century ago
When Gang No. 7 worked *hoe-hana* and *happai-ko* out near here,
Bending to weed the hoe rows or shouldering a 30# bundle of
   sticky cane,
Trying not to recall the fresh tubs of cold *tofu* lying on the wet
   plank floors in its grocery aisles
Or the money they owed for bags of rice, cans of Crisco, and
   moxa pellets
They used for flaming the skin on their backs at night, relieving
   aches with flashes of pain,
Remembering fire was for loneliness, smoke was for sorrow.

And, if I see a puffer fish, dried and lacquered, full of spikes and pride,
Suspended over a woodframe doorway as I glance back while
   driving by,
Or if the tall television actor with long blond hair and a cowboy's
   gait
Walks from the parking lot toward the picnic tables of the
   decrepit shrimp shack

Where the old icehouse used to be, where the cameras and film
    crew now stand,
I'm not going to lean forward into wanting or desire,
    amusements of my time,
But remember instead that Pine Boy died here one afternoon in 1925.

I know this because I count from the year my grandmother was
    born in 1910,
The year Twain died and the comet passed close to them sitting
    among the cane at night,
A pearly fireball and long trail of alabaster over the empty
    Hawaiian sea,
And forward to the story of how she was fifteen when the *lunas*
    called her to calm him.

Matsuo was her adopted brother, a foundling of Hawaiian blood
    raised Shigemitsu
And sent, at sixteen, to work the canefields with his brothers and
    uncles.
No incidents until the day the field bosses ordered cane fires to be
    lit,
Workers oiling the roots and grass, torchers coming through to
    light the cane,
Burn its leaves down to harvestable stalks that could be cut and
    stacked.

Something flamed in Matsuo, too, because he grabbed a *luna* and
    cut his throat,
Ran into the blazing fields, and could be heard whimpering
    jul'like one pig,
His cries coming through the rising smoke and crackle of the
    cane fires.

What words he said I've never been told—only that he moved
    within the fields,
Staying ahead or within the fire, and could not be coaxed out
                                    or pursued with dogs or on a horse.

Among the Gang, there was no one who doubted his own death

should they follow him.
But Tsuruko, his sister, was called, *tita* who had nursed with him,
Rushed out of school and brought in the manager's car out to the
  fields,
The man opening the door and taking her hand *as if she haole
  wahine ladat!*
As she stepped from the cab and onto the scorched plantation earth.

The image I have is of her walking over opened ground
  absolutely cleared of cane,
The brown and black earth mounded up around her as she stood
  among small hillocks
                              as if a score of graves had just been dug,
The soft, inconstant breezes pressing a thin cotton dress against
  her skin,
Her back to the crowd while she says something into the wind
  that only the cane and Matsuo could hear.

And then his crying ceased and he emerged magically from a
  curtain of smoke and cane,
His eyes tarred and patched with burnt oil and charcoaled with
  molasses.
He stood out for an instant, in front of wicking flames,
Then felt the bead of a rifle on him, and he slipped quickly back in,
The cane fires muffling whatever words he might have called as
  they took him.

The crouching lion of a lava bluff juts near the road,
And I know the jeep trail will come up next,
A cattle fence and white and brown military sign its marker.
It's where the radar station is, far past the fields and up-mountain
Where the sluice-waters start and the apples blossom,
Leaving white popcorn flowers dappling the mud with faint,
                              perishable relics of rage and beauty.

Aubade, Kawela

Drizzle of rain pattering on the dwarf palms, dark towers and
   blue parapets of clouds
Over the ruffled blue gingham of the sea, sweet scent of seawrack
   and fresh life borne on the wind
That ambles along the sands and sticks of drift like a nosing *poi*
   dog
Wig-wagging from the lava rock point along this thin scythe of a
   beach.

I'm home again, curling waves tossing their soaked white tresses
   to the skies,
Dropping them tendrilously around my ankles in a dancer's
   expert tease,
Pipers scooting like feathered gray racecars accelerating ahead,
The shark's fin-and-tail in the surf the first plainsong of the
   morning,
Gloria of the bobbing turtle just offshore the second.

I came here once when I was nineteen and near fully a Mainland
   kid by then,
Slept shrouded on the beach in a GI-surplus mosquito net,
                              smoked Camels and Marlboros
Days playing cards with cousins—nickel bets, peanuts, and *pidgin*
   all in the mix—
Dripping bottles of Primo beer our cold drink, raw fish salad our
   chaser.

Winter vacation sophomore year, I'd brought a blue Sears
   suitcase filled only with books—
Joyce, Beckett, Kawabata, Tillich, and Buber. Novels and baby
   theology.
I found something in them that drew an ache out of my heart,
Poultices of words, *pharmakoi* of pages flecked with angelic
   particles of sand,

As I read madly on the beach, dawn to dusk, frigate birds and
    gulls
Squawking overhead like schoolmates inviting me to leave studies
    behind
And sail with them in the gay, gusting winds, seek Amaryllis in
    the shaded seas.

But the most I would do was plunge in the surf when it got too
    hot,
Then stroke out past the shorebreaks to the dark ribbon of reef
                         a hundred yards out.
Along the way, warm waters would be sieved with the cool
From freshwater springs coming through the lagoon's sandy
    bottom.
I'd catch gray glimpses of mullet schools, yellow tangs, and eel-
    like, spotted *hinalea*—
Wrasses furling amid green corals and tentacled blooms of white
    anemonae.
And, if I flipped myself over like a contrarian seal, disporting on
    my back
And wanting to wail with the unsayable, I didn't know how to,
Except that aching had turned to resolve, the sun's scorn to
    imperative suggestion
As I floated along, catching my breath, feeling the wind's cool
    fingers
Tantalize along my trunks and wet skin of my arms and hairless
    chest.

Signature of all things I am here to read, thought Joyce's Daedalus,
Channeling Plato, himself derived from Heraclitan mystics
And yet their proud, sophistic apostate.
                    Unlike them, I had a place but no stories,
No tradition except utter silence like the deeps that fell away
    offshore,
Sixty feet to a sixty fathoms in a breath. What was there was more
    than mystery,
The dropoff past unportrayed even in lore and without
    unisonance,

The luminous and anecdotal cloaked in inky shrouds, absent my
   own conjured romances.

And yet the ache stayed, as if all the slate sky was a stone's weight
   on my chest,
Pressing me down beneath the waves for truth and a confession,
Pressure of the unspoken shorting my breath until vision and the
   epiphanic
Might distinguish themselves from delirium, sunshowers over the
   opened seas
An amber dazzle to the left of my rolling shoulder as I shrugged
   quickly over
And began my measured strophes back to the daedal shore.

A Child's Ark

Hot Los Angeles summer days, late '50's, a seven-year-old
Shut in the tiny, midtown apartment on South Kingsley Drive,
I'd flip on the TV to the black-and-white game shows,
Rerun comedies, and half-hour detective dramas,
Seeking company, avoiding the soaps, news, and cartoons.

One of my favorites for a while was a show called *Kideo Village*,
In which kids would wend their way through the attractive curves
Of a game path spooling through the sound studio and its faux
    lampposts,
Small minimalist archways, doors, pushcarts, and streetstands
Set up and interspersed along the telegenic route—
A bakery, a toy shop, the ice cream parlor, etc.
The tragedies strewn in the way would be a bookstore or piggy
    bank—
For one you'd have to lose a turn and stay inside to read a book,
For the other, you'd give up spending for a certificate of virtue.

The glory was a pet store of fluffy animals—
Nose-twitching rabbits bearing sachets of cash around their necks,
A dog hitched to a wagon filled with sacks of stage gold.
Wealth was the message, the child contestants obliged
To exercise the right energy and enterprise
To run themselves briskly through the board's intricate
    arrangement
Of pleasure, danger, and delight without risk,
Their assignment to luck into opportunities
That would set off crescendos of bells ringing,
Video paradisos of lights flashing through the transparent lucite
                                    under their feet.

Yet it was splendor and the minute articulations of a fantasy
    village's architecture
That mesmerized me, that a child could skip along in a moment's
    time

Without having to be put in a car or be handled by adults,
To a candy store, movie house, or shop full of cream puffs.
Glee and surprise were everywhere just on the next luminous
    square
Around the looping turn on the glittering game board.

When the power went out one day, or perhaps when the show
    was cancelled,
I got out scissors, paper, and pens, Crayolas arranged in stick
    puddles
On the dingy, carpeted floor of the apartment's living room,
Mapping out a village of my own on wax paper from a kitchen
    drawer.
I found empty green stationery boxes my mother brought home
    from work,
Tore the labels off, drew on them, marked rectangles for doors;
I cut windows, made folding blinds, used the leftover cutouts
To make counters and tables, a long, folded cardboard flume
For water to run in a sluice . . . the tofu-maker, the rows of shacks,
A union hall where my uncles would gather, my aunt's gas station
On the highway, clear glass medicine bottles for pumps,
The peaked roof of Kahuku Betsu-In, the barber's, the butcher's,
The Chinese Association . . .

This was the village we left behind—
And our apartment, the scatter of debris on its floor, my child's ark
                                                    of the lost world.

Vesuvius

Every morning in the hour before you wake,
when the sun squares off against the kitchen floor,
and the cups from last night still wear
necklaces of wine, stoles of milk,

I hear waves in the walls.

A tide swells from the corner
behind the fridge: crest and crash,
and that silty forgiveness of sand
sweeping back over sand and stone.

I won't tell you about this.
We are close to having children.
I can feel it in my ribs when I lie down
to sleep, and some nights I cannot
sleep, knowing the white paint
and plaster will be still as always,
the lint not drift below.

In the absence of dreams,
my memory sends me postcards:

One New Year's Eve off the coast
of Thailand, I stripped and swam
in the wet dust of phosphorus,
writing a message to time:
I am endless, brilliant, and small.

At the Celtic walls, I forgot
history and picked blueberries.

Was that really me
stepping over a puddle of melting
ice cream on the street
of the goldmakers?

Not so much later, I grew up
and met you,
tossed coins in a fountain,
thought up names.

I grow older thinking
of places we may never go:
a blue pagoda, the winter swamp
choked with swans.

For hundreds of years,
the citizens of Pompeii must've looked
upon their sturdy, imperfect city,
and found it beautiful
because it was theirs, and up to
the smoking mountain with a greater
tenderness, because it was not.

Rue de Poitiers

translated by Clare Cavanagh

Late afternoon, light snow.
The Musée d'Orsay is on strike, beside it
a gray lump huddled on the sidewalk's edge:
a bum curled in a ball (maybe a refugee
from some country caught in civil war)
still lying on the grate, packed in a quilt,
a scrap-heap sleeping bag, the right to life.
Yesterday his radio was playing.
Today coins cooling on a paper shape constellations,
nonexistent moons and planets.

Untitled

This year
I bore no fruit,

just leaves
that give no shadows

I am afraid, Rabbi,

I am afraid, Lord,

that I'll be cursed by him who hungers,

weary
on the endless road
to Jerusalem

Arrival & Departure

Arriving in December on a Greyhound
from Paducah, you saw the usual sun
rising on your right over the bowed houses
of Dearborn as a wafer of moon descended
on your left behind the steaming rail yards
wakening for work. "Where are we?" you asked.
In 1948 people still talked
to each other even when they had something
to say, so of course I answered. I wasn't
innocent exactly, nor experienced
either, just a kid; "Downtown," I said,
as the bus with its cargo of bad breath
pulled in behind the depot just off
Washington Boulevard. Had you been
a woman, even one with crooked teeth,
a tight smile, and no particular charm,
I would have offered you a place to stay,
but at 6′2″ and 185
with your raw Indian features and hands
twice the size of mine, you got only advice,
in the long run not very good advice.
I should have said, "Go home, this town
will break your heart," but what did I know
about your home on a hillside tobacco farm
in North Carolina? What do I know now
except the forests as you climb higher,
dotted here and there with weathered shacks
the color of lead, and the rising silence
of winter as the snow descends unstained
into the early dusk. There was snow here, too,
speckled with cinders, piss yellowed, tired,
and the smell of iron and ashes blowing
in from Canada, and you and I waiting

for a streetcar that finally arrived
jammed with the refuse of the nightshift
at Plymouth Assembly. I should have seen
where we were headed; even at twenty
it was mine to know. Like you I thought
2.35 an hour was money, I thought
we'd sign on for afternoons and harden
into men. Wasn't that the way it worked,
men sold themselves to redeem their lives?
If there was an answer I didn't get it.
Korea broke, I took off for anywhere
living where I could, one perfect season
in your mountains. The years passed,
suddenly I was old and full of new needs.
When I went back to find you I found
instead no one in the old neighborhood
who knew who I was asking for, the Sure Shot
had become a porno shop; the plating plant
on Trumbull had moved to Mexico
or heaven. In its space someone planted
oiled grass, stripped-down cars, milkweeds
shuddering in the traffic. The river was here,
still riding low and wrinkled toward a world
we never guessed was there, but still the same,
like you, faithful to the end. If your sister,
widowed now, should call today and ask
one more time, "Where is he at? I need him,
he needs me," what should I tell her?
He's in the wind, he's under someone's
boot-soles, he's in the spring grass, he lives
in us as long as we live. She won't buy it,
neither would you. You'd light a cigarette,
settle your great right hand behind my neck,
bow down forehead to forehead, your black hair
fallen across your eyes, and mutter something
consequential, "bullshit" or "god a-mighty"
or "the worst is still to come." You came north
to Detroit in winter. What were you thinking?

When He Described the Park

translated by Clare Cavanagh

When he described the park, the
path, sick fires glowed
in his cooling eyes, his voice
grew stronger and his hands tried
to be what they once were,
when deft squirrels trustingly
took sugar from them. Now
I'm here. And everything is as
he'd remembered: the yellow forsythia, the poplars'
shady tunnel, the insects' thrum, the cuckoo.
That place had entered him
for good, faithful to the smallest
leaf, that place, which holds
no trace of him. The inhuman,
perfect beauty he recalled while dying,
never needed him, then
or now. It needs no one. It is
and will remain the same: a quick squirrel
on the path, twenty generations
past the one he'd fed, flees,
mortally frightened
at my sight.

I Look into Her Face

I look into her face and see ever more clearly
time's subcutaneous machinations. Death's
terrifying progress. Which will alter
nothing in her features, her mouth's shape, the color
of her hair. Nothing, since so little: only
this light, this motion, this
warmth. Only what isn't actually there,
what can't be seen, truly is. And
will not be. This "and"
holds everything. And this moment.
And her. And me. And the way
I—knowing this—don't cry out or
plead, do nothing, as if
there were really nothing
to be done. And finally
my trembling heart which obeys no one,
which is to say only me.

Semper Augustus

Broken tulip, 17th-century Holland

The plain white petal between her finger and thumb
belled into a sail pregnant with nothing it could bear,
then split, dark seamed, its length. A whole fleet

foundered in the field around her: bands of white tulips,
red and yellow, diluted to shadow beneath
a setting moon splinted against the sky. Each spring,

they lost themselves, kiltered together, no longer
petal and flower but color and field that flared
in daylight and drew inward at night like shutters
no one looked out of. What shame to always wake

to the same thing, she thought. Elsewhere, tulips
turned wily, shot through with someone else's fortune,
but not here, not under her watch. Here,
nothing rivered or flamed, nothing streaked

wildly the way the horses, startled from the stable
last winter, shocked the field with their frantic darks,
giving up the names she and her husband called
as they ran for the canal and the year's first loss.

Once, she'd seen the famed Semper Augustus,
single white flower feathered with red, saw
how it moved, ravenous, starving for the eye.

It struck her the way whatever sent the horses
from their narrow stalls thrashed their tame hearts;
like seeing two worlds at once—a surface
she was meant to, an underneath she was not.

Even now she closed her eyes and saw the petals,
veined, corrupt—how they sickened her to look at them,
they were that beautiful. She'd even dreamed

the flower stricken by illness, its bulb split
into handfuls hollowing themselves into each late
and later flourish and reflected in a bank of mirrors
meant to multiply the owner's fortune

that for all their trouble would at last
duplicate his two hands plying wasted husks
from the soil. Semper Augustus, he'd named it,
and kept its generations mostly to himself,

but in her dream even his hands disappeared,
and any reason to look, the mirrors freezing over,
cracked piecemeal by the seasons into shard,
particle and glint, until nothing was left to show.

She'd awakened to a blear of color caught
from her window same as every morning,
spring after spring. How could the flowers in the field

not be the sick ones?—or the sickness itself, spread
as they were like an irritation. And when she knew
she'd lost the child, the name she'd meant for it
a husk on the tongue she couldn't quite swallow back,

she wanted something in the field to draw her eye,
its *now* erupted petal by petal so each flower
demanded its own attention, its intricate hour.
Better to be sick with beauty than despair.

She imagined she could wait for color to craze
the petals, feathering toward her outstretched hand,
imagined her husband at the window behind her,
watching what by will alone she'd drawn from the field.

But the tulips raised the same blank refusal
to rupture, to river and flame, to roil two bodies
into one. Want cannot give what won't come
even to its own name, hard lesson it takes too long to see.

She thought of how she ran through the field in winter,
casting her voice like rope at what wouldn't be saved:
ice splintered and yawed under one horse

crossing the canal; the other bloodied itself
going down, bloodied the ice veined like a widened eye,
the first horse looking back from the other side.

CATE MARVIN

Monsterful

We meet day-plain and inches away, faces
facing off in a garden,
                              kissing closed kisses,
solemn, bone-dry, and exquisite as the leaves
of our sweating faces
                              glisten, sheens giving
back each tree's green. *My greenery grows
untoward,*
                *branches burst windows, menace
doors, what sky is wide enough to house me?*
                              Breath labored, we meet
between noon and never,
in heat dense and coupled with rose scent.
                              Koi rise mouth-first
in a fountain's deep basin, bodies bone-white
and rust-flecked,
                              worn as worn dress gloves,
whiskered gapes funneling the water's glossy
surface. You water
                              my eyes with your eyes
and the plant of my gaze   climbs toward
your sky, wanting your mouth
                              to hatch into mine,
as a cloud contracts inside this evening's sky.
                Nights have me now think of how
we first met, not pressed
                              inside dream's tent,
but day-bright,   mouths soft as opiates.
In a gold pool poured
                              out your lit window,
chained to this lingering,
I stand so still my skin feels each spore settle.

To slip like a vapor
                    beneath your door, appear
in the cloud your breath presses to a mirror,
                    to read an evening paper
in your heart's anteroom. Necking in a cloud
bank,
          milking an hour's dew, hands roving
their devouring herd,
          you tongued my every sharp blade
soft, and I knew   the terrible suspense
of a hand's white claw push open
                    the heavy lid of my chest,
emerge a night terror: I have conceived
an impossible child,
                    now catalogue your words' hues
by density of violet, become altogether new
     and newly violent.

Set Theory

Number following number,
                    oscillations
Neatly described, heart's plunder
Or loss, following,
                    that old saw, *again and again,*
And the route taken always is the shortest
Between two points,
                    between what must be
And that lapsing cloud, a continental
Dimming, and then stillness,
                    and always the afterward,
Trying to place it, a landscape, verdigris,
Cerulean, lightened azure,
                    indigo the deepest point,
The sky beginning to open, if
We could see them, stars ascending
Serially, marking
                    time's season,
Boolean sets, you then not-you,
                    and that
Graphed line between, thin veil,
Memory lifted, lifting
                    over the garden's trees
An equation of synapses,
                    but now just that—

Before the beginning of darkness
Settling on
                    the leaves of hawthorns,
Carnelian fruit, neither

Loss nor gain, but that astonishment
You are here, between
This and what is
                    fired—cinnabar to cadmium—and gone.

Location, Location

A spider webbed the cellar doorway
the morning of my cleaning spree,
pale star with him floating at the center.
And for all his meanness, bigness,
blackness, I let him be, having once
squashed ants, crushed butterflies,
stalking field and sidewalk. Love,
come late in life, had softened all
my anger. His net spanned half
the upper frame, invisible as water,
and forgetting to bend I swept it
down with my hair. When I looked up,
he clung to wood by an arm like one
leapt to safety above the falls. Next day
he watched from his new web like an eye
as I remembered and ducked, but again
my head brushed his rigging down.
I wanted to flick or kick him, saying
(I did say) "You just can't live here now,"
or stomp and be done, but left him
gripping the lintel like a kitten.
On the third day he'd climbed onto
the propped screen door and strung
his web across its pane, tied prettily
to all four corners: safer, better off.
The way I see him now contents me,
swinging in his hammock as I gently
close the screen. Our bond's in where
we've come from, which makes
our current condition so sweet.

EUGENIO MONTEJO

Exit

translated by Kirk Nesset

I'll be an easy cadaver to carry
through woods and over the sea;
in a carriage, on a white ship,
as the oboe laments, or bassoon,
over the droning croaking of toads.

I'll be an innocent cadaver,
quietly regarding my remains,
while despite me a requiem sounds,
the moan of a lonely ghost
in the hooves of the old horse.

I'll be the cadaver I am now,
ponderous, engrossed in the holy,
though light and easy to carry:
in a carriage, on a white ship,
as the oboe laments, or bassoon,
over the droning croaking of toads.

Exclamation Point

It could come right now as a *dit-dah* of rain,
    mere pine needle lost in a tree-stack of beads,
        thorn expelled from red dot, print felt
            an inch from a finger, pursed lips speaking in tears.

It makes you look dotty. Easily amused. It *starts*
    like a Spanish ¡—down on your luck on your back. Like a baby's,
        your weak arms reach up. Heads near the ceiling shake.
            Everything's
                high. To the point. Up *there*. Outside, gothic pillars of
                trees sway

when you see their full height, small sun. They take thin wedges
            of light away. It's now,
    you know. You're fading. You focus one moment on
                squirrels—how they leap
        as if trees were solid. Scamper as if *up* were *onward*. Then
            pain, which was rising,
                fades, too. As you float, you find you can fall *up there*.
                Don't worry!

you want to exclaim, *I'm above it all. It's easy!*
    But the biggest point of your life soars unnoticed, free
        of clamor, of gesture, of flesh. No hint of tomorrow's vibrancy.
            When someone attends to your body (not you), it says
            something else: *help me!*

Every Night

Federal holding cell, Hughes County jail

Fights. Never quiet—like years back
with the folks, but ratcheted-up, bloodied,
multiplied, till the badge writes the last two
shovers up, says he'll do the same for all of us
if we can't keep the crybabies smothered
I WANT SOME PEACE,
SLEEP, NO MORE GETTING
OUT OF THE CHAIR, IT'S BAD ENOUGH
WATCHING YOU IDIOTS ON
THE MONITOR, NEXT TIME I'LL SHUT
THE TV OFF IN HERE FOR YOU,
GIVE YOU A REASON TO COMPLAIN

—do that. Myron's flat voice from under
his blanket above me, only sound from up
there in two days except his creaking down
for hot-dog chow or a crap—only guy no one
yells at when he's on the shitcan—what a
display, someone every hour stinking this cage
of sixteen waiting to be shipped, strung out,
on top of each other every minute—bunk,
shower, shitter, picnic table, TV remote to
fight over, that's it. I thought machinery'd
ruined my ears already, but 24/7 banging and
shouting has them way more gone. Maybe
Myron's working on hearing nothing. Finally
weather over 75, so they were herding us out
thirty minutes a day to watch a 20 x 20 patch
of sky framed by concertina, till one guy's pal
tossed a pack of Pall Malls over and that was it
for light and air—*leave the cigs alone,* Myron
growled. Stupid joes got us all shaken down.

Now tonight they throw in a fish, kidnapped
his own kid or something *HOW*
CAN THEY TAKE HER slamming
his arms at the bars till they're bleeding,
then old Buffalo yelling *AIDS! GIT 'IM*
OUTA HERE—hammers his own fists
on the steel for the hack to come, clank in,
lock the TV off, and turn his back on
two bulldogs in the corner working
the fresh guy over—*SHE'S MY KID,*
FOR GOD'S SAKE—FORGET GOD
DIPSHIT, YOU'RE IN NOW, YOU'RE
A GONER and Buffalo cranking the shower
STOP THE BLOOD, THROW 'IM IN
THE SLIME, I TELL YA, KEEP
'IM AWAY FROM ME
till Fuzzy pulls a shank and shuts him up.

Myron groans, rolls over, whacked-out Scott
snores on, *peace, sleep, chair,* the turnkey's
words echo long after his last shudder of the bars
—it's all I wanted too, to find the stuff that would
take me out—*peace, sleep, chair,* close as it gets
to lullaby in here, close as any of us ever
got maybe—TV black, our own soundtrack
jagging and vibrating till God knows when.

JIRI ORTEN

Wounded

translated by Lyn Coffin, with Leda Pugh

The earth opened wide.
Rain, a doctor, dripped remedies.
All night, moving down the mountainsides
were molten seas.

You, my fevered country, now must spend
your last moments caught in delirium's coil—
peacefully, tenderly, you ask at the end:
Where's the boil?

2
My soul, your wind died away.
Silence fell on the mills like a stone.
I lost, like a deer gone wildly astray,
my home.

I run into sharp edges and I feel
revenge would be a painful, faithful start:
but my particular Achilles heel
is in my heart.

Goodbye Letter #6

Oh, pain will die, I swear, when I succeed
in making a Myshkin of these tears
to master agony, quietly, there
where I burn with beautiful helpless need,

where voices go mute, and feelings wake late,
before finally disbanding.
To smile (to reach understanding)
just as He said. And not to wait.

So it's far. At a higher elevation
than the rise and fall of simple speech.
Who can't write his way to conciliation
lived for the coffin. He should be betrayed.

And that's me, woman, that's me,
fullness rotting and being dispersed
and all that was suffered for will go
there where you wounded me the worst

where the fragrance of kisses is laid
where the ones who've been tried are made
to love what terribly isn't so
about which I endlessly know.

Dead of the Night

For once, no flowers. Past midnight, and very quiet along this corridor. The clock on the opposite wall is round, a cartoon clock. Funny, the idea of *keeping time,* here of all places. Beneath the clock, a square tablet announces in bold what is now the wrong date, April 3.

I could walk over, just a few steps, tear the page away from the calendar, and make it today, April 4. But that would cause a ripping sound, and I'd have to let go of her hand. So, leave it. In this room it's yesterday. We won't reach today until this is over, the time warp we entered three days ago. She'd appreciate that, irony being her last grasp on reality.

"This time," the doctor said in the hallway last night—it might have been two nights ago—"you understand this time, this is it?"

Five years ago I had faced him wild-eyed in the ER after her first stroke. "What do you want us to do?" he had asked.

What do *I* want you to do? I have a graduate degree in lyric poetry, what do I know? But I heard myself say in a commanding voice, "Treat her like a sixteen-year-old who's just crashed on her boyfriend's motorcycle."

And he did. They did. The whole high-tech array of surgical, medical, therapeutic systems revved into high gear.

But this time I don't try to save her. I look at the doctor, by now my accomplice, and I say *Oh yes* when he says *You understand this is it,* eager to prove myself no trouble, a maker of no fuss. Not something she could be accused of. "I get the feeling your mother doesn't...like me," he confided a year ago, this mild man of goodwill and even better bedside manner. "I walk in the room, and she scowls. As if she *hates* me."

You got that right. I experience a surge of perverse pride at her capacity to alienate those with power over her, the self-immolating integrity of her fury. Her essential unfairness, throwing guilt like a girl, underhand. For her, no such thing as an innocent bystander. Cross her path, and the poisoned dart springs from the quiver of her heart. *The look.* Narrowed eyes, pinched disdainful mouth, brilliant mime of venomous dislike. I know it well, doctor. "You goody two-shoes," she spit out once when I was cleaning her apartment, mopping up cigarette ash around her chair. She didn't bother to disguise her contempt for me as a non-smoker—obviously, I didn't know how to enjoy life.

But that sour face of her elderly fury keeps disappearing just as she is disappearing. Even this latest face, the one propped on the hospital pillow, the hieratic visage that seems polished and will soon be an object, even this one is hard to keep in focus. I'm sitting here, holding her hand, but it's that ardent face from 1936 that keeps appearing, the face in the photograph that was propped above the piano all the years of my girlhood and beyond. Heart-shaped with high cheekbones and eyes set wonderfully wide, it is the face of a romantic lead.

Not because she was beautiful—she wasn't beautiful. She was seriously pretty, the way Scott Fitzgerald described the real heartbreakers. The slightly dazzled eyes (she refused to wear her glasses) looked out with a shyness clearly feigned. That was the entrancing part—you could tell she wasn't really shy. She was happy. And a little startled by it. She couldn't keep the happiness of her body and soul off her face. Neither could my father—because of course he's standing next to her. Though not yet my father, not yet her husband.

Both of them look directly at the camera, standing by a cottonwood tree on a sandy bank of the Mississippi. Springtime from the look of the tree, site of a picnic, no doubt. She leans her trim self in a stylish slouch, just touching his lean body. A claim being made. She's happy and he looks—proud. They both have that slightly abashed shyness stamped on their faces. Good-lookers. They're stepping into their future, he in an open-neck shirt, she in jodhpurs and a little leather jacket. Depression-era sweethearts with nothing to lose. It's their first picture together.

I stared at it all my girlhood as if at a problem to be solved—who *are* these people?—while I tooled my way through a Chopin mazurka, a Bach prelude, under the erotic glory of two kids crazy in love who gazed at me from another planet, not the one we inhabited together in our bungalow on Linwood Ave.

"The nurses can set up a cot for you," the doctor said last night.

The low cot is wedged next to her now; I'm perched on the edge, barely hoisted above the floor, a supplicant crouched below the elevated royal bed. I gaze up at the tiny body, the porcelain face. There's a yellow legal pad on my lap. I'm a note-taker from long habit.

It's her habit, in fact, one I borrowed or inherited or stole from her. Note-taking, newspaper-clipping, file-making, all the librarian traits of wordiness and archival passion she displayed. Her favorite books were biographies (how smoothly the past tense inserts itself, already), big thumpers of Dolley Madison and Abigail Adams on the American history side, Parnell and Wolfe Tone for the Irish obsession. And now on the yellow legal pad, the beginning of hers:

HAMPL, Mary Marum
Age 85
Mary Catherine Ann Teresa Eleanor Marum Hampl born July 26, 1917 in St Peter, MN, to Martha Smith and Joseph Marum. The family moved to St Paul when she was five, and she lived the rest of her life in this city she loved, in "God's country," as she always called Minnesota. A 1935 graduate of Mechanic Arts High School, she married her classmate Stanislaus Hampl in 1940 in the St Paul Cathedral. They were together 58 years until Stan's death in 1998.

That's as far as I've gotten, having made the first artistic decision—loading on all the pretty names. They make her sound like a crowned head. I always wondered if she conferred most of them on herself.

I should probably put in her astrological sign. She was always glad to give it, raising her flyaway mane imperiously above her petite frame to say, "I'm Leo—the Lion." She liked to read my horoscope aloud (placid Pisces) in the morning after she read hers, and my father's and brother's (both the Bull, as men should be), to see how we were all doing, cosmically speaking. "Too bad," she would say sympathetically after giving me the wan future Jeanne Dixon so often predicted for my watery self.

Not until the night nurse stops in and glances down does it occur to me that composing my mother's obit with my left hand as I hold her unconscious hand with my right might strike an outsider as offensive. Not to *her,* I want to protest. She would have expected nothing less, the dutiful writer-daughter scribbling in the half-light, holding the dying hand while hitting the high points of her subject's allegedly ordinary life that is finally going to see print. For a great reader, this is a great death.

She's glad I'm her daughter ("I'm proud of you," she says with some frequency), but for this I'm required to play my role, to be The Writer ("Are you working?" she asks, ever aware of any slacking off). Writing is my vocation—her word, the word of my upwardly mobile Catholic childhood. She really thought being a librarian would have been the better choice: nicer to spend a lifetime reading than tied to a desk forever doing homework—because what else is writing?

She stands by this spiritual time clock waiting for me to punch in. And I do. I want to. On this we can agree. The roller ball moves smoothly now across the blue lines, over the conveyer belt of the yellow paper. I look up briefly and smile at the night nurse.

But for once the nurse doesn't smile back, doesn't ask gently if she can get me something, coffee, a cookie. She touches the porcelain forehead, straightens the already smooth cotton blanket, walks out without a word, the frown hardened, the lips pursed.

A lifelong people-pleaser, I find I'm glad to be disapproved of. And who does this remind me of? *I don't give a damn,* she's often said these last lost years. *I'm going down the drain, kid. Let's have a cig.*

I put in how she wrote to-the-barricades letters to the *St. Paul Pioneer Press Mailbag* (the dual erosions of progressive politics and correct grammar usage were her chief concerns for Minnesota civilization, and *not* unrelated in her view). I'm pleased, on rereading, with the reference to "God's country," her little riff about Minnesota. I note that she was devoted to the Rosary. But I won't mention that she was fiercely anti-abortion. A little censorship to keep the liberal politics undiluted by her priest-pleasing orthodoxy. *I'm praying for you,* she would say to me, eyes narrowed witchily. A hex, a jinx. *If I'd been for abortion, where would you be? Ha-ha!*

Her hand gives back no pressure, but it's pleasantly cool. My hand is bigger than hers now, but it—my hand, not myself—*remembers* her hand, how it felt to be enclosed in hers, walking down Wabasha, as she strode along, not looking down at me, head held high, Leo the Lion negotiating the crowded summer sidewalk downtown. There's even a photograph of this moment, taken by one of the roving photographers of the 1950's who snapped candid shots on the street and then ran after you to sell them for a dollar. Strange to think she bought such a thing, she who watched every penny.

We're in front of Birdie's, where my Czech grandmother "marketed," though my mother wouldn't be caught dead shopping there. "Birdie's is *filthy*," she said. Maybe she's just said that as the photographer snapped the picture because her face has a severe, disapproving look. Or maybe I mistake as disapproval her purposeful expression as she rushes through the downtown crowd, me trailing beside her, clearly straining to keep up. But it's a remark I heard more than once—*Birdie's is filthy.* An oblique Irish swipe at the Czech side of the family. *A mixed marriage,* one of the Irish great-aunts said. *She was meant for an Irish boy, a college boy. Your father had quite the movie-star looks. She went for the looks, doncha know.*

At Birdie's, shiny tumescent fish lay on crushed ice next to mounds of bruised pears. Heavy green flies lofted above the stand. A man in a soiled white apron waved a northern pike in the air to clear the flies before he slapped the fish on butcher paper and wrapped it, marking the price with the oil pen he kept tucked behind his ear. I wanted to stop, poke the fish with an index finger as my Czech grandmother did. But the cool, utilitarian handholding of my young mother was pulling me away. I was an appendage, dragging at the side of her swishing skirt. She was keeping me from all this dirt, this *filth*.

I was magnetized by the word *filth*, or maybe by her disgust, which was charged with relish when she uttered it. The smell of fish, jeweled flies fussing over warm offal, the crush of people, and the casual rot that real life can't rid itself of—that was the future I aspired to. This dirt was more than a covert emblem of sex. It was the insignia of escape, the promise of liberation from the enclosure of the cool, purposeful hand of my mother. *Don't call it dirt,* one of the old Austrian growers said when I was playing near the mound of potting soil at the greenhouse where my father worked. *This here is soil, it's earth, this here.*

Maybe from that greenhouse reverence I sensed that filth was the essence of the Great World I longed for. I was meant for New York. And places like New York—Paris, of course, and Prague, where the other side of family had come from, Africa and Asia in general, and San Francisco because it had a Chinatown.

I knew instinctively a real city had to be a mess if it counted at all. St. Paul was out of the running. *Yours from this hell-hole of life & time,* Scott Fitzgerald, my first literary hero, signed a letter when he was stranded at home in St. Paul to Edmund Wilson, who existed on high in blessed Greenwich Village. My true destination, too. Just give me my ticket out.

So how is it I never got away? Strange—that I, the family hippie, one-time pot smoker, and strident feminist who refused for years to marry, living in laidback communes or (*in sin*—my mother's voice) with the draft resister (*dodger,* my brother, scowling) my family never liked but was faultlessly polite to—that this person, me myself in middle age and for years now happily married (*thank God,* my mother crowing) to *a good guy* (my father laconically okaying my true love)—that I ended up being the caretaker of my frail, failing parents. I who for so long made every effort to be selfish, to be unfettered (no marriage, no children), to organize my energies around poetry and travel, who spoke with august certitude about "my work" before there even was any, I who meant to *get out of here.*

But here I am, still dragging at the side of her hand, still living in the same old St. Paul neighborhood. Never have had anything but a Minnesota driver's license, never have lived more than a long walk from my girlhood home. Still a daughter, an aging ingénue. But soon, in hours apparently, I'll be nobody's daughter.

For years now I've sat in doctors' offices, waiting for my father or my mother, as they are dealt with by their medical handlers. I read magazines I would never read otherwise, *Ladies' Home Journal, Family Circle.* I seem to zero in on the articles on "parenting" (a word my own parents never used). Relentlessly bland narratives, replete with common sense or its obverse, tedious reassurance. I read them with rapt attention, especially those on the rebellious adolescent child, I who have no children.

It is "natural," also "inevitable," I read again and again, that the child must grow away from ("reject" is the preferred word) the parent. It's the backdrop of the deeply held postmodern faith, the religion of self-realization I've tried to practice all my adult life—you must abandon ship in order to . . . what? To exist, to be a "self."

Becoming a person was the point. Being a child—a daughter—that's an interim position, a form of failure, really, a stunted condition. I've sat in the cardiologist's waiting room, in the neurologist's waiting room, attentively reading therapeutic bromides, as if I might finally get the message. Somewhere along the line, it seems, I neglected to *break away*. I remained The Daughter. *Boy, I don't envy you,* my oral surgeon brother says from his safe perch on the West Coast where he's lived for decades.

Still holding her hand now, I glance away from the figurine my mother has become. I turn to the big window that is black and gives me nothing but my own face. Then I turn to the walls, the cartoon clock, the square calendar: the full compass of these days in this shadowy room. I'm waiting for light to break. It'll be another long night. The last one, probably.

In the dark, if I stare hard enough, the city reconfigures out the window, a ghostly replica of itself, shapes cast against the darkness. I can make out the form of the History Center. Beyond the History Center, the Cathedral that, from a different angle, I see from my own house. I'm close to home here, always.

From the top window of the narrow brownstone where I live in this town I've never managed to escape, the illuminated dome of the St. Paul Cathedral rests top-heavy on the city's dominant hill, an improbable Jules Verne spaceship poised to observe the earthlings. The theatrical lighting also comes to us courtesy of the St. Paul Archdiocese that has decided, either out of civic generosity or from sheer self-regard, to indulge in the expense of the display.

Either way, thank you, thank you very much.

That's where they started it all. It was an August wedding because my florist father preferred summer, the growing season. Mother, the darker soul, favored late September, falling leaves, the first killing frost.

Did she ever get her way? Not then, not during her sweetheart period, not till later when she mastered the fine art of being impossible.

They settled on the thirty-first, as close to September as you could get without actually giving over to it. An overcast day, she used to say, as if in retrospect this augured poorly.

The Cathedral was her family parish, the Irish lighting candles before the altar of the Virgin Mother. He had no parish. His father, the Czech immigrant, growled through his stutter, *Priests are c-c-rooks.* But the Irish grandfather was an usher at Sunday Mass, *a pillar of the church,* as the Irish great-aunts said.

On the arm of her father, the pillar, on the last day of August 1940, my mother came down the yawning center aisle of the bombastic nave whose immensity made even a nice crowd of family and friends look skimpy. A hired photographer documented all this. Big eight-by-ten glossies in a leatherette album fastened in place by black tabs, pictures so primal they're glued in mind more powerfully than memory itself, as if the twentieth century gave everybody an extra kit-bag of memories, your own flimsy, inexact ones, and the incontrovertible evidence of photo albums, image upon unsorted image documenting your life before you existed.

She was dressed in a chalk-white gown, the skirt formed by rows of lace flounces, the bodice topped with a mandarin collar and sprouting gossamer cap sleeves. She held no bouquet. She preferred to carry a book, as if she already divined her years as a library file clerk that lay ahead. The white kid-leather prayer book trailed satin streamers punctuated by stephanotis blossoms that her florist bridegroom had ingeniously wired to the ribbons. The dress was a knockoff of the one Vivian Leigh wears in the opening scene of *Gone with the Wind.* It had been mass-produced for the brides of 1940. She was one of many Scarlett O'Haras that year.

Later, the dress, folded in sky-blue tissue paper, lived in a large waxed cardboard box pushed to the back of their closet where, over the course of my girlhood, it grayed into a strange yellow like an old bruise. It wasn't just a dress but something hallowed and creepy—a relic, the bleached bone of a saint. When I learned in school about the Shroud of Turin, the disintegrating gown sprang to mind, dreadful in the dark of their airless closet, lying in its waxed box the size of a child's casket.

But why should it—they—matter? Except to me, of course. We're all allowed to make much of our parents in this super-psychologized culture. A whole proliferating profession caters to *the wounded child*, disabled veterans of the civil wars of the middle-class family who hunch forward, talking fast and furious from low-slung leather chairs in the faux living rooms of therapists' offices across the land.

Not that. Mine isn't the aggrieved story of the misunderstood or mistreated. I was spoiled with devotion.

My mother, with her fey clairvoyance and oracular readings from the newspaper horoscope, conscripted me to eternal daughterdom: *A son is a son until he takes a wife. A daughter is a daughter all her life.* Remember the note of triumph when she recited that rhyme? And my father's soft brown eyes apologetically radiating weightless decency like vast wealth he wished to settle on me, though, like all wealth, it came freighted with responsibility: *A guy has to do the right thing, no matter what the other guy is doing.*

These allegedly ordinary people in our ordinary town, living faultlessly ordinary lives—and believing themselves to be ordinary—why do I persist in thinking—knowing—they weren't ordinary at all?

What's back there? *Back there,* I say, as if the past were a location, geographic rather than temporal, lost in the recesses of old St. Paul. And how did it become "old St. Paul," the way I habitually think of it now, as if in my lifetime the provincial Midwestern capital had lifted off the planet and become a figment of history, and from there had ceased to exist except as an invention of memory? And all the more potent for that, the way our lives become imaginary when we try most strenuously to make sense of them.

It was a world, old St. Paul. And now it's gone. But I still live in it.

Nostalgia, someone will say. A sneer accompanies the word, meaning that to be fascinated by what is gone and lost is to be easily seduced by sentiment. A shameful undertaking. But nostalgia shares the shame of the other good sins, the way lust is shameful or drink or gluttony, or sloth. It doesn't belong to the desiccated sins of the soul—pride, envy. To the sweet sins of the body, add nostalgia. The sin of memory.

Nostalgia is really a kind of loyalty—also a sin when misapplied, as it so often is. But it's the engine, not the enemy, of history. It feeds on detail, the protein of accuracy. Or maybe nostalgia is a form of longing. It aches for history. In its cloudy wistfulness, nostalgia fuels the spark of significance. My place. My people.

Another old St. Paul way of thinking: Mother talking about her *people*, meaning not the nation, but the clutch of family streaming back to illiterate Kilkenny, her Irish grandfather who wouldn't take up a gun during the Traverse des Sioux "Indian Uprising" (*I couldn't shoot. I played with those boys*), her mother one of "the seven beautiful Smith girls, tall as men," and their one lone brother, feeble-minded, wandering the street with a small tin drum. And he the handsomest of them all. Pity, pity.

Or she would say *my folks*, that mild Midwestern descriptor. My people, my folks, Mother and Dad—M&D in the private patois of the fervent journals I've kept all these years as if I were doing research for a historical novel, forever incomplete because the research keeps proliferating. Until now. Now the research is almost done.

All these scattered bits I've collected that wait patiently, perfectly willing to be ignored, this being St. Paul, this being my folks.

But there's no ignoring it all now. No more clinging to duty in the old world with its humid kitchens and gossipy neighborhoods, its impacted furies and proud silences. Time's up, the wages of daughterhood are almost over. But I'm still stuck, trying to sort out the welter of inner and outer photographs where their faces peer, mute and demanding, from the wedding album, from the piano where I only seemed to be practicing Chopin, gazing back at their mysterious faces that should be the most familiar faces in the world to me.

Nothing is harder to grasp than a relentlessly modest life.

I've done the research. I've got the evidence. Pick any of the notebooks off the shelf—each one covertly turning to dust as old books and old dresses do. Moments, episodes, frustrations, exquisitely rendered injustices, scalpel-sharp character studies that draw a bead of blood along the line of a paragraph—they're packed away in old journals, left in my own airless closet as if swathed in blue tissue paper.

This one from April 1981 will do. She and I are walking past the flower shop downtown. Maybe we were going to stop by to say hello to Dad. I can't remember that and didn't record it. We'd been to lunch at the River Room in Dayton's department store.

I'm already past thirty, but we've been going to the River Room since I was six when she advised, *Order the Russian salad, darling.* The Russian salad had two anchovies laid across it in a limp salty X. *You should know what an anchovy is.* She, too, had an instinct for the Great World where anchovies might be encountered from time to time. In spite of indenturing me (...*a daughter's a daughter*...), she didn't expect I'd be stranded here in this proud Catholic town of fish sticks and "Friday menus" posted at the Grand Avenue restaurants. Without Minneapolis, we read with humiliation, what would we be? A cold Omaha.

But by 1981 even St. Paul had entered the new world order of quiche and croissants. The Russian salad of the Joe McCarthy years was off the menu, taking with it the risky glamour of pinko food. The new Frenchy *cuisine* had no such illicit allure. St. Paul took to it overnight. Glass of wine, too, another nouvelle touch. "Take your mother to lunch," my father said about that time. "She gets lonely." Both of them were starting to "doctor," as Mother said, the beginning of their long endings.

Maybe it was the glass of wine she'd had. Well, two. Maybe her new frailty. Suddenly she was on the sidewalk, had fallen somehow. Just collapsed. She howled in pain, clasped her arm. It was broken. Many bones would break before the end.

In my notebook I reported to myself: *Then she started sobbing, "I wish I were dead, I wish I were dead," right there on the sidewalk. People walked around us. Later, when he came to St. Joe's Hospital where I took her, D looked down and rubbed his bruised knuckle. He hurt it when he'd moved a wedding palm at the greenhouse. I wanted to sob—that he rubbed his knuckle. For her I felt—what did I feel? Nothing, just nothing. That can't be right, to feel nothing when she's crying she wants to die. No, I did feel something, I thought: she's lying, she doesn't want to die. A cold feeling, as if she ought to mean it.*

An ordinary middle-class Midwestern family, in other words. A cozy setting for heartlessness. Work hard, please your customers, believe in decency, make an honest buck, watch love sobbing it wishes it were dead. My father's story, cutting to the chase—the honorable man almost done in by cheats.

My mother's story—my mother's case, I almost said—the furious believer fighting legions of enemies all the way back to Kilkenny. He loses his shirt, she loses her mind.

Such people, modest to a fault, assume they're unremarkable even in their passion, even as they go down in licks of flame. They think they're leaving themselves to silence and forgetting. That's okay, they don't mind. Isn't that what death is, anyway? And isn't that what an ordinary, decent life is?

They expect to be forgotten.

But they aren't forgotten. They're less gone now than they were in their prime. Now that he's gone and she barely lingers, they're everywhere, bits of mica glinting off the Cathedral granite.

From time to time someone asks where I live. "In the shadow of the Cathedral," I say automatically, as if to say "near the Cathedral" wouldn't give the exact location. In the shadow of the Cathedral, the shadow of their long lives.

Six bells, tall as persons, are housed in the massive belfry. They bang out the quarter-hour. On the hour they make a bigger commotion. Living a block away, it's impossible to forget the Cathedral. It's always remarking on itself.

Inside people light candles, mostly by the Blessed Mother's altar. Weekday afternoons, an organ student sometimes gets permission to practice in the choir loft. You can feel the bass notes in your body. Much Bach, some Buxtehude, dogged repetition of difficult phrasing, the complications of a fugue abandoned, a folding chair scraping the stone floor.

Occasionally someone will set up an easel, trying to get on canvas the rose window or the complex perspective of the place. I've seen people settled into the pews as if on a davenport at home, reading novels—Judith Krantz, Elmore Leonard. Here and there, scattered figures kneel, fingers skimming their beads. A few homeless people catnap in prudently chosen side pews.

But in these off-hours most people just stroll through, heads thrown back to take in the astonishing vault of the dome. It's riveted at the compass points with the four principal virtues, spelled out in massive gilt letters as if they held up the entire enterprise: Fortitude, Tolerance, Prudence, Justice. Midwestern virtues, especially the first three. The fourth is what we like to believe we're capable of. Or, the real believers, like my father, think Justice is what life is poised upon, the impenetrable primer coat of existence that protects life from rust and decay, cynicism and greed, the vast uncaring clawing away at human endeavor.

A bronze commemorative plaque is affixed to a pew just below the raised pulpit. In this pew, it reads, sat John F. Kennedy, President of the United States of America, when he attended the eleven o'clock Mass, October 7, 1962. Some of the front center pews still carry small metal nameplates. These are even older, left over from the age of pew rental, my Irish grandfather's era, the pillar who wore in his buttonhole a white carnation that gave off the sharp scent of clove, as he moved up the aisle with the red velvet-lined collection plate on its long wooden handle.

"Of course we couldn't give *that* kind of money," my mother said. "We never had a nameplate." Always eager to assure me of our modesty, our middling safety in the middle of the continent in the middle of the century. *You were born after the War, you're a peace baby,"* she would say, securing my well-being not only in life but in history. She even wanted me to understand that, according to my third-grade teacher, I was neither brilliant nor stupid. "You're in the middle," she said with obvious relief. The best place to be: the middle. No harm done there. That's us: smart enough, middle-class, Midwestern, mid-century—middle everything. Safe, safe, safe.

The preferred pews of the upper classes belong now to nobody. Except to memory, if tarnished metal bearing a name that no longer brings anyone to mind is memory.

Just as they bequeathed themselves to the adored child they made sure to educate out of silence, past their own modesty, the sweet safe middle they clung to and urged upon me as the paradisal place. The place I was determined to escape.

I've long been acquainted with the alien anchovy, and I was already jaded when she could hardly wait to introduce me to the croissant during its debut at the River Room.

It was the beginning of trying to get the story straight, the day she admitted she wished she were dead, the day she revealed to me my cold heart.

Goat

Mrs. Venkataraman had never seen a black man before. There they were in the arrival lounge at Murtala Muhammad Airport, with their coal-black skins and eyes, pawing through their passports, looking for the residence visas her husband's university had obtained for them, shaking their heads and laughing loudly, saying *Eh-hehn Eh-hehn* over and over again. Perhaps they were joking about her and Murthi, her husband. Their loud squeals of laughter reverberated through the folds of her Madras silk sari as she pulled its drapes tighter around her shoulders. *Eh-hehn.* What did it mean? She watched the Nigerians warily, feeling the cracked cement floor through her thin leather chappals, the sweat stains spreading under her arms, and wondered sadly what had made them leave their beloved home in India to come here, to live among these strange noisy people.

They must also seem strange to the Nigerians, she realized, with her limited knowledge of strangeness and otherness. Her husband was a tall thin man, his trousers held up by tan cloth suspenders, his thick black-rimmed glasses perched on his nose, leaning eagerly over the wooden dais towards the immigration official, trying to explain he had come to teach mathematics at the University of Lagos at the invitation of the chancellor himself. He attempted to make himself heard, but the official was thumbing through the pages of her passport, clearly not interested in anything her husband had to say. The man looked at her, and she shrank back a little. What a full face he had, jowly and creased, his eyes hard with suspicion as he noted her alarm. "Who is she?" he boomed. Perspiration broke out on her upper lip; the man could read right there in the passport, see her picture taken only ten days ago at Mr. Murali Sankara's photo shop in Madras. Mrs. Venkataraman—the professor's wife.

Professor Venkataraman blinked behind his heavy glasses as he explained, "My wife. This is my good wife." *Eh-hehn.* The man laughed again. He was scrutinizing her: a short, deep-brown, plump woman encircled in yards of gray and white silk, her hair tied back in a bun, a large red dot in the middle of her forehead. Her chubby hands were pressing into her tummy, the bejeweled fingers interlaced across the sari folds. She was aware of her stern, unsmiling face as she watched him inspect her. Then, to her surprise, he slapped her passport shut and jovially ushered them on. "Welcome to Nigeria," he said.

Mrs. Venkataraman often thought of those first few moments in the country, before they had even set foot in it: how bleak things had seemed, how she had sat in silence all the way from the airport to their home. In the rearview mirror she saw her small puckered walnut-shell of a face, reflecting her inner misery. The university had sent a car to receive them, and as they got out of the airport, the driver turned on the radio. "What is the band?" her husband asked. The driver said it was High-life. Sunny Ade, he said. Mrs. Venkataraman stared at her husband. What business was it of his what music this man was listening to? She was shocked to see him move his shoulders and his head in tune to the rhythm. They had passed a market along the roadside, large black women in bras and wrappers, yelling out the prices of the tomatoes, yams, dried fish, and plastic goods they had displayed in front of them. "Like India," her husband had said, smiling out of the car window. How could he say those women blatantly baring their breasts were like India? And those men, bantering, touching the women up...how could he say *that* was like India? She turned her head away from him and looked rigidly out of the window. Even the very generously laid-out home they had been given by their hosts had failed to cheer her up. She had slid, simply, into a quiet simmer.

At night she slept restlessly, unable to tune out the constant shrieking of Danfo buses on the Apapa-Ilupeju flyover nearby— *peenh peenh,* they went all night—and the deafening chorus of crickets from the swamps at the back of the house. Everything about the place had got on her nerves very quickly—the Hausa night-watch saying his prayers every evening on a rug facing Mecca; the constant tap-tap-tap from noon to three of Baba Lému up in the palm trees, filling his calabashes with the sap for palm wine; the shrieking parrots that flew out of the swamps at the back of the house and attacked the red chilies she had laid out for drying; Mr. Ikkimikki's goats eating her marigolds. Murthi would say only, It is so much like India, especially the south. She disagreed.

She liked the highways, only recently built, and the big new glass buildings that were going up everywhere. It was an oil-rich country, and its wealth showed. Murthi had been to neighboring Ghana, for the University of Accra, too, had been interested in offering him a post, and had paid for a two-week trip for him to go there in order to decide. Though she had not gone with him, she could tell from his lack of enthusiasm that democratic Nigeria had struck him as more vibrant, more the place to be. She had gone along with his decision—Accra, Lagos, or Timbuktu, it was all the same to her.

Mrs. Venkataraman came from a long line of Brahmin priests, her husband from a long line of Sanskrit scholars and academics. One of her husband's forebears had been a world-renowned astrophysicist and had finally ended up at NASA in America. She held on to all their family traditions proudly. But the priestly line she was descended from was her greatest joy. She was a proud Brahmin woman and scrupulously followed every ritual, from being strictly vegetarian to not allowing meat-eaters into their house. And this last was already causing some serious problems.

"Amma, some revision is in order, no?" her husband would plead, trying to cajole her into doing some entertaining at home. "How I am going to keep a good face with all the others, when my wife will not allow them to come to my house? How I can manage in this country if you are so strict?"

But Amma was firm. "You say revision, revision. Little bit here, little bit there... but where will it stop? Think carefully, Murthi. If you pollute your body, everything is finished. We cannot have anything to do with these meat-eaters. You must tell them, no? It is against our religion."

"What?" Murthi Venkataraman glared at her. "What is against our religion?"

"Meat-eaters," she replied, without batting an eyelid.

What is it like over there? her sisters, her aunts asked in letters. What is Africa like? At the first faculty dinner she had attended with Murthi, an Englishman—a longtime resident in Nigeria—had looked at her with his malaria-yellow eyes and said, "Some people come to Lagos to die, some to dream." It had alerted her quickly to the extremes of living in the city, made her even more guarded. Now, locked in a world of her own making, she lacked the words to describe the place. Come to us and see it, she said finally. Come yourself and see.

For two long years no one bothered to come. Then suddenly came a letter from her Guru, a wise young man who lived near Madras. He said that Africa had been very much on his mind. Why? she wondered, frowning as she looked up from the neat typescript. What is there over here that it should be on his mind? She wrote instantly to say he must come and make their home his. Everything was to be at his disposal. She would try to introduce him to some of their African friends, if it was Africans he was wanting. But there are many Indians here, she added, devout Hindus who will await your trip with much anticipation and joy. You can count on a good number of devotees here, she said, thinking of the Reddys, the Srinivasans, the Ramaswamys, the Pillais—conservative Hindus like them and big-hearted. Oh, he would have a fine time with them all. Wildly happy at the thought of seeing his beloved face again, she swore she would obey every command of his, even those she was reluctant to follow. She referred here obliquely to the time he had asked her to get out of her car in Madras and apologize to the washerwoman she had sacked for destroying her new polycotton sheets, which had come all the way from America, a gift from her sister. It had hurt her to bow and scrape before the careless woman, but she had done it for her Guru's sake. Now, too, she said, his wish would be her command.

And for the time he was here, she would try to forget this horrible country, with its inedible food, its beer drinkers, its loud nasty music, its armed robbers, its poisonous snakes and lizards—"we have these in India, too," her husband said. "Ours are not like theirs," she replied. "Ours will not kill you." What about our cobras, he wanted to say, but one look at her face with its deep treacly folds, its sternly pursed lips, and he dropped it.

She prepared for his visit with care. She laid fresh rush matting in his room; she added a layer of foam to the bed, and placed a coverlet she had embroidered herself over it. Uttapam, rasam, coconut chutneys, and raw mango pickles—she stayed up for nights cooking, freezing, and bottling the things she had made so that she could attend wholly to her Guru's needs while he was here.

In some ways, her husband admitted, she had made some concessions to her new life. She had learnt to shop at Jankara Market without his help, haggle with the bra-clad women for better prices, and knew the names of most things. She had picked up the language a little.

"*Oyinbo, oyinbo,*" naked children dancing to music from transistor radios would yell out at her. Foreigner, foreigner. In her madras silk, she went from display to display, the trailing edges of the sari scraping the ground, picking up the red dirt of Lagos, which no amount of washing could get rid of.

"Wish kein paw-paw?" she asked, picking up large orange papayas.

"Na Kano paw-paw," the woman replied, holding one up to her nose. "Hear di smell na. Sweet sweet."

"How much?"

"Na, fifty kobo."

"Eh-hehn," she would say, directing Sunday, the house steward who accompanied her on these jaunts, to place them in her bag. Guavas, beans, okra, tomatoes, all found their way in with a little haggling, a little bantering here and there.

She managed such transactions adequately, but, in her heart of hearts, the people remained strange to her, and she didn't trust their ways.

"Milk no born yet," Sunday announced the morning of the Guru's arrival.

"What?"

"Milk don't go to sleep, now."

"Oh, Sunday," she yelled at him. "How the milk no go sleep?"

Yogurt. Her Guru ate a lot of it, and here was Sunday telling her that it hadn't set yet. She sighed. This country. These people.

He looked small and frail next to the large dashiki-clad Nigerians who came out of the plane with him. She banged on the glass door, trying to get his attention, and when he saw her, he smiled. She took Murthi's arm and went and stood by the door of the arrivals lounge, radiant and smiling happily by the side of her husband.

Some considered him a saint, this man who had converted from Islam to Hinduism. He believed he was an incarnation of Sai Baba, the most revered living saint in Hinduism. He was called to the faith, he said, when asked about his Muslim origins.

People had testified to the many miracles he had performed. Sick children were cured, infertile women got pregnant and delivered healthy babies, and spinsters found spouses. He was a miracle worker, all his followers said. Mr. and Mrs. Venkataraman had been his devotees since he had been "discovered" at the age of eight, a recent convert to Hinduism but already revered as one of the chosen disciples of God. He was now twenty-five, but his demeanor was that of an old sage; he held a saffron-colored shawl close to his chest and walked slowly, hands held before him in blessing.

The immigration officials in the lounge, amid stamping passports and sending arriving passengers on their way, threw curious looks at the saffron-clad man waiting in the queue. At his side was a tall dark woman—her long black hair streaming down her back, her pretty long face partly obscured by the long locks. She was wearing a short black skirt, white fitted jacket, and high heels, like a British Airways airhostess, Mrs. Venkataraman observed. She stared at the woman, immediately suspicious. "Look at the woman," she said to her husband.

"Where?"

She nudged him with her elbow, pointed with her eyes. "You can't see her? There—that giraffe by his side."

"Oh," he said, adjusting his glasses on his nose. "She must be helping him with the papers and all that. He doesn't know about these things."

"Maybe." She watched the woman take his arm and lead him out of the hall.

In a few minutes, the two were outside. Mrs. Venkataraman ran to her Guru and fell at his feet. "Long live Satya Sai Baba," she said. He lifted her up with some difficulty, then accepted the same greeting from her husband. "Come, come," Mrs. Venkataraman said. "The driver will get your luggage."

The Guru said, "I want you to meet Delphine D'Silva. She traveled with me here all the way from Delhi. She is meeting her fiancé. Where is he, my friend?" he asked.

The young woman scanned the visitors' lounge. "He must be here," she said, her eyes peering into the farthest corners of the room.

When her fiancé couldn't be found, the Guru suggested that Delphine go home with them. Mrs. Venkataraman was dismayed. She said, "Guru, I don't have enough—"

"It is not the size of the house but the size of the heart that matters," he pronounced.

Murthi nodded. "We will make room," he said. "Come, let us find your luggage."

The bags loaded into the car, Delphine, Mrs. Venkataraman, and the Guru got in at the back. Murthi sat in the front with the driver.

Mrs. Venkataraman was suddenly silenced by the turn in events. She breathed in the woman's heavy scent and fumed silently. She had planned the evening down to the last detail. She would feed him, bathe him, ring some of their Indian neighbors so they could come to pay their respects. They would sleep early and talk about his plans in the morning over breakfast. She stared at Delphine. What a tall girl she was, a meat-eater without question. Where was she going to put her in their unpolluted home? But she had sworn in her letter to do as her Guru asked. Tomorrow they would clear the house of these undesirable influences with incense and prayer.

Stuck in a go-slow, she looked out of the window. Suddenly Delphine let out a scream, and her hand flew to her mouth. "Oh my God," she said. "Oh my God." They all craned their necks, following her gaze. On the side of the road lay a rotting corpse, stripped of everything but the shoes. "Armed robbers," Murthi said grimly. "This city breeds them like rats, bored young men with guns from the Biafran war. Soldiers, now turned into thugs." A tense silence filled the car. Men in the front seat of the Danfo bus next to their car looked back at them balefully, their eyes reddened from too much kola nut and too little sleep. Trigger-happy men, Mrs. Venkataraman saw, their guns lying across their laps, ready to shoot at the slightest provocation. Her Guru was looking at the men with a bemused expression on his face. *Move*, she prayed, *move now.* Fearfully, she looked away as their car surged forward. As they entered the faculty compound, Murthi announced, "We're nearly home."

"I need a drink," Delphine said.

Delphine D'Silva was not an easy guest. She asked for lime juice, for ice. She produced a bottle of vodka and asked them all to join her. Mrs. Venkataraman wanted to say that no alcohol was allowed in their house, but her Guru was smiling affably at the woman, saying, "You go ahead, child." Child. Mrs. Venkataraman was seething. Then Murthi, seeing that she would be drinking alone, said that he would keep her company.

As he was cracking the ice cubes out of the tray in the kitchen, Mrs. Venkataraman appeared by his side and whispered in his ear, "There is no need to be so hospitable. Think of *him*—drinking in front of him."

Murthi paused for a moment. Then he said, "He would stop me, no, if he wanted. Why do you try to think for everyone else?"

She gave up and went back into the sitting room. Delphine was telling the Guru about her fiancé. She had met him at medical college in Madras, and they had fallen in love. "He is a very good man—he wants to get married, but you can't just get married like that. So I came all the way to see whether we are compatible. You know, it is a long way from my home in Goa. My mother will be very sad to lose me."

The lights suddenly flickered. "We have blackouts here," Murthi was explaining when the electricity suddenly went. "NEPA, don't die," Sunday said loudly, coming in with lit candles and Tiger brand mosquito coils. "Nigerian Electrical Power Authority," Murthi explained.

"Or Never Enough Power Anytime," Mrs. Venkataraman said.

"Ha, ha, that's a good one, Mrs. Venkataraman," Delphine said, her shoulders heaving with laughter. "Very funny." She had taken off her high heels, and her toenails, painted with a frosty white polish, glittered in the candlelit dark. She slapped her palms against her bare calves, brushing off the mosquitoes she killed. Her face was shiny with makeup and sweat. She was like a luminous African bat that had accidentally flown into their home. Mrs. Venkataraman observed her carefully.

When Murthi came in with a refilled glass tinkling with ice, she took it from his hands, saying, "Enough now. Time for sleep." She picked up a candle and led them all up the stairs, the Guru holding on to Delphine's arm, Murthi following behind like a mindful sentry.

The next morning, Delphine was all packed and waiting by the door. "My fiancé is coming for me," she explained to Mrs. Venkataraman. She drank the cup of Madrasi coffee Mrs. Venkataraman offered her but declined her offer of breakfast. Some minutes later, a large blue Mercedes came up to the house, and a tall black man hopped out. "My darling," he said, taking large strides towards Delphine, who ran to him. They all stared—the Guru, Murthi, and Mrs. Venkataraman. It was a while after the two had left that the truth sank in: Delphine D'Silva was going to marry a black man.

He had come to help the African people find peace within themselves, the Guru explained to his number one devotee, Mrs. Venkataraman. I want to reach them, he said. Mrs. Venkataraman said, "But there are many Indians here who are waiting to meet you. They have planned lunches and dinners. Everyone has already booked all the days that you will be here. I don't—"

"Murthi, can you arrange with your university to hire their largest hall?"

Mr. Venkataraman looked at the Guru in shock. "You have come to convert the Nigerians to Hinduism?" he asked.

"I want to tell them about Hinduism," he said. "Our faith is simple and healing for our times."

Murthi looked into the distance; a deep crease had appeared in his forehead, as if he was pondering a difficult mathematical problem. "I respect you with my whole heart," he finally said. "But I don't think this is such a good idea."

But the Guru had decided, and things fell into place immediately. The university agreed to let Murthi have the use of the hall for one evening. With a capacity of a thousand, Murthi wondered where they would find the people to fill up a quarter of the hall. Neither he nor his wife had the skills the Guru needed to advertise the event or to set up private sessions with him for individuals. "You need a secretary," Murthi announced.

Mrs. Venkataraman said, "I was thinking that only this morning. You don't have to worry, I have found her already," she said triumphantly.

"Whom have you found?" the Guru asked, an amused expression on his face.

"Sheela, the Sankarans' daughter. She has come from Kaniyakumari to spend a year here with her parents before the boy she is marrying can come here. She is a very sweet, very devoted girl. She can do all your work for you, so you don't worry," Mrs. Venkataraman said.

"Amma," the Guru said sternly. "Did I ask you to do this for me?"

She stopped and stared at him. "Did I?" he repeated.

"No."

"In future, if I don't ask you to do something for me, you leave me to take care of my own things."

"Yes, Guruji," she said, contrite but puzzled by his sharpness.

"I have found my secretary. She will be reporting for work this afternoon."

"Who is she?" Mrs. Venkataraman asked hesitantly.

"Delphine," the Guru replied. "She and her fiancé, Tony, are helping. He has already told many people about my lecture. He says the hall will be full."

Mrs. Venkataraman backed out of the room, disappointment filling her heart.

Tony Olatunji had printed up fliers, which stated that the holy man from India was a miracle worker. The fliers pictured the Guru's face and contained the headline "Miracle Man" right at the top. All you had to do, the fliers said, was to come and listen to him, and your problems would melt away. They were pasted onto the sides of roadside stalls everywhere. Tony's houseboys had also been busy leafletting shoppers outside the big supermarkets like Leventis, UTC, and Kingsway. They had trotted through Jankara Market, handing them out to curious passersby. "You don't worry," Tony told Murthi. "Your hall will be full."

* * *

The hall was in Apapa, some distance away from Ilupeju, where they lived. There was a long line of cars parked outside the hall hours before the Guru's lecture, and seeing the crowd, Mrs. Venkataraman thought Tony Olatunji's big talk might have something to it. As the Guru came onstage, there was a deafening round of applause. People had gathered in the aisles and at the back of the hall, where they stood three rows deep. The Indian contingent was grouped in one small section of the hall, surrounded by Nigerians of all stripes—Hausas, Ibos, Yorubas, Fulanis, Calabaris, Christians—people with long tribal memories and scores of all kinds to settle. Every time Mrs. Venkataraman turned around to look at the hall, shivers ran down her spine. It seemed to her as if all of Nigeria had come to hear her Guru speak.

He spoke to them in parables that fitted the context of their lives. Of a man who was very kind to his neighbor, and offered him every kind of help, showing him how to grow better yams and raise healthier chickens and goats. One day, the man comes home to find that his prized goat has been stolen. He does not know who has done it, but when his neighbor avoids him, he begins suspecting him of the deed. He begins to hate his neighbor, the very man he had once been happy to have at his table and to break bread with him at his. What can save this man from his hate? the Guru asked. Only tolerance and compassion. He said: When others are not like yourself, and when they do things you don't understand, you are angry and surprised. But you must learn to love them, because only then can you see God. The key, he said, is tolerance and compassion.

At question time, a man from the back raised his hand. "Oga, my friend, a hungry man is a angry man, no bi so? How you go tell a hungry man no make trouble? He no fit listen. His belly trouble am too much."

Someone translated the pidgin. The Guru said, "The hunger of the heart is bigger than the hunger of the belly. If the man punishes his neighbor, then his neighbor will find a reason to punish him again. It will go on and on. And the heart becomes more and more hungry. You must listen to the hunger of the heart before you listen to the hunger of the belly."

Another man raised his hand. "Ifin you do all dis ting, you no can see God," he said, glowering at the Guru.

"You can see God," the Guru claimed, "if you look hard and long enough."

Whether or not they were convinced by his message, all joined him in clapping hands and repeating the lines of bhajans after him. At one point, Mrs. Venkataraman stuffed her pudgy fingers into her ears. The words were heaven, but the noise was deafening. When she looked back, the women in their embroidered wrappers and bubas, the men in their elaborate dashikis and gleaming gold watches, all had risen to their feet, and many were gyrating to the rhythms and clapping their hands. Radhe Krishna, Radhe Krishna, Krishna Krishna, Radhe Radhe. Mrs. Venkataraman, stunned, simply looked on. It was like a dream.

Delphine had effectively taken over. Tony's driver would drop her off in the mornings, and as she came in she would say good morning to Mrs. Venkataraman and make a pretense of lingering, but her eyes were on the staircase that led up to his room. Mrs. Venkataraman watched her go up with hate in her heart. Her gods, her room, her house—and this woman walked in and went up to him as if it was all hers. She fixed a tray of tomato roti, yogurt, a potato vegetable, and a coconut green bean salad. In another stainless-steel container she put skinned, cut slices of apple and mango, and finally set a steel mug of hot tea on the tray. She climbed the steps slowly, for the tray was heavy. She stopped outside his door. Laughter reached her—his high-pitched cackle, her peals. She could barely breathe. She pushed the door open with her bare foot and went inside. He was seated cross-legged on the floor; Delphine was at his side, pressing his feet. Her skirt had risen to an unseemly level up her thighs, and her hair was a little askew. Mrs. Venkataraman placed the tray on the floor and hurried out of the room. What was going on, her pounding heart demanded, what was happening here, under her own roof?

When Delphine left that evening, Mrs. Venkataraman went up, as was her usual custom, to sit with him and meditate for a while. She sat cross-legged on the rush matting, pulling her sari border over her head to cover it in a traditional gesture of respect. He wanted to talk.

"Delphine is getting married," he said.

"Oh?"

"Yes, next week. She and Tony have asked me to marry them. They have invited two hundred people to the reception party afterwards, and they have invited you and Murthi also."

"Will you marry them?" she asked.

He smiled at her knowingly. "Why do you ask?"

"Because they are not Hindus. She is a Christian, and he is—I don't know what he is. Yoruba, I think. They have their own gods," she said, definitively. "Their gods are not like ours," she said.

He nodded his head. "Yes, I thought that would be your answer."

"Will you marry them?" she asked again.

"I will meditate to see what I should do," he said.

"Their party—"

"Yes, what about their party?"

"You cannot go because there will be only goat to eat. The Nigerians do not eat vegetables."

"I see," he said. And that was all.

He did marry them, after all, in a traditional Hindu ceremony. She wore a red sari, he yellow and gold embroidered pants and long tunic and matching headdress. It was a small gathering, and she, Murthi, the Guru, and Delphine were the only Indians in the room. Mrs. Venkataraman heard her Guru recite the familiar Hindu wedding scriptures and nudged her husband. "Nobody here knows what these words mean. Even Tony won't know what the Guru is saying. What kind of a wedding is this?" she whispered to him. He put his finger on his lips and said, "Chup." Shut up. She pursed her lips and looked away.

When the bride walked around a lit fire in a small brazier seven times, and when her sari was tied to his tunic, Mrs. Venkataraman felt as if some sacred and ancient order was being perverted under her eyes.

At the reception party, she sat silently watching the goat being brought in, turned on its spit, roasted at an open fire. The air was filled with the stench of roasting flesh. She held a hanky to her nose. Bottles of Guinness, Heineken, and Johnnie Walker Black sat at each table. Boys darted around, fetching ice and soda, paper plates and forks. There was their strange food: moin-moin, jollof rice, fu-fu, dodo, roasted corn. She ate the corn and drank some Fanta, but touched nothing else. The air thickened, lights grew brighter as the dense African night covered them like a fog. She was watching her husband carefully, for he was displaying an unnatural interest in the goat turning on the spit. If he eats it, I will kill myself, she vowed.

When the dancing began, she asked Murthi to take her home. He wanted to stay, she could see it on his face. But her Guru had taken her aside and told her he was leaving for India the next day. "Delphine and Tony will accompany me back," he said. "They are coming to my ashram for their honeymoon."

Mrs. Venkataraman had a vision of them standing by the open door of the plane, she flanking him on one side, her big black husband on the other, and it was enough to make her feel sick. "Take me home, please," she said to her husband. "Please take me home."

JOYCE CAROL OATES

Hi Howya Doin

Good-looking husky guy six-foot-four in late twenties or early thirties, Caucasian male, as the initial police report will note, he's solid-built as a fire hydrant, carries himself like an athlete, or an ex-athlete just perceptibly thickening at the waist, otherwise in terrific condition like a bronze figure in motion, sinewy arms pumping as he runs, long muscled legs, chiseled-muscled calves, he's hurtling along the moist woodchip path at the western edge of the university arboretum at approximately six p.m., Thursday evening, and there comes, from the other direction, a woman jogger on the path, female in her late thirties, flushed face, down-turned eyes, dark hair threaded with gray like cobwebs, an awkward runner, fleshy lips parted, holds her arms stiff at her sides, in a shrunken pullover shirt with a faded tiger cat on its front, not-large but sizable breasts shaking as she runs, mimicked in the slight shaking of her cheeks, and her hips in carrot-colored sweatpants, this is Madeline Hersey frowning at the woodchip path before her, Madeline's exasperating habit of staring at the ground when she runs, oblivious of the arboretum, though at this time in May it's dazzling with white dogwood, pink dogwood, vivid yellow forsythia, Madeline is a lab technician at Squibb, lost in a labyrinth of her own tangled thoughts (career, lover, lover's "learning disabled" child), startled out of her reverie by the loud aggressive-friendly greeting *Hi! Howya doin!* flung out at her like a playful slap on the buttocks as the tall husky jogger passes Madeline with the most fleeting of glances, big-toothed bemused smile, and Madeline loses her stride, in a faltering voice *Fine— thank you*—but the other jogger is past, unhearing and now on the gravel path behind the university hospital, now on the grassy towpath beside the old canal, in the greenly lushness of University Dells Park where, in the late afternoon, into dusk joggers are running singly and in couples, in groups of three or more, track-team runners from the local high school, college students, white-haired older runners both male and female, to these the husky jogger in

skin-tight mustard-yellow T-shirt, short navy-blue shorts show-
ing his chiseled thigh muscles, size-twelve Nikes calls out *Hi
Howya doin* in a big bland booming voice, *Hi Howya doin* and a
flash of big horsy teeth, long pumping legs, pumping arms, it's his
practice to come up close behind a solitary jogger, a woman
maybe, a girl, or an older man, so many "older" men (forties,
fifties, sixties, and beyond) in the university community, some-
times a younger guy who's sweated through his clothes, beginning
to breathe through his mouth, size-twelve Nikes striking the earth
like mallets, *Hi! Howya doin!* jolting Kyle Lindeman out of
dreamy-sexy thoughts, jolting Michelle Rossley out of snarled
anxious thoughts, there's Diane Hendricks who'd been an athlete
in high school now twenty pounds overweight, divorced, no kid,
replaying in her head a quarrel she'd had with a woman friend,
goddamn she's angry! goddamn she's not going to call Ginny
back, this time! trying to calm her rush of thoughts like churning
roiling water, trying to measure her breaths Zen-fashion, inhale,
exhale, inhale and out of nowhere into this reverie a tall husky
hurtling figure bears down upon her, toward her, veering into her
line of vision, instinctively Diane bears to the right to give him
plenty of room to pass her, hopes this is no one she knows from
work, no one who knows her, trying not to look up at him, tall
guy, husky, must weigh two-twenty, works out, has got to be an
athlete, or ex-athlete, a pang of sexual excitement courses through
her, or is it sexual dread even as *Hi! Howya doin!* rings out loud
and bemused like an elbow in Diane's left breast as the stranger
pounds past her, in his wake an odor of male sweat, acrid-briny
male sweat and an impression of big glistening teeth bared in a
brainless grin or is it a mock-grin, death's-head grin?—thrown
off stride, self-conscious and stumbling, Diane manages to stam-
mer *Fine—I'm fine* as if the stranger brushing past her is interest-
ed in her, or in her well-being, in the slightest, what a fool Diane
is!—yet another day, moist-bright morning in the university dells
along the path beside the seed-stippled lagoon where amorous-
combative male mallard ducks are pursuing female ducks with
much squawking, flapping of wings, and splashing water, there
comes the tall husky jogger, Caucasian male six-foot-four, two-
twenty pounds, no ID as the initial police report will note, on this
occasion the jogger is wearing a skin-tight black Judas Priest T-

shirt, very short white-nylon shorts revealing every surge, ripple, sheen of chiseled thigh muscles, emerging out of a shadowy pathway at the edge of the birch woods to approach Dr. Rausch of the university's geology department, older man, just slightly vain of being "fit," dark-tinted aviator glasses riding the bridge of his perspiring nose, Dr. Rausch panting as he runs, not running so fast as he'd like, rivulets of sweat like melting grease down his back, sides, sweating through his shirt, in baggy khaki shorts to the knee, Dr. Rausch grinding his jaws in thought (departmental budget cuts! his youngest daughter's wrecked marriage! his wife's biopsy next morning at seven a.m., he will drive her to the medical center and wait for her, return her home and yet somehow get to the tenure committee meeting he's chairing at eleven a.m.) when *Hi! Howya doin!* jolts Dr. Rausch as if the husky jogger in the black Judas Priest T-shirt has extended a playful size-twelve foot into Dr. Rausch's path to trip him, suddenly he's thrown off-stride, poor old guy, hasn't always been sixty-four years old, sunken-chested, skinny white legs sprouting individual hairs like wires, hard little pot belly straining at the unbelted waistline of the khaki shorts, Dr. Rausch looks up squinting, is this someone he knows? should know? who knows *him*? across the vertiginous span of thirty years in the geology department Dr. Rausch has had so many students, but before he can see who this is, or make a panting effort to reply in the quick-casual way of youthful joggers, the husky jogger has passed by Dr. Rausch without a second glance, legs like pistons of muscle, shimmering sweat-film like a halo about his body, fair-brown, russet-brown hair in curls like wood shavings lifting halo-like from his large uplifted head, big toothy smile, large broad nose made for deep breathing, enormous dark nostrils that look as if thumbs have been shoved into them, soon again this shimmering male figure appears on the far side of the dells, another afternoon on the Institute grounds, hard-pounding feet, muscled arms pumping, on this day a navy blue T-shirt faded from numerous launderings, another time the very short navy-blue shorts, as he runs he exudes a yeasty body odor, sighting a solitary male jogger ahead he quickens his pace to overtake him, guy in his early twenties, university student, no athlete, about five-eight, skinny guy, running with some effort, breathing through his mouth, and in his head a swirl of numerals, symbols, equations, quantum optics, quantum noise, into this reverie *Hi! Howya doin* is like a firecracker tossed by a prankish kid, snappishly the younger jogger replies *I'm okay* as his face flushes, how like high school, junior high kids pushing him around, in that instant he's remembering, almost now limping, lost the stride, now life seems pointless, you know it's pointless, you live, you die, look how his grandfather died, what's the point, there is none, as next day, next week, late Friday afternoon of the final week in May along the canal towpath past Linden Road where there are fewer joggers looming up suddenly in your line of vision, approaching you, a tall husky male jogger running in the center of the path, instinctively you bear to the right, instinctively you turn your gaze downward, no eye contact on the towpath, you've been lost in thought, coils of thought like electric currents burning-hot, scalding-hot, the very pain, anguish, futility of your thoughts, for what is your soul but your thoughts, upright flame cupped between your hands silently pleading *Don't speak to me, respect my privacy please* even as the oncoming jogger continues to approach, in the center of the path, inexorably, unstoppably, curly hairs on his arms shimmering with a bronze-roseate glow, big teeth bared in a smile *Hi! Howya doing!* loud and bland and booming mock-friendly, and out of the pocket of your nylon jacket you fumble to remove the snub-nosed, twenty-two-caliber Smith & Wesson revolver you'd stolen from your stepfather's lodge in Jackson Hole, Wyoming, three years before, hateful of the old drunk asshole you'd waited for him to ask if you'd taken it, were you the one to take his gun that's unlicensed, and your stepfather never asked, and you never told, and you lift the toy-like gun in a hand trembling with excitement, with trepidation, with anticipation, aim at the face looming at you like a balloon-face up close and fire and the bullet leaps like magic from the toy-weapon with unexpected force and short-range accuracy and enters the face at the forehead directly above the big-nostriled nose, in an instant the husky jogger in the mustard-yellow T-shirt drops to his knees on the path, already the mustard-yellow T-shirt is splashed with blood, on his belly now and brawny arms outspread, face flattened against the path fallen silent and limp as a cloth puppet when the puppeteer has lost interest and dropped the puppet, he's dead, *That's how I'm doin.*

Cherries

There's mercy in the decades as they pass,
reducing years of ache to a single afternoon
beneath a cherry tree in a terraced garden:
the cherries seem to ripen while we gaze,
darkening as sunlight starts to fade.
You're talking; I'm waiting for you to realize
what you won't admit for another decade:
love is not a word I wouldn't use
you'll say once I've had daughters, you, a son.
Now there's another decade gone
and I have yet to hear of love
without some qualifier, some double negative.
Perhaps I've stifled it? It's getting late;
no sign of ripeness, just failing light.

The Asexual Reproduction of Ferns

This is my father bent like a Michelangelo prophet
over a tray of spore, showing me how
to pour boiling water over the soil
to eradicate fungi, etc.
I stand beside him ignoring his lecture.
Instead watch steam from his coffee cup curl
into the blue of the tubular daylight bulbs.

This is my brother in our empty school car park
crouched like Stig of the Dump
over the cradled engine of his '61 Chevy
on wet afternoons. "Tinkering," he calls it:
I call it, "Catching a cold."
Soon I'll learn all about his innards
from some old anatomy chart
and frighten him with gall bladders
and chambers in the heart.

The men in my family are squeamish
about softness in themselves.
But they scoff sausages and chops and steaks
briskly like huskies.

And when I was small I had them
carry me up mountains.
Summers they'd grapple with bracken
to make me a bed with the skylarks.
Winters they'd pull me for miles across snow
bound like a baby Inuit
they knew they must never eat.

SUE OWEN

A House Sparrow

Sometimes I've wondered why
it seems happy enough.
It hangs around like a meek
reminder of smallness,

and chirps its slight sound,
and flashes its dull brown,
in the vague green of summer.
And it must think that

there in the spread of leaf,
where it pauses on a branch,
it is hardly ever noticed,
which is almost true.

But today as I stare at it
and think of all things small,
the dust, flies, and stars,
the house sparrow's hopping

seems to matter as one
small detail that is always
there to prove a larger point,
one addition to the day.

And it must like to belong
there with the wind and sun.
It must somehow know
it is important and that

itself must make it glad
to go on and sing for us,
against the sky, that one
repeated syllable of its note.

The Van

In the van we are as corks in water, bobbing, filled with air.
Earplugs jam up my ears with the simple fact that a secret music
    illuminates
the window-better from my side of the inside seat, crammed
up against a housewife, cow-like from Des Moines with wads
of Kleenex in her fist, arriving with Broadway tickets, a scar in
    her heart.
She says we can stop at the hospital first, as the young lovers
from San Francisco unburden themselves of additional gravity
by linking mouths opened to each other. I've jet-hopped here
like a woman on burning sand with bare feet, having jolted up in
    the morning
to minister to my dying mother who does not believe in dying.
All of us passengers bounce, up down up down,
wedged and resectioned in air like a cancerous lung made clean,
balloon-like and full of memory, our very living actions.
The lack of suspension cures us of our various human maladies
as we huddle together on this fair ride down the Long Island
    Expressway.
The East Indian driver proselytizes to us with his grip and jerk of
    the wheel,
a sort of prayer wheel as it cuts, swerves, swears in tongues as if to
    exorcize
us of that mortal willpower we each hold so tightly like our bags,
we clutch it like desire. Our feeble wills, floating and descending,
    orbs
in space. All of us give over to it, we are thrusting into New York,
which begins to emerge on the left side of the van like a heaven
we've all been traveling toward, stripped of all control, we dream
of beds, restrooms, loved ones, lunch, different lives
waiting there for us, the ones we know or the ones we've yet to meet.
The van's buoyancy and lift propulsion understands romantic
    love, the redemption

of fate. We haven't crossed the city line, gone up York Avenue
toward the opulent garden of the cancer ward where people
become trellises of their bodies' own hatred, yet
still the skyline beckons us as we feel the lift and letdown
of a hill, just as we did as children. I can't help but see
what's missing in the skyline, the holding spaces,
the enigma that I drive toward that settles no doubt but makes
    me see
the rumble and movement that propels me to something beyond
    this city
into the darkening of question of who will survive, how we
    mingle
and bump not only into each other but this feeling of air
that wants to astound us and lovingly lift us apart
until we are sick to our stomachs and dizzy
and say we have done it out of duty, yes, but also
a love of travel. There are no shock absorbers, we're resigned to
    that now,
and determined, albeit sickly, and can imagine no other way.

The Failed Trick

The white mouse went first, pink eyes, pink feet,
then the ace of hearts, the quarter and half-dollar,
    the pigeon, the cat,
once the dog, who didn't howl for a good hour,
    wherever he was,
our old man's hands faster than our eyes
as we lined up on the picnic table seat
to watch him toss the black cape on whatever
    came into range,
once getting our mother under that dark,
her blue bathrobe and red lips, the pink rollers
sticking out at all angles with twirls of hair,
    while he waved his hands above her,
chanting words we'd never understand,
    and then the tap of the wand,
the side of the box flipped up, flipped down
    to show her still doubled over,
looking at us to see if we could see her
under the clothesline sagged with underwear,
    socks, shirts, and pants
she would soon enough have to unclip and fold
    in the blue basket,
our mother touching her arms and legs to make sure
    she was all there,
uncoiling slowly in the sun with both feet on the ground
where she walked in one great circle around us
    without a word
before disappearing into the shadowed door of the house.

Three Lanterns

There's our son at the end of my hook
    riding over the Detroit River

where Tecumseh's still rowing
    towards his oblivion.

This boy we're casting to the land
    of the leaping frogs.

My lass lives on the floor
    where the fish are frying,

her spine snapped in half
    the way a Milky Way might.

She squares her thumbs and fingers together,
    frames for our son

a picture window to climb through.
    *

Eighteen months with us
    and our dark-skinned son

still has pockets sewn over his clothes.
    They're filled with stones

that keep a boy underwater,
    his vowels bubbling up to us.

With our brooms and hockey sticks,
    we're swatting away

city streetlights that followed him here,
 those bulbs that bow

and peck at his back.

 *

My love's trying to stop the chiming,
 her fingers so singular

since that one dark bell
 is ringing again in her neck.

I hollow this house while she sleeps,
 take my time and chisel

the proper curve so our canoe
 cuts easy through rough water.

My lass is a sweet tomahawk
 for the scalping

of moons and runaway boys.

 *

We press four hands over our son's
 mouth when he sleeps

so his body blows up and floats.
 We nail our stakes in the yard

to keep him
 tethered to this world.

See how he splashes
 in summer when he knocks

his mouth against moon water.
 See how we paint with one finger

bright horses across his ribs,
    and rivers on the outside

streaming down his arms.
    *

Sometimes we sketch with smoke
    a door just over

that rock in our boy's chest. You can hear it
    rusty when he knocks

on our bedroom door. We take the scent
    that falls from him—

baby powder, gun powder—into our skulls
    because we live in an empty house,

and in each bedroom there's a bell
    ringing under the covers

where a child might live.
    *

We sledge the stake in our yard,
    then let the line out slowly

until our son's way up there
    where the moon makes

a lovely mess of him.
    When my wife and I

are overwhelmed with this,
    we beat our skulls upon the moon,

and it empties over the earth.
    I tell you, when we kiss,

even the little bell in my love's neck
   jingles, it rhythms,

it makes a lovely sound.

Telephone Call

Put your pain on one side,
it is unwelcome tonight,
we have guests,
dinner is to be served,
the pain must wait.
I am sorry, do not be angry,
do not hate, put your pain away
for a more convenient day.
The telephone rang with need,
your hurt was huge,
it was not unrecognized,
but pain must know its place.
The food is ready, the wine just poured,
please understand your pain
was not ignored. It just arrived
as other guests waited to be heard.

PHILIP SCHULTZ

Specimen

I turned sixty in Paris last year.
We stayed at the Lutetia,
where the Gestapo headquartered
during the war, my wife, two boys, and me,
and several old Vietnamese ladies
carrying poodles with diamond collars.

Once my father caught a man
stealing cigarettes out of one
of his vending machines.
He didn't stop choking him
until the pool hall stunk of excrement,
and the body dropped to the floor
like a judgment.

When I was last in Paris,
I was dirt-poor, hiding
from the Vietnam War.
One night, in an old church,
I considered taking my life.
I didn't know how to be so young
and not belong anywhere, stuck
among so many perplexing melodies.

I loved the low white buildings,
the ingratiating colors, the ancient light.
We couldn't afford such luxury.
It was a matter of pride.
My father died bankrupt one week
before his sixtieth birthday.
I didn't expect to have a family;
I didn't expect happiness.

At the Lutetia everyone
dressed themselves like specimens
they'd loved all their lives.
Everyone floated down
red velvet hallways
like scintillating music
you hear only once or twice.

Driving home, my father said,
"Let anyone steal from you
and you're not fit to live."
I sat there, sliced by traffic lights,
not belonging to what he said.
I belonged to a scintillating
and perplexing music
I didn't expect to hear.

Guide for the Perplexed

The bedroom slippers' silk linings.
The dressing gown of brocade, stitched with the zodiac.
The pajamas underneath also made out of silk,
for which how many individuals of the species *B. mori,*
having munched the succulent, pale-green mulberry leaves
and insinuated a sack wherein to magnify themselves,
were steamed to death from the inside out?
The delicate fibers are intact.
He feels their ripeness on his skin.
He listens deeply into the night, which listens back.
The birch log pops in the fireplace.
The fetishes brood on the mantelpiece.
The ice melts in the gin.
And yellower and deeper than dandelion yellow,
yellower and stronger than Moroccan yellow,
the color, almost, of a yellow marigold, is
the yellow silk kimono she wears to greet the floating world.
Moths on the wing clutter the starlight.
Ghosts of dead moths are on the windowpane and
knee-deep in the ballroom,
in social clubs and places of worship.
They are proof, if anyone still needs proof, that
awesome are the powers of humankind,
who have taken this selfsame moth
and endowed it with a gene from the jellyfish
so as to produce fluorescent silk!
And all in the interests of beauty!
(I shall spare you, by the way,
my exhaustive researches into the history
of the Silk Road.)

JASON SHINDER

Hospital

While the machine sucks the black suds

from my mother's blood and then sends it back
stinking clean into the pistol-tube nailed down

into her chest, I climb out of my shoes and slip

a cotton swab of water between her teeth,
her dentures sliding off the back porch

of her mouth. Nobody knows, never knows,

how she has to pee, wrapped in a diaper.
But can't. The yellow eggs she ate one hour ago

already the shit in her bowels. And lonely,

head-hanging-from-the-balcony-of-her-body lonely,
darkest-passage-from-the-hairless-vagina lonely.

But brave. But lonely. Because I did not stay all night.

Because I won't. Because I'm going to pull out
the one bone that hurts her the most and break the back

of every word I ever said to her. The world is evil, Mother,

and I am, too.

Under the Pergola

An Adirondack chair, painted in a primary color,
in one corner, under the pergola, the blooming vine
appealing above—people an abundance
of themselves, prodigal in sunglasses, in the shade.

Will I speak to him, and if so, do I call him
"Mr. Secretary"? He groans into his chair,
opens the *Times,* reads, then glances at me,
and I stare over the edge of my Asian novel.

Many years after the war he speed-walked
through the streets of Hanoi in his jogging suit,
then around the Lake of the Restored Sword.
Nine years ago, but now he struggles atop his cane.

Between my life, wedged in this chair,
and the stories offered to explain
both that life and the pastoral freedom
packaged with the chair, there is a chasm.

There is a chasm between what I know
of the body and the nerveless force of history,
between the partial replies of ancient minds
and conclusions of quartermasters and cover girls.

Anything to fill that desolate space.
This is why we follow a man who describes
what seems to be occurring in the plosive world,
who paints the face of evil on a three-minute egg.

The old man's wife sits in the third chair,
the nurse dozes in the fourth corner. "Bobby,

come sit *here,* in the shady corner," and so he lifts
himself up painfully, shuffles across, and sags

with a wailing sound. Nine years ago,
before meeting with his former enemies,
he walked around the Lake of the Restored Sword—
where the fisherman Le Loi long ago found

a magical sword in his net, swung it three times
above his head, and led his people to throw
the Chinese out of Vietnam. When he returned
to thank the spirit of the lake, a giant tortoise

made off with the sword. The Emperor Le Loi
stared into the depths of the lake, two passive eyes
returned his gaze, during the liquid hour of peace,
and the weeks of warm memories of war.

ANN SNODGRASS

As Nooteboom Would Have It

Basho neither trusted nor distrusted the reeds.

He was simply a poet on the way north.
And being on the way north, he could choose

to ignore them. That sound, after all—

wind through them—was not the voice
of a master. If there had been

a master once, he was gone.

Ah, to have loved what turquoise waves
erase—to find beneath a pebble beach's pain.

And to go on. In the distance

are the "cherry blossoms of Yoshino."
In the distance.

As for travel, it just means being

where one may never be again.
Often for the first time, too.

So Basho may have gone north

in search of the departed
that still had not been named.

Unnamed, it left no tracks or memory.

Ah, to love what turquoise waves erase.
There are secrets, as a poet, a man keeps.

We know so little of him really.

What has vanished still exists as the vanished.
But when he passed, he passed forever.

SUSAN STEWART

Black Walnut

There's a kind of leaving when you arrive
even though it's the place you've come from—
how love can be alive

There, though not for you, and while it's like none
of the first feelings, a recognition of what is passing
flashes, itself passing—there were more deaths, but now there's
  only one,

And what you are learning will be lasting,
you already know. Even so, it's hard to tell
how long the feeling will be gone before it comes again, tasting

Like regret. Too late, too far, waiting, expecting, the certainty fell
"with a thud," you said—like the walnuts too hard
for bothering. Come down to earth, she said, so many things to sell

To want, to buy, coming down and going on, a yard
of this or that stored up, sometimes you'd say it was too much
  trouble
to remember, and of course there was the guard

Of conscience and the border of the heart itself, an edge so subtle
it only evoked a limit you'd rather forget.
Expecting, waiting, she expected you and you expected so little

In return and then there was even less. You had your heart set
on a meaning, a catch or harvest. The green
leaves came and went, came and went, wet

Then yellow in the black rains. Do you remember that other
  yellow, yellow-green

hull, the shell stonier than any stone,
and inside, the dark nut, so bitter it seemed to have gleaned

All the bitterness of the world—you nurtured it there in the dark
    while the sun shone
every summer day, and other children laughed and ran in the
    fields,
and you waited in the kitchen, puzzled, puzzling, why was it
    yours alone?

DAN STRYK

Reading the Torah

Sometimes in the fading winter light
    that streaks my desk by six o'clock
        revealing grains in aging oak, like desert

sands, I imagine, before leaving my
    shelved books to laze with those I love
        before the easy flicker of some talk show

on TV, that I stay back *this time,*
    forgetting them, to light my taper, blend
        in secrecy into the holy night, and *there*

pick one small passage from the plush-
    bound, dog-eared book that's gathered
        dust for years since settling, by chance,

upon my shelf, remnant of vague whispers
    of my family's Hebraic past—pick that
        isolated passage meant for me, which

grasped, would lead me like those fallen
    flakes of manna—cleansing sweetness
        on the spirit and the tongue—to Jobean

acceptance of my lethargy, late evening's
    mix of daily love and pain, the wish
        to be, and not to be, or wrestling life's

angel, suddenly exalt myself, for once
    and all released, ascend the dusty
        ladder of my life into a greater bliss.

Neglect

translated by Clare Cavanagh and Stanislaw Baranczak

I misbehaved in the cosmos yesterday,
a day and night without a single question,
surprised by nothing.

I performed my ordinary chores,
as if nothing more were required.

Inhale, exhale, step by step, tasks and errands,
and not a single thought beyond
setting out and getting home again.

The world might have been taken for insane,
but I took it for daily use only.

Not a single what or wherefore,
and how it got that way,
and why it needs so many restless details.

I was like a nail hammered too flat against the wall
or
(insert comparison I couldn't find)

One change slipped by after another,
even within the blinking of an eye.

Yesterday's bread standing on a younger table
sliced differently with a hand younger by a day.

Unprecedented clouds producing unprecedented rain,
since it fell with different drops.

The earth rotated on its axis
but in a space that's passed forever.

This all took a good 24 hours.
A 1,440-minute occasion.
86,400 seconds for inspection.

The cosmic savoir-vivre,
although it's silent on our subject,
still makes its demands on us:

a little attention, a few phrases from Pascal,
some stunned participation in a game
whose rules remain unknown.

DANIEL TOBIN

Fall Day

after Rilke

It's time, Lord. The summer was so immense.
Now on the sundials your shadows stretch their lengths
And across the meadows you release the winds.

Command the last fruits to swell with life,
Grant them still a few days of florid sun,
Press them to completion, and like a hunter
Chase the fleeting sweetness into full-bodied wine.

Whoever has none now will never have a home,
Whoever is alone now will grow lonelier,
Will grow sleepless, reading, scribbling ponderous notes,
And will wander back and forth along the avenues
Restlessly, among the leaves dry and driven.

DAVID   WAGONER

Night Song from the Apartment Below

The argument begins. One voice is overcoming
another because it's had it, it's had enough
of all this shit and, unaccompanied, rises
to the edge of screaming and past it
till the column of air in that throat has nearly abandoned
everything under it. Only the vault of the forehead
and the bridge of the nose are left to resonate.

An abrupt pause. A brief intermission.

Lotte Lehmann, who knew all there was to know
about singing, said in the upper register
one should always have two notes in reserve
which one never uses.
                              And now the second voice
comes lurching up and out of the dungeon
beneath the memory of the other, from as deep
as the torture chamber of the diaphragm,
offering to surrender everything
imaginable, hope, wine, money, love,
credit cards, even the need to be touched.

In the following silence, the long silence,
those of us already lying down
in our own forms of darkness are listening
in the name of mercy for the next wrong note.

He Won't Go to Sleep Without Me

I like to say. I must like to; I say it all the time, leaving
parties early, acting put-upon. My little boy sucks blood
out of my social life, friendships draining like my hopes
to pitch for the Yankees, or find important fossils in my yard.

Still, I love knowing my son won't let sleep's towel
cover his head until he hears my tiptoed footsteps,
throws open his door, and squawks, "Daddy! Hug!"
Non-parents may think he's a Mars-sized ball-&-chain—

a tackler like Mean Joe Green rattling my brains each time
I try to throw a pass—a bungee that, just as I'm set
to plunge into some cool pool of adult delight, yanks me
back to the *Teletubby* night. Jim Sweet described kids

that way as we fished, up to our onions in trout stream.
His girlfriend, Jan, laughed—high and clear as a coloratura,
frank as two dogs in the street. On their first date,
when a broken high heel dumped her on the floor,

she laughed so hard she peed, then couldn't stand,
since her dress hid the evidence, which made her laugh
and pee some more. She must have loved that story;
she told it all the time, laughing as Jim steamed. Her bathroom

humor no more fit Jim's image of *wife* than his image
of *life* held trusted friends. He'd get suspicious of me,
stay away for weeks, then show up with a book
on steelheading I had to see. "I've never trusted anyone

as much as you," he said so often, he must have liked to say it.
Wading the Skagit one day, I slipped and current

caught me. Two guys had drowned in the same place,
the same way: their waders filled and dragged them down.

But Jim shoved his new rod at me. "Grab on!"
he yelled. I cracked the rod, but it deflected me enough
to let Jim drag me, half-frozen, to shore.
Another time, at Lenice Lake, a rattler slid across our path.

"Let's go," I said when only slither-marks remained.
Out bulled the secret Jim had kept penned up for years:
"I'm scared of snakes." Big Jim, who'd flown army
choppers, couldn't step where the rattler had been.

So, piggyback, the way Dad used to carry me,
I carried him. Afraid-of-nothing Jim. Never-trust-
anybody Jim Sweet trusted me—then, afterwards,
was certain I'd tell everyone. After he married Jan

and had a little girl, he moved away, wrote once,
and stopped. I think of him when I piggyback my son
to bed: all that hope and trust and life riding
                                                    on me.

GEORGE WITTE

Does She Have a Name?

The intern's wand assayed your abdomen
with wavelengths   sounding the nocturnal pool
she swam within   pale cave dweller   tipped down
to pass between existences   asleep
forehead globed beneath her body's question
There she is   Everything's okay   except
the blood   a sudden flux enriched your gown
tear in the placental wall   *Nothing wrong*
the intern said   no sign of fetal stress
no reason to disturb the resident
who slept until his presence was required
your labor quickened   *Progressing nicely*
the intern mumbled under breath   then left
you to progress   bleeding out   unaware
how close death brushed   our cells a poisoned fruit
the cure expulsion or delivery
whatever's first   the monitors conferred
in secret tongues   regarding fetal heart
and lungs   the intern strode in   discomposed
by mystery   her printout bucketing
you felt the urge to urinate   sat up
and at that moment the placenta ripped
abrupted   peeled away   the intern burst
your sac to fix a lead into her skull
your water gushed rust brown   the lead relayed
a thready beat that flickered out   flatlined
one nurse slammed a hand against the desk call
She's going brady get him in here now
and so the resident emerged   blinking
in fluorescence   confused   torn raw from dream's
nutritious tissue   she drowned inside you
while he scrubbed   counting minutes to himself
the anesthesia pulled you under   *Now*

he cut   digging through your ravaged garden
then lifted her   our daughter   limp and blue
while you lay gutted   sewn in senselessness
the NICU team convened its ministry
a laying on of hands and oxygen
revived her from baptism into breath
one asked me for her name   to humanize
the sum of their procedure   revenant
in limbo   comatose   alive   *Helen*

VALERIE WOHLFELD

Poppies

Clashing paper umbrellas of red
and orange. The fur of the moth's eye-
spot centered: wind shakes the poppy, and the poppy shakes the head
of the pod shapely as Egyptian skull, bone-dry.

Spliced spore, sap and milk: tiny black seeds
seamed inside; like the pocket walls' little wooden veins
holding the paper umbrellas up. Every cocktail cherry bleeds,
stemmed, swirled, colors real as unreal rains

glassed in grenadine. Drowned pulp, poppy petals
never color-fast; meant for show: quickly red
abandons the poppy, and the flesh mummifies the shell's
seeded Pharaonic head. The living, the dead,

grow side by side in every soil-bed. Breath comes cheap
to Morpheus as to the ancient poppies' silent shackled sleep.

KEVIN YOUNG

Ode to Greens

You are never what you seem.
Like barbeque, you tell me time
doesn't matter, that all
things wait. You take long
as it takes. Wife
to worry, you can sit
forever, stewing, grown
angrier by the hour.
Like ribs you are better
the day after, when all
is forgiven. Death's daughter,
you are often cross—bitter
as mustard, sweet
when collared—yet no one
can make you lose
all your cool, what strength
you started with. Mama's
boy, medicine woman,
you tell me things end
far from where
they begin, that forgiven
is not always forgotten.
One day the waters will part.
One day my heart will stop & still
you'll be here dark
green as heaven.

ADAM ZAGAJEWSKI

Kantor

translated by Clare Cavanagh

He dressed in black,
like a clerk at an insurance bureau
who specializes in lost causes.
I'd spot him on Urzednicza
rushing for a streetcar,
and at Krzysztofory as he solemnly discharged
his duties, receiving other artists dressed in black.
I dismissed him with the pride
of someone who's done nothing himself
and despises the flaws of finished things.
Much later, though,
I saw *The Dead Class* and other plays,
and fell silent with fear and admiration—
I witnessed systematic dying,
decline, I saw how time
works on us, time stitched into clothes or rags,
into the face's slipping features, I saw
the work of tears and laughter, the gnashing of teeth,
I saw boredom and yearning at work, and how
prayer might live in us, if we would let it,
what blowhard military marches really are,
what killing is, and smiling,
and what wars are, seen or unseen, just or not,
what it means to be a Jew, a German, or
a Pole, or maybe just human,
why the elderly are childish,
and children dwell in aging bodies
on a high floor with no elevator and try
to tell us something, let us know, but it's useless,
in vain they wave gray handkerchiefs
stretching from their school desks cut with penknives
—they already know that they have only

the countless ways of letting go,
the pathos of helpless smiles,
the innumerable ways of taking leave,
and they don't even hear the dirty stage sets
singing with them, singing shyly
and perhaps ascending into heaven.

Pleasure Boating in Lituya Bay

Two and a half weeks after I was born, on July 9th, 1958, the plates that make up the Fairweather Range in the Alaskan panhandle apparently slipped twenty-one feet on either side of the Fairweather fault, the northern end of a major league instability that runs the length of North America. The thinking now is that the southwest side and bottom of the inlets at the head of Lituya Bay jolted upwards and to the northwest, and the northeast shore and head of the bay jolted downward and to the southeast. One way or the other, the result registered 8.3 on the Richter scale.

The bay is T-shaped and seven miles long and two wide, and according to those who were there it went from a glassy smoothness to a full churn, a giant's Jacuzzi. Mountains twelve to fifteen thousand feet high next to it twisted into themselves and lurched in contrary directions. In Juneau, a hundred and twenty-two miles to the southeast, people who'd turned in early were pitched from their beds. The shock waves wiped out bottom-dwelling marine life throughout the panhandle. In Seattle, a thousand miles away, the University of Washington's seismograph needle was jarred completely off its graph. And meanwhile, back at the head of the bay, a spur of mountain and glacier the size of a half-mile-wide city park—forty million cubic yards in volume—broke off and dropped three thousand feet down the northeast cliff into the water.

This is all by way of saying that it was one of the greatest spasms, when it came to the release of destructive energy, in recorded history. It happened around 10:16 p.m. At that latitude and time of year, still light out. There were three small boats, carrying six people, anchored in the south end of the bay.

The rumbling from the earthquake generated vibrations that the occupants of the boats could feel on their skin like electric shock. The impact of the rockfall that followed made a sound like Canada exploding. There were two women, three men, and a seven-year-old boy in the three boats. They looked up to see a wave breaking *over* the seventeen-hundred-foot-high southwest edge of Gilbert Inlet and heading for the opposite slope. What they were looking at was the largest wave ever recorded by human beings. It scythed off three-hundred-year-old pines and cedars and spruce, some of them with trunks three or four feet thick, along a trimline of 1,720 feet. That's a wave crest five hundred feet higher than the Empire State Building.

Fill your bathtub. Hold a football at shoulder height and drop it into the water. Imagine the height of the tub above the water-line to be two thousand feet. Scale the height of the initial splash up, appropriately.

When I was two years old, my mother decided she'd had enough of my father and hunted down an old high school girl-friend who'd wandered so far west that she'd taken a job teaching in a grammar school in Hawaii. The school was in a little town called Pepeekeo. All of this was told to me later by my mother's older sister. My mother and I moved in with the friend, who lived in a little beach cottage on the north shore of the island near an old mill, Pepeekeo Mill. We were about twelve miles north of Hilo. This was in 1960.

The friend's name was Chuck. Her real name was Charlotte something, but everyone apparently called her Chuck. My aunt had a photo she showed me of me playing in the sand with some breakers in the background. I'm wearing something that looks like overalls put on backwards. Chuck's drinking beer from a can.

And one morning Chuck woke my mother and me up and asked if we wanted to see a tidal wave. I don't remember any of this. I was in pajamas and my mother put a robe on me and we trotted down the beach and looked around the point to the north. I told my mother I was scared and she said we'd go back to the house if the water got too high. We saw the ocean suck itself out to sea smoothly and quietly, and the muck of the sand and some flipping and turning white-bellied fish that had been left behind. Then we saw it come back, without any surf or real noise, like the tide coming in in time-lapse photography. It came past the high tide mark and just up to our toes. Then it receded again. "Some wave," my mother told me. She lifted me up so I could see the end of it. Some older boys who lived on Mamalahoa Highway sprinted past us, chasing the water. They got way out, the mud spraying up behind their heels. And the water came back again, this time even smaller. The boys, as far out as they were, were still only up to their waists. We could hear how happy they were. Chuck told us the show was over and we headed up the beach to the house. My mother wanted me to walk but I wanted her to carry me. We heard a noise and when we looked we saw the third wave. It was already the size of the lighthouse out at Wailea. They got me into the cottage and halfway up the stairs to the second floor when the walls blew in. My mother managed to slide me onto a corner of the roof that was spinning half a foot above the water. Chuck went under and didn't come up again. My mother was carried out to sea, still hanging on to me and the roof chunk. She'd broken her hip and bitten through her lower lip. We were picked up later that day by a little boat near Honohina.

She was never the same after that, my aunt told me. This was maybe by way of explaining why I'd been put up for adoption a few months later. My mother had gone to teach somewhere in Alaska. Somewhere away from the coast, my aunt added with a smile. She pretended she didn't know exactly where. I'd been left with the Franciscan Sisters at the Catholic orphanage in Kahili. On the day of my graduation from the orphanage school, one of the sisters who'd taken an interest in me grabbed me by both shoulders and shook me and said, "What is it you *want*? What's the *matter* with you?" They weren't bad questions, as far as I was concerned.

I saw my aunt that once, the year before college. My fiancée, many years later, asked if we were going to invite her to the wedding, and then later that night said, "I guess you're not going to answer, huh?"

Who decides when the time's right to have kids? Who decides how many kids to have? Who decides how they're going to be brought up? Who decides when the parents are going to stop having sex, and stop listening to one another? Who decides when everyone's not just going to walk out on everyone else? These are all group decisions. Mutual decisions. Decisions that a couple makes *in consultation with one another.*

I'm stressing that because it doesn't always work that way.

My wife's goal-oriented. Sometimes I can see on her face her *To Do* list when she looks at me. It makes me think she doesn't want me anymore, and the idea is so paralyzing and maddening that I lose track of myself: I just step in place and forget where I am for a minute or two. "What're you doing?" she asked once, outside a restaurant.

And of course I can't tell her. Because then what do I do with whatever follows?

We have one kid, Donald, named for the single greatest man my wife has ever known. That would be her father. Donald's seven. When he's in a good mood he finds me in the house and wraps his arms around me, his chin on my hip. When he's in a bad mood I have to turn off the TV to get him to answer. He has a good arm and good hand-eye coordination but he gets easily frustrated. "Who's *that* sound like?" my wife always says when I point it out.

He loses everything. He loses stuff even if you physically put it in his hands when he's on his way home. Gloves, hats, knapsacks, lunch money, a bicycle, homework, pencils, pens, his dog, his friends, his way. Sometimes he doesn't worry about it; sometimes he's distraught. If he starts out not worrying about it, sometimes I make him distraught. When I tell these stories, I'm Mr. Glass Half Empty. Which is all by way of getting around to what my wife calls the central subject, which is my ingratitude. Do I always have to start with the negatives? Don't I think he *knows* when I always talk about him that way?

"She says you're too harsh," is the way my father-in-law put it. At the time he was sitting on my front porch and sucking down my beer. He said he thought of it as a kind of mean-spiritedness.

I had no comeback for him at the time. "You weren't very nice to my parents," my wife mentioned when they left.

Friends commiserate with her on the phone.

My father-in-law's a circuit court judge. I run a seaplane charter out of Ketchikan. Wild Wings Aviation. My wife snorts when I answer the phone that way. My father-in-law tells her, who knows, maybe I'll make a go of it. And if the thing does go under, I can always fly geologists around for one of the energy companies.

Even knowing what I make, he says that.

Number one on her *To Do* list is another kid. She says Donald very much wants a little brother. I haven't really heard him address the subject. She wants to know what *I* want. She asks with her mouth set, like she's already figured the odds that I'm going to let her down. It makes me what she calls unresponsive.

She's been after me about it for a year, now. And two months ago, after three straight days of our being polite to one another— Good morning. How'd you sleep?—and avoiding brushing even shoulders when passing through doorways, I made an appointment with a Dr. Calvin at Bartlett Regional about a vasectomy. "Normally, couples come in together," he told me at the initial consult.

"This whole thing's been pretty hard on her," I told him.

Apparently it's an outpatient thing, and if I opt for the simpler procedure I could be out of his office and home in forty-five minutes. He quoted me a thousand dollars, but not much out of pocket, because our health insurance should cover most of it. I was told to go off and give it some thought and get back in touch if and when I was ready to schedule it. I called back two days later and scheduled it for the day before Memorial Day. "That'll give you some time to rest up afterwards," the girl who did the scheduling pointed out.

"He *had* a pretty big trauma when he was a baby," my wife reminded her mom a few weeks ago. They didn't realize I was at the kitchen window. "A couple of traumas, actually." She said it like she understood that it was going to be a perennial on her *To Do* list.

So for the last two months I've gone around the house like a demolition expert who's already wired the entire thing to blow and keeps rechecking the charges and connections.

It was actually flying some geologists around that got me going on Lituya Bay in the first place. I flew in a couple of guys from ExxonMobil who taught me more than I wanted to know about Tertiary rocks and why they always got people salivating when it came to what they called petroleum investigations. But one of the guys also told the story of what happened there in 1958. He was the one who didn't want to camp in the bay. His buddy made serious fun of him. The next time I flew them in I'd done my research, and we talked about what a crazy place it was. I was staying overnight with them, because they could pay for it, and they had to be out at like dawn the next morning.

However you measure things like that, it has to be one of the most dangerous bodies of water on earth. It feels freakish even when you first see it. It's a tidal inlet that's hugely deep—I think at its center it's seven hundred feet—but at its entrance there's barely enough draft for a small boat. So at high and low tides the water moves through the bottleneck like a blast from a fire hose. That twilight we watched a piece of driftwood *keep up* with a tern that was gliding with the wind. The whole bay is huge but the entrance is only eighty yards wide and broken up by boulders. Stuff coming in on the high tide might as well be on the world's largest water slide. And when the tide running out hits the ocean swells, it's as if surf's up on the North Shore of Hawaii from both directions at once. We were two hundred yards away and had to shout over the noise. The Frenchman who discovered the bay lost twenty-one men and three boats at the entrance. The Tlingits lost so many people over the course of their time there that they named it *Channel of the Water-Eyes,* "water eyes" being their word for the drowned.

But the scared guy had me motor him up to the head of the bay and showed me the other problem, the one I'd already read about: as he put it, stupefyingly large and highly fractured rocks standing at vertiginous angles over deep water in an active fault zone. On top of that, their having absorbed heavy rainfall and constant freezing and thawing. The earthquakes on this fault were as violent as anywhere else in the world, and they'd be shaking unstable cliffs over a deep and tightly enclosed body of water.

"Yeah yeah yeah," his buddy said, passing around beef jerky from the back seat. I was putt-putting the seaplane back and forth as our water taxi at the top of the T. Forested cliffs went straight up five to six thousand feet all around us. I don't even know how trees that size grew like that.

"You have any kids?" the scared guy asked, out of nowhere. I said yeah. He said he did, too, and started hunting up a photo.

"Well, what's a body to do when millions of tons avalanche into it?" his buddy in the back asked.

The scared guy couldn't find the photo. He made a face at his wallet, like what else was new. "Make waves," he said. "Gi-nor-mous waves."

While we crossed from shore to shore they pointed out some of the trimlines I'd read about. The lines went back as far as the middle of the 1800's. The experts figure the dates by cutting down trees and looking at the growth rings. The lines look like rows of plantings in a field, except we're talking about fifty-degree slopes and trees eighty to ninety feet high. There are five lines, and their heights are the heights of the waves. One from 1854 at three hundred and ninety-five feet. One twenty years later at eighty feet. One twenty-five years after that at two hundred feet. One from 1936 at four hundred and ninety feet. And one from 1958 at 1,720 feet.

That's five events in the last hundred years, or one every twenty. It's not hard to do the math, in terms of whether or not the bay's currently overdue.

In fact, that night we did the math, after lights-out in our little three-man tent. The scared guy's buddy was skeptical. He was still eating, having moved on to something called Moose Munch. We could hear the rustling of the bag and the crunching in the dark. He said that given that the waves occurred every twenty years, the odds of one occurring on any single day in the bay were about eight thousand to one. There was a plunk down by the shore when something jumped. After we were quiet for a minute, he joked, "That's one of the first signs."

The odds were way smaller than that, the scared guy finally answered. He asked his buddy to think about how much unstable slope they'd already seen from the air. All of that had been exposed by the last wave. And it had now been exposed almost fifty years, he said. There were open fractures that were already visible.

So what did *he* think the odds were? his buddy wanted to know.

Double digits, the scared guy said. The low double digits.

"If I thought they were in the double digits, I wouldn't be here," his buddy said.

"Yeah, well," the scared guy said. "What about you?" he asked me. It took me a minute to realize it, since we were lying in the dark.

"What about me?" I said.

"You ever notice anything out here?" he asked. "Any evidence of recent rockfalls or slides? Changes in the gravel deltas at the feet of the glaciers?"

"I only get out here once a year, if that," I told him. "It's not a big destination for people." I started going over in my head what I remembered, which was nothing.

"That's 'cause they're smart," the scared guy said.

"That's 'cause there's nothing here," his buddy answered.

"Well, there's a reason for that," the scared guy said. He told us he'd come across two censuses of the Tlingit tribes living in the bay from when the Russians owned the area. The populations had been listed as two hundred and forty-one in 1853 and zero a year later.

"Good night," his buddy told him.

"Good night," the scared guy said.

"What was that? You feel that?" his buddy asked him.

"Aw, shut up," the scared guy said.

What's this thing about putting people to *use*? What's that all about? What happened to just loving being *around* someone? Once I got Donald up off his butt and made him throw the base-ball around with me, and asked that out loud. I only knew I'd done it when he said, "*I* don't know." Then he asked if we could quit now.

"Did you ever really think you'd find someone that you weren't in some ways cynical about?" my wife asked the night we'd decided we were in love. I was flying for somebody else and we were lying under the wing of the Piper that we'd run up onto a beach. I'd been God's lonely man for however many years—twelve in the orphanage, four in high school, four in college, a hundred after that—and she was someone that I wanted to pour myself down into. I was having trouble communicating how unusual that was.

That morning she'd watched me load a family I didn't like into a twin-engine and I'd done this shoulder shake I do before something unpleasant. And she'd caught me, and her expression had given me a lift that carried me through the afternoon. That night back in my room she made a list of other things I did or thought, any one of which was proof she paid more attention than anyone else ever had. She held parts of me like she had never seen anything so beautiful. At three or four in the morning she used her arms to tent herself up over me and asked, "Don't we have to sleep?" and then answered her own question.

Around noon we woke up spooning and when I held on when she tried to head to the bathroom, we slid down the sheets to the floor. She finally lost me by crawling on all fours to the bathroom door.

"Well, she's as happy as *I've* ever seen her," her father told me at the rehearsal dinner. Twenty-three people had been invited and twenty-one were her family and friends.

"It's *so nice* to see her like this," her mother told me at the same dinner.

When I toasted her, she teared up. When she toasted me, she said only, "I never thought I would feel like this," and then sat down.

We honeymooned in San Francisco. Here's what that was like for me: I still root for that city's teams.

I've always been interested in the unprecedented. I just never got to experience it that often.

Her family is Juneau society, to the extent that such a thing exists. One brother's the arts editor for the *Juneau Empire;* another works for Bauer & Gates Real Estate, selling half-million-dollar wilderness vacation homes to second-tier Hollywood stars. Another, go figure, is a lawyer. On holidays they give each other things like Arctic Cats. Happy Birthday: here's a new 650 4 x 4. The real estate brother was 11–1 as a starter and team MVP for JDHS the year they won the State Finals. The parents serve on every board there is. Their daughter when she turned sixteen was named Queen of the Spring Salmon Derby. She still has the tiara with the leaping sockeye.

They didn't stand in the way of our romance. That's what her dad told anyone who asked. Our wedding announcement said that the bride-elect was the daughter of Donald and Nila Bell and that she'd graduated from the University of Alaska summa cum laude and was a first-year account executive for Sitka Communications Systems. It said that the groom-elect was a meat cutter for the Super Bear supermarket. I'd done that before I'd gotten my pilot's license, when I'd first gotten to town, and the guy doing the article had fucked up.

"You don't think he could have *checked* something like that?" my wife wanted to know after she saw the paper. She was so upset on my behalf that I couldn't really complain.

It's not like I never had any advantages. I got a full ride, or nearly a full ride, at St. Mary's in Moraga, near Oakland. I liked science and what math I took, though I never really, as one teacher put it, found myself while I was there. A friend offered me a summer job as one of his family's set-net fishermen my junior year, and I liked it enough to go back. The friend's family got me some supermarket work to tide me over in the winter, and it turned out that meat cutting paid more than boning fish. "What do you *want* to do?" a girl at the checkout asked me one day, like if she heard me bitch about it once more she was going to pull all her hair out, and that afternoon I signed up at Fly Alaska and Bigfoot Air, and I got my commercial and multi-engine, and two years later had my float rating. I hooked on with a local outfit and the year after that bought the business, which meant a three-room hut with a stove, a van, the name, and the client list. Now I lease two 206's and two 172's on EDO 2130 floats, have two other pilots working under me, and get fourteen to fifteen hundred dollars a load for roundtrip flights in the area. Want an Arctic Cat? I can buy one out of petty cash. At least in the high season.

"So are we not going to talk about this?" my wife asked last week after her parents had been over for dinner. We'd had crab and her dad had been in a funk for most of the night, who knew why. We'd said good night and handled the cleanup and now I was lunging around on my knees trying to cover my son in nerf basketball. He always turned into Game Fanatic at bedtime. We'd hung a nerf hoop over the inside of the back door to accommodate that need. He took advantage of my distraction to try and drive the baseline but I funneled him into the doorknob.

"I'm ready to talk," I told her. "Let's talk."

She sat on one of the kitchen chairs with her hands together on her knees, willing to wait. Her hair wasn't having the best day and it was bothering her. She kept slipping it back behind her ear.

"You can't just stay around the basket," Donald complained, trying to lure me out so he could blow by me. He was a little teary with frustration.

"I was going to talk to Daddy about having another baby," she told him. His mind was pretty intensively elsewhere.

"Do you *want* a baby brother?" she asked.

"Not right now," he said.

"If you're not having fun, you shouldn't play," she told him.

That night in bed she was lying on her back with her hands behind her head. "I love you a lot," she said, when I finally got under the covers next to her. "But sometimes you just make it so hard."

"What do I do?" I asked her. This was one of the many times I could have told her. I could have even just told her I'd been thinking about making the initial appointment. "What do I do?" I asked again. I sounded mad but I wanted to know.

"What do you do," she said, like I had just proven her point.

"I think about you all the time," I said. "I feel like *you're* losing interest in *me*." Even saying that much was humiliating. The appointment at times like that seemed like a small but hard thing that I could hold on to.

She cleared her throat and pulled a hand from behind her head and wiped her eyes with it.

"I hate making you sad," I told her.

"I hate being made sad," she said.

It was only when she said things like that and I had to deal with it that I realized how much I depended on having made her happy. And how much all of that shook when she whacked at it. *Tell her,* I thought, with enough intensity that I thought she might've heard me.

"I don't *want* another kid," Donald called from his room. The panel doors in our bedrooms weren't great, in terms of privacy.

"Go to sleep," his mother called back.

We lay there waiting for him to go back to sleep. *Tell her you changed your mind,* I thought. *Tell her you want to make a kid, right now. Show her.* I had a hand on her thigh and she had her palm cupped over my crotch, as if that, at least, was on her side. "Shh," she said, and reached her other hand to my forehead and smoothed away my hair.

Set-net fishermen mostly work for families that hold the fishing permits and leases, which are not easy to get. The families sell during the season to vendors who buy fish along the beach. The season runs from mid-June to late July. We fished at Coffee Point on Bristol Bay. Two people lived there: a three-hundred-pound white guy and his mail-order bride. The bride was from the Philippines and didn't seem to know what had hit her. Nobody could pronounce her name. The town nearest the Point had a phone book that was a single mimeographed sheet with thirty-two names and numbers on it. The road signs were hand-painted, but it had a liquor store and a grocery store and a superhardened airstrip that looked capable of landing 747's, because the bigger companies had started figuring out how much money there was in shipping mass quantities of flash-frozen salmon.

We strung fifty-foot nets perpendicular to the shore just south of the King Salmon River, cork floats on top, lead weights on the bottom, and pickers like me rubber-rafted our way along the cork floats, hauling in a little net, freeing the salmon's snagged gills, and filling the raft at our feet. When we had enough we paddled ashore and emptied the rafts and started all over again.

Everybody knew what they were doing but me. And in that water with that much protective gear, people drowned when things went wrong. Learning the ropes meant figuring out what the real fishermen wanted, and the real fishermen never said boo. It was like I was in the land of the deaf and dumb and a million messages were going by. Someone might squint at me, or give me a look, and I'd give him a look back, and finally someone else would say to me, "That's too *tight*." It was nice training on how you could get in the way even when your help was essential.

How could you *do* such a thing if you love her so much? I think to myself with some regularity, lying there in bed. Well, that's the question, isn't it? is usually my next thought. "What's the day before Memorial Day circled for?" my wife asked a week ago, standing near our kitchen calendar. Memorial Day at that point stood two weeks off. The whole extended family would be showing up at Don and Nila's for a cookout. I'd probably be a little hobbled when it came to the annual volleyball game.

"Should you even *have* kids? Should you even have a wife?" my wife asked, once, after our first real fight. I'd taken a charter all the way up to Dry Bay and had stayed a couple of extra nights and hadn't called. I hadn't even called in to the office. She'd been beside herself with worry and then with anger. I'd told her to call me back before I'd left and then when she hadn't, I'd been like, Okay, if you don't want to talk, you don't want to talk. I'd left my cellphone off. *That* I'm not supposed to do. The office even thought about calling Air-Sea Rescue.

"Bad move, chief," even Doris, our girl working the phones, told me when I got back.

"So I'm wondering if I should go back to work," my wife tells me today. We're eating something she whipped up in her new wok. It's an off day—nothing scheduled until tomorrow, except some maintenance paperwork—and I was slow getting out of the house and she invited me to lunch. She was distracted during the rinsing the greens part, and every bite reminds me of a trip to the beach. She must notice the grit. She hates stuff like that more than I do.

"They still need someone to help out with the online accounts," she says. She has an expression like every single thing today has gone wrong.

"Do you want to go back to work?" I ask her. "Do you miss it?"

"I don't know if I *miss* it," she says. She adds something in a lower voice that I can't hear because of the crunch of the grit. She seems bothered that I don't respond.

"I think it's more, you know, if we're not going to do the other thing," she says. "Have the baby." She keeps herself from looking away, as if she wants to make clear that I'm not the only one humiliated by talks like this.

I push some spinach around and she pushes some spinach around. "I feel like first we need to talk about us," I finally tell her. I put my fork down and she puts her fork down.

"All right," she says. She turns both her palms up and raises her eyebrows, like: *Here I am.*

One time she came and found me at two o'clock in the afternoon in one of the hangars and turned me around by the shoulders and pinned me to one of the workstations with her kiss. A plane two hangars down warmed up, taxied over, and took off while we kissed. She kissed me the way lost people must act when they find water in the desert.

"Do you think about me the way you used to think about me?" I ask her.

She gives me a look. "How did I used to think about you?" she wants to know.

There aren't any particular ways of describing it that occur to me. I imagine myself saying with a pitiful voice, "Remember that time in the hangar?"

She looks at me, waiting. Lately that look has had a quality to it. One time in Ketchikan one of my pilots and me saw a drunk who'd spilled his Seven and Seven on the bar lapping some of it up off the wood. *That* look: the look we gave each other.

This is ridiculous. I rub my eyes.

"Is this taxing for you?" she wants to know, and her impatience makes me madder, too.

"No, it isn't taxing for me," I tell her.

She gets up and dumps her dish in the sink and goes down the cellar. I can hear her rooting around in our big meat freezer for a popsicle for dessert.

The phone rings and I don't get up. The answering machine takes over and Dr. Calvin's office leaves a message reminding me about my Friday appointment. The machine switches off. I don't get to it before my wife comes back upstairs.

She unwraps her popsicle and slides it into her mouth. It's grape.

"You want one?" she asks.

"No," I tell her. I put my hands on the table and off again. They're not staying still. It's like they're about to go off.

"I should've asked when I was down there," she tells me.

She slurps on it a little, quietly. I push my plate away.

"You going to the doctor?" she says.

Outside a big terrier that's new to me is taking a dump near our hibachi. He's moving forward in little steps while he's doing it. "Goddamn," I say to myself. I sound like someone who's come home from a twelve-hour shift and still has to shovel his driveway.

"What's wrong with Moser?" she wants to know. Moser's our regular doctor.

"That was Moser," I tell her. "That was his office."

"It was?" she says.

"Yes, it was," I tell her.

"Put your dish in the sink," she reminds me. I put the dish in the sink and head into the living room and drop onto the couch.

"Checkup?" she calls from the kitchen.

"Pilot physical," I tell her. All she has to do is play the message.

She wanders into the living room without the popsicle. Her lips are darker from it. She waits a minute near the couch and then drops down next to me. She leans forward, looking at me, and then leans into me. Her lips touch mine, and press, and then lift off and stay so close it's hard to know if they're touching or not. Mine are still moist from hers.

"Come upstairs," she whispers. "Come upstairs and show me what you're worried about." She puts three fingers on my erection and rides them along it until she stops on my belly.

"I love you so much," I tell her. That much is true.

"Come upstairs and show me," she tells me back.

That night in 1958 undersea communications cables from Anchorage to Seattle went dead. Boats at sea recorded a shocking hammering on their hulls. In Ketchikan and Anchorage, people ran into the streets. In Juneau, streetlights toppled and breakfronts emptied their contents. The eastern shore of Disenchantment Bay lifted itself forty-two feet out of the sea, the dead barnacles still visible there, impossibly high up on the rock faces. And at Yakutat, a postmaster in a skiff happened to be watching a cannery operator and his wife pick strawberries on a sandy point near a harbor navigation light, and the entire point with the light pitched into the air and then flushed itself as though driven underwater. The postmaster barely stayed in his skiff, and paddling around the whirlpools and junk waves afterwards, found only the woman's hat.

"You know, I made some sacrifices here," my wife mentions to me later that same day. We're naked and both on the floor on our backs but our feet are still up on the bed. One of hers is twisted in the sheets. The room seems darker and I don't know if that's a change in the weather or we've just been here forever. One of our kisses was such a submersion that when we finally stopped we needed to lie still for a minute, holding on to each other, to recover.

JIM SHEPARD

"You mean as in having married me?" I ask her. Our skin is air-drying but still mostly sticky.

"I mean as in having married you," she says. Then she pulls her foot free of the sheets and rolls over me.

She told me as she was first easing me down onto the bed that she'd gone off the pill but that it was going to take at least a few weeks before she'd be ready. "So you know why I'm doing this?" she asked. She slid both thighs across me, her mouth at my ear. "I'm doing this because it's *amazing*."

We're still sticky and she's looking down into my face with her most serious expression. "I mean, you're a meat cutter," she says, fitting me inside of her again. The next time we do this, I'll have had the operation. And despite everything, it's still the most amazing feeling of closeness.

"Why are you *crying*?" she whispers. Then she whispers, lowering her mouth to mine, "Shhh. Shhh."

Howard Ulrich and his little boy, Sonny, entered Lituya Bay at eight the night of the wave, and anchored on the south shore near the entrance. He wrote about it afterwards. Their fishing boat had a high bow, a single mast, and a pilothouse the size of a Port-o-San. Before they turned in, two other boats had followed them in and anchored even nearer the entrance. It was totally quiet. The water was a pane of glass from shore to shore. Small icebergs seemed to just sit in place. The gulls and terns that they usually saw circling Cenotaph Island in the middle of the bay were hunkered down on the shore. Sonny said it looked like they were waiting for something. His dad tucked him in bed just about ten, around sunset. He'd just climbed in himself when the boat started pitching and jerking against its anchor chain. He ran up on deck in his underwear and saw the mountains heaving themselves around and avalanching. Clouds of snow and rocks shot up high into the air. He said it looked like they were being shelled. Sonny came up on deck in his PJs, which had alternating wagon wheels and square-knotted ropes. He rubbed his eyes. Ninety million tons of rock dropped into Gilbert Inlet as a unit. The sonic concussion of the rock hitting the water knocked them both onto their backs on the deck.

It took the wave about two and a half minutes to cover the seven miles to their boat. In that time Sonny's dad tried to weigh anchor and discovered that he couldn't, the anchor stuck fast, so he let out the anchor chain as far as he could, anyway, got a life preserver onto Sonny, and managed to turn his bow into the wave. As it passed Cenotaph Island it was still over a hundred feet high and extending from shore to shore, a wave front two miles wide.

The front was unbelievably steep and when it hit, the anchor chain snapped immediately, whipping around the pilothouse and smashing the windows. The boat arrowed seventy-five feet up into the curl like they were climbing in an elevator. Their backs impacted the pilothouse wall like they'd been tilted back in barber's chairs. The wave's face was a wall of green taking them up into the sky. They were carried high over the south shore. Sixty-foot trees down below disappeared. Then they were pitched up over the crest and down the back slope, and the backwash spun them off again into the center of the bay.

Another couple, the Swansons, had also turned into the wave and had had their boat surfboard a quarter mile out to sea, and when the wave crest broke, the boat pitch-poled and hit bottom. They managed to find and float their emergency skiff in the debris afterwards. The third couple, the Wagners, tried to make a run for the harbor entrance and were never seen again.

Four-foot-wide trees were washed away, along with the topsoil and everything else. Slopes were washed down to bedrock. Bigger trunks were snapped off at ground level. Trees at the edge of the trimline had their bark removed by the water pressure.

Sonny's dad was still in his underwear, teeth chattering, and Sonny was washing around on his side in some icy bilge water, making noises like a jungle bird. The sun was down by this point. Backwash and wavelets twenty feet high were crisscrossing the bay, spinning house-sized chunks of glacier ice that collided against each other. Clean-peeled tree trunks like pickup sticks knitted and upended, pitching and rolling. Water was still pouring down the slopes on both sides of the bay. The smell was like they were face-down in the dirt under an upended tree. And Sonny's dad said that that time afterwards—when they'd realized that they'd survived, but still had to navigate through everything pinballing around them in the dark to get out of the bay—was worse than riding the wave itself.

A day or two later the geologists started arriving. No one believed the height of the wave at first. People thought that the devastation that high on the slopes had to have been caused by landslides. But they came around.

My wife fell asleep beside me, wrapped over me to keep me warm. We're still on the floor and now it really is dark. We've got to be late in terms of picking up Donald from his playdate, but if his friend's parents called, I didn't hear the phone.

One of my professors at St. Mary's had this habit of finishing each class with four or five questions, none of which anyone could answer. It was a class called The Philosophy of Life. I got a C. If I took it now, I'd do even worse. I'd sit there hoping he wouldn't see me and try not to let my mouth hang open while he fired off the questions. What makes us threaten the things we want most? What makes us so devoted to the comfort of the inadvertent? What makes us unwilling to gamble on the non-cataclysmic?

Sonny's dad was famous for a while, telling stories for magazines like *Alaska Sportsman* and *Reader's Digest* with titles like "My Night of Terror." I read one or two of them to Donald, which my wife didn't like. "Do *you* like these stories?" he asked me that night. In the stories, Sonny's mom never gets mentioned. Whether she was mad or dead or divorced or proud never comes up. In one Sonny's dad talks about having jammed a life preserver over Sonny's head and then having forgotten about him entirely. In another he says something like, in that minute before it all happened, he'd never felt so alone. I imagine Sonny reading that a year or two later and going, Thanks, Dad. I imagine him looking at his dad later on, at times when his dad doesn't know he's watching, and thinking of all that his dad gave him and of all that he didn't. I imagine him never really figuring out what came between them. I imagine years later people saying about him that that was the thing about Sonny: the kid was just like the old man.

Dressing Up

"Just in time for cocktails!" our mother's mother, Gran, says, obviously exasperated, coming to meet us out on the drive. We were supposed to be there for lunch. Now, dressed in her cocktail clothes—white pants, a silk smock, gold shoes, and jewelry—after perfunctory kisses hello (she's irritated) and the quickest sizing up of our mother's boyfriend extricating himself from the car (he's enormous, dwarfing our grandmother, covered with hair), she's already heading back to the house. "I have a guest!" she says. Her step's a little wobbly. She places her feet somewhat far apart. "He's rich!" she calls over her shoulder. "Recently divorced!"

Our mother, her eyes already more squinted than usual, busies herself unloading the bags. We four kids pile out of the car. Clyde reels around on the pavement, his sweaty hair plastered to his face. He's been sleeping. Lu has a headache because she's been trying to read. She presses her palm to the side of her head. Tuck and I have been playing bloody knuckles. We both have one very sore hand. Each hauling a suitcase, we straggle inside.

We visit our grandmother twice a year, once in winter, once in summer. This is our summer visit, mid-July. Our grandmother's house on Long Island is flat, one level, with red-tiled floors, and divided into adult and children's quarters. In the children's quarters are two bedrooms furnished with twin or bunk beds, above which hang sets of engravings of white men chasing Indians or the reverse. Lu and I, the oldest, always take the room with the twin beds covered with blue-and-white-striped bedcovers, while Tuck and Clyde are in the bunk beds.

For cocktails at our grandmother's we always have to dress. This is by far the fanciest event in our lives. Lu and I open our suitcases and take out our best clothes. Our mother always brings her dress-up clothes, too, but they're still hippie clothes. With our grandmother, she's forever between obedience and rebellion. Is our mother's boyfriend, Chester, going to change? We've never seen him wearing anything but what he has on now, blue jeans, a

T-shirt, and lace-up boots. He keeps his hair in a ponytail. We first saw him speaking at anti-nuclear rallies, where they introduced him as Dr. Kemp. Even now when we hear him talking, his low full voice coming out of his beard, it sounds like he's speaking into a microphone.

I put on my dress and sandals. Lu does, too. We look at ourselves in the mirror. As always, we're worried that our grandmother will find us dirty or without manners or not dressed right.

There's a step up into the part of the house where the adults reign, the dining room, with its gleaming appointments, the living room, the bedrooms further back. The kitchen is hidden away, shunned, like in a restaurant. We never go there. Cocktails are served in the living room. Everything is slick and polished, the cocktail table, the cocktail tray. Our grandmother doesn't own particularly valuable things. What she can't abide by are nicks and stains. Anything nicked or stained is quickly thrown away. Two porcelain elephants stand by the fireplace. Through the living room windows, you can look out and see the swimming pool, shaped like a kidney. To one side of the pool is a dog kennel filled with spotted hunting dogs.

Kneeling on the floor, dressed in our fancy clothes, we gobble down all the hors d'oeuvres, scallops wrapped in bacon, tiny sausages in rolls, shrimp dipped in cocktail sauce, clams on the half shell.

"My Gawd!" our grandmother says, in her mid-Atlantic drawl, having looked away and then back to find the plates empty. She, as usual, is horrified at our appetites.

Our mother and her boyfriend sit on the couch. Our mother wears an Indian dress with fringes on it. Chester has put on a button-down shirt. He's not a drinker but a pot smoker—he grows his own plants—but he's taken a gin and tonic all the same. Our mother has one, too. Suddenly, after admiring our grandmother's slender gold cocktail shoes, I glance down and see our mother's feet, her toenails full of dirt from working in the garden. I look up quickly at our grandmother's face. Has she seen?

Our grandmother lights a cigarette.

"Alec was a star athlete at Princeton," she says, referring to her guest.

Alec laughs. He has a straight, perfectly shaped nose. He's debonair, just what our grandmother likes, a man who drinks cocktails, wears clean, pressed clothes, combs his pressed wet-looking hair back from his forehead. "You put the left-hand shot in the right-hand corner," he says.

Our mother's squinted gaze is just polite. Of course we know that she'd never like this man, not in a million years. But our grandmother doesn't see it.

Chester leans forward, taking a long abrupt sip of the drink he doesn't want.

This gives me an idea. "Gran," I say, when she gets back, "can we have Shirley Temples?" She's the person who introduced us to Shirley Temples.

"Of course, darling. Alec, fix the children Shirley Temples."

Alec gets up quickly to oblige.

"We were just talking about the Jockey Club when you arrived, Faye," our grandmother says. "It seems your old beau Roger has been trying to get in."

"Of course we didn't let him," Alec says. The cocktail tray has wheels. He's standing in front of it, back turned, fixing our drinks.

"Why not?" our mother asks.

"Well," Alec says, turning, "to start with he's an activist."

"An activist?" our mother says. She laughs. "Since when is Roger an activist?" She turns to Chester. "You should see this guy."

"Oh, that's right," Alec says, as if mildly embarrassed, addressing Chester. "Because you, I understand, are the real thing."

Chester smiles, dryly amused.

"Chester also does research," our mother says. "He's a radiation chemist." It's not clear what she means, where she's heading with this. She looks irritated, distracted, as if she herself doesn't know what she wants.

"Oh, really? What sort of research?" Alec asks, distributing the Shirley Temples. I eat my cherry right away. Lu dunks hers, turning her whole glass rosy.

"Radiation tests. We study the effects of radiation, even low-level radiation, on thyroid function and mental development. The results are indisputable, not to mention the higher rates of infant mortality, miscarriages, and deaths by cancer in areas surrounding a nuclear power plant."

"Gawd." Our grandmother finds anything to do with study or the academic life profoundly boring. She holds out her glass to Alec. Her drink is a bullshot, beef broth, Worcestershire sauce, vodka, and lime. Alec's drinking the same. Still at the bar, he refreshes both their glasses.

"We're not even talking about accidents here," Chester goes on. "That's a whole other story. But of course it's all covered up. The figures the government was spouting following the Three Mile Island meltdown were way off."

"They left," our grandmother says to Alec, the judgment clear but unspoken behind the words. "Faye took the children out of school."

It was actually Chester who came in the middle of the day to take us out of school. He said there had been an accident at a nuclear power plant not far away and we had to get out of there fast. At home, our mother told us to pack a few things we really loved, because we might not ever come back to this house again.

"Why wouldn't we?" Lu asked. She was wearing by chance that day her "Stop Nuclear Power" T-shirt.

"Because," our mother said, "we don't know what's going to happen. We'll just have to see."

I couldn't think of what to bring. I looked through the things I had—my terrarium? my cactus plants? I packed some polished rocks. They didn't take much room. I could hold all four of them in the palm of my hand.

It was a hasty departure. Within an hour we were gone.

"Hold your breath," Lu said, as we were going out to the car.

"Why?" I asked.

"Because the air's poisonous now."

I held my breath between the front door and the car.

We drove south with our mother. Chester, not trusting the official meters, stayed behind to take radiation readings downwind of the plant. He would join us when he was done. The landscape was unfamiliar, Maryland, green horse pastures, white fences, Virginia. As we drove, we kept the radio on for news of the accident.

"Why aren't the other kids at school leaving, too?" Tuck asked.

"Because they don't know," our mother said. "Nobody knows

the truth. The government always lies about these things." From the driver's seat, she turned away, then back. "But everything might also be just fine."

We drove all day. By nightfall, we had made it as far as Tennessee. We stopped in a little town at the base of the Blue Ridge Mountains, checked into a motel, and went to a restaurant to eat. In the restaurant, there was a row of deer heads with full antlers over the bar.

We all slept in one room in the motel, our mother and Lu in the bed, the rest of us on the floor in our sleeping bags. The next morning, when we stepped out, we saw that there was a plastic swimming pool in the parking lot with a high curved slide. We hadn't noticed it the night before in the dark. Lu, Tuck, and I went over to look. But there was no water in the pool. Its sides were plastered with fallen brown leaves.

The days went by slowly. With the pool empty, there wasn't much to do around the motel. In front of it were a parking lot and a road. In back was a fence and behind the fence a brick building. If you went around the other side, you saw that in the brick building were a sneaker shop and a liquor store. We loitered in the parking lot. We played cards. Our mother called Chester to tell him where we were. She listened to the radio and watched the news on the motel TV. It was funny to see our mother watching TV. We didn't have a TV at our house. We kids also watched, hypnotized. But there was hardly any more news about the accident.

A week later, Chester joined us. He had been supposed to appear on TV himself, following the accident, but his appearance had been cancelled at the last minute when they found out what he was going to say. He made a lot of calls from the motel room. They were planning the next big anti-nuke rally, and he was going to speak.

We spoke to our father on the phone. Our mother took us on wildflower walks in the hills. A guide told us all about the mountain flowers. We were missing school. I worried about the tests I wasn't taking and the prizes I would now never win. At night, lying on the floor in my sleeping bag, unable to sleep, I pictured our house perched on the hill, empty, its windows staring out. The trees around it were all dead, the creek below dry and brown.

But when we finally did come back, everything was still alive.

The creek was rippling, the apple trees in bloom. The blossoms smelled sweet as ever. But were they poisoned? Would we be able to eat the fruit? I walked around looking, not touching things.

Our grandmother turns to Lu. "How long were you away from school?"

But Lu doesn't budge. She's on our mother's side. She shrugs. Our grandmother, annoyed, turns to me.

"Three weeks," I say.

"Three weeks!" she says, reporting, triumphant.

"Wasn't that a bit alarmist?" Alec asks.

"Well, actually, no," Chester says. "Not if you knew what was really going on." He begins to recite figures. He looks gigantic, imperturbable. His voice is deep, far off, as if he were once again addressing crowds. The hors d'oeuvres are gone. Outside in the dark the pool is glowing. There are lights on the floor of it. I picture jumping in, the way the water jets stream out at you underneath the surface. It would be cool but not too cool. It would be nice to step out of our fancy clothes.

"Now Clyde," our grandmother asks, "what would your favorite meal be?" We've moved into the dining room. The dining room table is made of dark polished wood. You can see the knots far beneath the polish gleaming. The silverware feels large and heavy in our hands. "Starting with the appetizer." Although the food she serves is rich and delicious, a crabmeat appetizer, sole with potatoes seeped in butter, our grandmother eats almost nothing herself, a hard-boiled egg at lunchtime, a few bites at dinner. "You can choose both a meat and a fish." Clyde doesn't know what she's talking about. "And then the dessert." She hasn't had dessert, we've heard, in thirty years. She used to be chubby, our mother tells us, when our mother was growing up, but since then our grandmother decided, with the same relentless determination with which she holds her opinions, never to be "fat" again.

"Pork chops," Clyde says.

Lu starts laughing.

"Good for you," Alec says. "A meat and potatoes man." He seems to be drunker. There's sweat on his brow. Both he and our grandmother have brought their drinks to the table.

Our grandmother turns to our mother. "So Faye, dear, tell us about the addition. Faye's building a wonderful new addition," she explains to Alec. "She's been living for years with a dirt floor in the kitchen. Dirt! Can you imagine? You dropped an egg, and there it was. There was nothing to do but rub it into the dirt." She rubs her gold sandal in a circle on the floor.

"I really enjoy the countryside," Alec says to our mother. "I have a country place myself."

"You do?" our mother asks.

"Sure! I like to go out walking or I shoot. I've got a little firing range set up."

"You hunt?" our mother asks.

"No, not much. But I like to shoot."

"That's wonderful," our grandmother says.

Our mother persists. "Why is that wonderful?"

She's thinking of the hunters who come onto our land and who, one year, shot our dogs.

"Well, shooting is wonderful, of course!" our grandmother says. "Everyone should know how to shoot."

Our grandmother has these implacable rules. Everyone should drink. A woman should marry rich. Everyone should know how to shoot. Sometimes in the afternoon she takes us out to shoot clay pigeons with her. She wears tan pants with leather bits sewn on them in the front. Standing there, her blond hair pulled back in a headband, she looks down the sights of her rifle, one eye squinted, and fires. Or she takes us to the horse races where we place bets. Once a visit we go with her to see her jeweler. We peer out into the yard by the pool to see if our mother wants to come. But she's not interested. She never wears jewelry, anyway. We're all dressed up, the best we can do, to go out with our grandmother. "Bye, Faye," our grandmother calls. What's our mother doing? Is she digging up the plants? Is she painting? She has her easel set up, so she must be painting. Her hands are dirty. She wears cutoff shorts. She has paint on her legs. Although in our normal life our mother is always dressed like this and always outdoors working with her hands, in this moment we look at her from where we're standing by the glass door with our grandmother's implacable gaze. Why doesn't our mother clean herself up, wear some decent clothes? It's an embarrassment. What's she thinking, behaving like this?

Our grandmother's car is dark green and shiny, with monograms on the doors. Once in town, we follow her, tap-tap, along the sidewalk. She wears beautifully cut pants, low flat shoes. She's tan—she always seems to be tan—and smells of perfume. We're allowed to choose something, a stone for a pendant, nothing too precious, or maybe a watch. Then we follow her, tap-tap, back along the sidewalk to the car.

We're just finishing the chocolate mousse. They're talking about our aunt's wedding, our mother's sister, the second time around, which we all went to a month or so ago. "Why couldn't they just have a normal wedding?" our grandmother asks. "Hmm? A normal wedding, a lovely white cake?"

The wedding was outside, and our mother acted as priest. She stood with two tall reeds stuck in the ground on either side of her. Then everyone sat down in a circle on the ground. A musician played the sitar. A woman in a green dress, our aunt's best friend, sang.

Our mother stiffens. She doesn't say anything. Then she does. "Because they didn't want that, Mum."

Our grandmother looks at her, as if not understanding. Blank, child eyes. The thing is not understandable.

Chester is quiet. This is what happens when he starts to get in a bad mood. He has a dry sort of humor when he's feeling all right, but when he gets in a bad mood he turns silent. He sinks further and further, often not speaking for days. Our mother stays clear of him and tells us to, too.

Our grandmother turns to Alec. "And then they served pasta." She says "pasta" with a short *a*, like "cat."

"What's wrong with pasta?" Alec asks, already amused.

Our grandmother takes another sip of her drink. She has that light in her eyes. This is when she starts getting outrageous. "What's wrong with it? What *is* it? Flour and water, flour and water!"

Alec laughs appreciatively.

Chester gets up from the table. "Excuse me," he says and leaves.

Alec turns and smiles at our mother, raising his glass. "The face that launched a thousand ships," he says.

Our mother's flattered. She can't help it. Having grown up in a house with girls—her father died young—she can never get enough attention from men.

"You should see Faye's work," our grandmother says. "She's a marvelous painter."

What our mother won't do, though, is please her mother. She stands up abruptly to clear the plates.

"No, no, Faye, leave it," our grandmother says.

I've been thinking again about the pool. I can tell Tuck and Lu have been eyeing it, too. Now Tuck asks what's in all our heads. "Mom, can we go swimming?"

Back in our rooms, we shed our fancy clothes as fast as we can and pull on our bathing suits. Racing each other, we dash back through the house, out the sliding glass doors, and jump into the pool. The jets along the sides shoot out silver bubbles. It's bright blue, deliciously cool. Tuck and Clyde play with the jets. Lu likes to dive down and skim the bottom.

Soon we're taking turns climbing out of the pool, running, and doing dives or leaps of different kinds. I step behind a set of low bushes, thinking I'll add a variation by leaping over the bushes and then taking my dive. But there's something there in the dark, a long shape on the grass. It's a person, Chester, lying down. He's smoking a joint, looking up at the sky. He turns his head and sees me, but doesn't say anything. I don't say anything, either.

A little while later, our grandmother and Alec step out of the house, fresh drinks in hand. Our grandmother, it seems, is on a roll.

"Charles Manson was a sex symbol, of course he was!"

Alec's delighted. "But Rosie, really, how can you say that?"

"It's obvious! Just look at all those beautiful gurls he had."

Alec, chortling, totters over to pee in the bushes.

Our mother comes outside, too, and looks around for Chester. She calls out his name.

Suddenly Chester gets up, right near where Alec is peeing—I can see his dark towering shape—and, silent and furious, walks away.

Our mother starts to follow him, but Alec, returning, cuts her off. Shirt untucked, standing on the flagstones around the pool, he does a little dance step in front of her. "The one-step, two-step Fred Astaire," he says.

Our grandmother laughs, her whole body collapsing entirely, charmingly, the way our mother's does, too, when she laughs. But our mother's not laughing now. She looks confused. It's as if she can't afford the luxury of frolicking. She wants a world where things mean something.

The night air has turned cool.

"I'm going to ask," Lu says to me, shivering. Beside her, Clyde is clinging to the edge of the pool, teeth chattering.

Our grandmother and Alec are now sitting at an iron table out on the flagstones. Lu pulls herself up out of the water and walks over to them.

"The face that launched a thousand ships," Alec says as she arrives.

"Gran," Lu says, ignoring him, "can we take a bath?"

"Of course, darling," our grandmother says.

Dripping and shivering, the four of us follow our grandmother into the house. She walks ahead of us jerkily, placing her feet far apart. We pass the kitchen, then bedrooms, going further and further into the adult side. At the far end is the bathroom, tiled in salmon-pink tile, the seat in our minds of all the mysterious glamorous magic that goes on in this house. One half of it consists of the bathtub itself, enormous, step-in, square, and deep. All four of us can fit into it easily at once. On a counter below the mirror are perfume bottles of different shapes with different shades of gold liquid inside, Mary Chess ("French," our grandmother says, her hand on the bottle, "very hard to find"), Opium, Chanel No. 5. To one side there's a bidet that intrigues us. Later, once our grandmother's gone, we'll play with it, spraying it up, the sudden flowering burst of cold between your legs. Along one wall hang lacy white nightgowns, dozens, it seems, soaked in perfume. Our grandmother puts the bath water on and pours in bubble bath. She turns and picks out two of the nightgowns. "Here, gurls, these are for you."

Later, waterlogged after hours in the pool, another long hour in the bath, dizzy with the smell of our perfume-soaked nightgowns, our stomachs gorged with rich food, Lu and I lie in our twin beds with the engravings of white men chasing Indians hanging above us on the wall.

Our mother comes in in her dress with fringes. The lamp is out, but there's light coming through the doorway. Chester has already gone to bed. In the background, out again by the pool, we can still hear Alec's voice. "You put the left-hand shot in the right-hand corner." Our mother sits down. She's about to say something, but then we hear our grandmother in the corridor.

"Faye, are you there?"

Our mother hesitates for a second. "Yeah, here, Mum."

Our grandmother appears in the bedroom doorway. "Oh," she says. She teeters there for a second, awkwardly, as if she might come in, but no one invites her. "Is everything okay?" she asks.

"Yeah, yeah, fine," our mother says.

"All right, then." Our grandmother, hesitating, turns away.

Our mother waits for a moment. Stiff, girl-like, in her Indian dress, she's sitting on the edge of my bed, but looking over at Lu, really talking to her. "She never, not once, tried to understand us," she says. "Why did she never once try to understand us?"

ABOUT EDWARD HIRSCH

A Profile by Brian Barker

In 2003, Edward Hirsch left his eighteen-year teaching post at the University of Houston and moved to New York City to become the president of the John Simon Guggenheim Memorial Foundation. At the time, his decision to accept such a position surprised many of his colleagues and students, who knew him as a generous, passionate, and natural teacher, and an integral force in building the UH Creative Writing Program into one of the elite writing programs in the country. But the move also made perfect sense, as the *Houston Chronicle* recognized, announcing that Hirsch had "found a bigger bully pulpit."

Hirsch, whose own lyric poetry yokes together an intrinsic intellect and a profound emotional depth, has been an unflagging advocate for the art. For more than twenty-five years—in essays and newspaper columns, at conferences and festivals, in classrooms and auditoriums, at galas and fundraisers—he has proselytized, taught, and championed poets and poetry of every ethnic and aesthetic stripe. "If you think that poetry—American poetry and poetry from other countries—has something to offer the larger culture," he says, "then poetry needs some people who are willing to speak on its behalf and to do the work of not only devoting themselves to their own poems, but also taking up the cause of poetry's place in the culture. Some people are called to do that and others are not. I don't think that there's a hierarchy here. But I do think that American poetry suffers if *everyone* turns away from these larger tasks." The fact that Hirsch has turned to these larger tasks speaks volumes about the man and the poet: his deep-seated sense of *civitas* within the world of poetry, his ebullient spirit, and his lifelong love affair with his art.

Born in 1950 in Chicago, Hirsch's first initiation into poetry came at the age of eight. As the story goes, he was picking through a box of musty books in the basement of his home when he opened an anthology to an anonymous poem. What he read— Emily Brontë's "Spellbound," he would discover years later—

immediately arrested him. In his book *How to Read a Poem and Fall in Love with Poetry,* he describes this first brush with the ecstatic powers of poetry: "I suppose that in some sense I never really shut that worn anthology of poetry again because it had opened up an unembarrassed space in me that would never be closed. I had stumbled into the sublime. I had been initiated into the poetry of awe." Despite this early encounter with poetry, Hirsch describes himself as an emotional and distracted child, obsessed with sports, who didn't naturally gravitate towards reading, but had to be coaxed by his mother. She encouraged him with books about sports, and something took hold.

By the seventh grade he was deep in *Crime and Punishment* and *Wuthering Heights* and never turned back. His grandfather, too, was an important figure during his childhood, an abiding presence of affection and tenderness, and an early source of language and poetic possibility. "I adored my grandfather," Hirsch says. "He came from Latvia and had Old World manners. He was wry, witty, affectionate, displaced. He never quite adjusted to the American marketplace, never quite figured out how to earn a living. I seem always to have been aware that he wrote poetry. He copied his poems down in the backs of his books, which didn't strike me as strange until I was much older. He wrote from right to left in Hebrew, and I had no idea what his poems were like. He also quoted poetry to me—Shakespeare and Keats—without ever identifying it. I just thought of it as part of the pool of the English language." His grandfather's native language and European sensibilities would inform both Hirsch's own poetry and his love, as a reader, for poetry from other countries. He acknowledges, in fact, hearing his grandfather's accents and tonalities in the Eastern European poetry he began to discover in his early twenties. "It felt like I was recognizing something, and it called to me," he says. "It spoke to something in me that I didn't hear in English and American poetry. I loved the combination that I found of high intellect and great tenderness."

Hirsch attended Grinnell College in Iowa, where he played baseball (outfield) and football (tight end), earning Academic All-American honors. After Grinnell, he went on to complete a Ph.D. in Folklore at the University of Pennsylvania. His first book, *For the Sleepwalkers,* appeared in 1981, a highly praised debut that

Evin Thayer

received the Lavan Younger Poets Award from the Academy of American Poets and the Delmore Schwartz Memorial Award from New York University. His career catapulted from there. His second collection, *Wild Gratitude* (1986), won the National Book Critics Circle Award. Four more volumes of poetry have followed since—*The Night Parade* (1989); *Earthly Measures* (1994); *On Love* (1998); and *Lay Back the Darkness* (2003)—and four astute and appreciative books of criticism on poetry and art—*Responsive Reading* (1999); *How to Read a Poem and Fall in Love with Poetry* (1999); *The Demon and the Angel: Searching for the Source of Artistic Inspiration* (2002); and *Poet's Choice* (2006). Hirsch has been honored with many of the most prestigious awards in letters, including fellowships from the Guggenheim and MacArthur foundations, an Ingram Merrill Foundation Award, a National Endowment for the Arts Fellowship, an American Academy of Arts and Letters Award, the Rome Prize from the American Academy in Rome, and a Lila Wallace–Reader's Digest Writers' Award.

At a time when so many poets whittle themselves down into defining personal styles and subjects—into what the Polish poet Adam Zagajewski has dubbed "deft miniaturists of a single theme"—Hirsch has remained remarkably open, a restless, questing, and ravenous poet of the world. Formally, his poems resist being pigeonholed, but there's never any doubt that they've been shaped by a rigorous maker, proving solid enough to bear strong emotional swells and supple enough to follow the quick movements of a keen mind. Hirsch is a poet as comfortable and capable in the fixed form of a villanelle (see the exquisite and moving "Ocean of Grass" in *On Love*) as he is in the unpredictable cadences and movements of a dramatic monologue (see the whole sequence of monologues in, again, *On Love*), or of an elliptical and lean lyric sequence (see the fabulous ekphrastic poems in *Lay Back the Darkness*—"The Horizontal Line," "Evanescence," and "Two Suitcases of Children's Drawings"—which insistently circle their subject matter and illuminate it from various angles).

This terrific formal scope reflects the wanderings of a poet who travels vast distances in his poems, inward and outward, across time and space, between praise and lamentation. Hirsch has written elegiac and tender poems about his childhood, his family, and his Jewish heritage. He has also written poems that wield a shrewd historical consciousness, taking on such subjects as the devastating European plague of the fourteenth century, torture in the twentieth century, and the Chicago fire of 1871. His poems have traversed the gritty, urban decay of the American city; the sunstruck peaks of Greece; the windswept, scoured absence of the early plains; and numerous other real, imagined, and mythic landscapes. He has written heartrending elegies and soaring homages to artistic geniuses as varied as Art Pepper, Paul Celan, and Georgia O'Keefe. In fact, Hirsch's poetry tends to be a gathering place for a whole cast of literary and cultural figures, from Simone Weil to Henry James, from Wallace Stevens to Orpheus.

When asked about these writers and thinkers that often appear in his poems, Hirsch says, "They're not just literary figures to me. I like to try to remember that poetry is made by flesh-and-blood human beings. It's a human art. When you're reading poets or thinkers deeply, you feel as if you know them better than the people around you. I've never quite understood when critical readers take them to be academic performances. The work by the figures I'm writing about is work that I've always experienced very intimately." Perhaps the strongest testament to this feeling manifests in the sequence of monologues in *On Love,* where a pantheon of literary figures speak on Eros. Amongst such notables as Charles Baudelaire, Zora Neale Hurston, and Colette appears Oscar Ginsburg, Hirsch's beloved grandfather. It's a symbolic gesture that simultaneously elevates the grandfather into this gallery of luminaries while drawing the literary giants down into the real world, into the flesh-and-blood family.

At mid-career, Hirsch's body of work and cache of distinguished awards would already add up to a tremendous lifetime of achievements for many poets. What's even more remarkable, and admirable, in Hirsch's case, is that he's been able to achieve so much with his own poetry while persistently acting as an unfaltering voice of advocacy on behalf of the art. Those lucky enough to have encountered him in a class, or on the lecture circuit, or even in one of his books of criticism, have been inspired time and again by his infectious enthusiasm. The way he speaks and writes about poetry—unpretentiously, with immediacy, with unfeigned candor and feeling, and with unwavering intelligence—moves against the current of so much of the chilly, jargon-ridden, and hyper-specialized literary criticism that's in vogue. It's a fact that's not lost on Hirsch. "At a certain point I decided—because I was frustrated by criticism and a little appalled by the way that poets had turned over the craft to literary theorists without advocating on behalf of their own art themselves—to change how I myself write about poetry," he says. "I wanted to see what would happen if when you wrote about poetry you were always emotionally present without any sacrifice of critical apparatus or intelligence or erudition. And I wanted to see if I could write about poetry in a way that would speak to two audiences: those who are initiated into poetry and knew a lot about it, and those who are not initiated into poetry, those who didn't know much about it. I wanted to see if you could write in a democratic way that would welcome people to poetry without any lowering of your standards."

This approach worked. *How to Read a Poem and Fall in Love with Poetry* was a national bestseller and captured the attention of scores of readers, new and old alike, with its powerful explorations of the lyric and narrative modes, and poetry's relationship to grief, ecstasy, history, praise, and prayer—to name a few of its many subjects. In *The Demon and the Angel,* Hirsch refined this critical style and extended it to other art forms, including film, dance, music, and painting, as he engaged the concept of *duende* and delved into the impetus of creativity, vision, and imagination, examining artistic examples as various as Robert Motherwell, Martha Graham, Charlie Parker, William Blake, and Federico García Lorca.

His latest endeavor, *Poet's Choice,* gathers together most of the pieces written during his three-year tenure for *The Washington Post Book World* poetry column. He writes on more than one hundred thirty poets from Asia, the Middle East, Europe, Latin America, and the United States in short entries, most of which top out at three or four pages. Though brief, these pieces are replete with Hirsch's characteristic warmth and sharp insights. Hirsch began the *Book World* column shortly after September 11, 2001, and though the book is not arranged chronologically, the historical weight of the moment is often palpable. There are pieces on poetry and suffering, women and war, protest poetry, and poets from all over the world who have written from the abyss of tyrannical violence or war. The ground note for the whole mood of this new book is struck in an introduction that hovers somewhere between a prayer and a call to action:

> Poetry is a means of exchange, a form of reciprocity, a magic to be shared, a gift. There has never been a civilization without it. That's why I consider poetry—which is, after all, created out of a mouthful of air—a human fundamental, like music. It saves something precious in the world from vanishing. It sacramentalizes experience.... Poetry speaks with the greatest intensity against the effacement of individuals, the obliteration of communities, the destruction of nature. It tries to keep the world from ending by positing itself against oblivion. The words are marks against erasure. I believe that something in our natures is realized when we use language as an art to confront and redeem our mortality. We need poems now as much as ever. We need these voices to restore us to ourselves in an alienating world.

In the book as a whole, as he does here, Hirsch reminds us of the redemptive and necessary power of poetry, of its ability to nourish us in the darkest of times.

Hirsch recently began his fourth year as the President of the Guggenheim Foundation, and when asked how things are going, he speaks of the deep gratification he derives from guiding an organization that supports the lives of individual artists and scientists. "It's thrilling to be able to support people to do their work. And it's also very exciting to watch their professional lives get a big boost. Often, people change levels, and that's really a pleasure. It's nice to be part of that." Luckily, too, the demands of the job have not eclipsed his writing time. He's completing his seventh book of poetry at the moment, titled *Special Orders,* and expects it to be published in the spring of 2008. When asked if he still thinks of himself as a teacher, he answers emphatically: "Oh, yeah. I think part of my writing about poetry is the same project as my teaching. I mean, I run the Foundation, but my inner life remains part of the culture of poetry. And teaching poetry is very much on my mind. Sometimes it's not in classrooms now, but my writing about poetry is meant to be in the same spirit as my teaching." We can be glad for that. In the ever-deafening buzz of our contemporary culture, we're lucky to have a voice like Hirsch's that keeps calling us back to poetry—a voice that keeps calling us back to the life of the mind, the life of the heart.

Brian Barker is the author of a book of poems, The Animal Gospels, *winner of the Editors' Prize from Tupelo Press. His poems, reviews, and interviews have appeared in such journals as* Poetry, Agni, The Indiana Review, *and* Blackbird. *He is an Assistant Professor and Coordinator of Undergraduate Creative Writing at Murray State University in Kentucky.*

Books Recommended by
Our Staff Editors

Radio Crackling, Radio Gone, *poems by Lisa Olstein* (Copper Canyon): Olstein's first book weaves its reader into a sensual and fibrous dreamscape inhabited by totem animals, somnambulist lovers hypnotic with longing, and symbols boldly acknowledged for their inherent duplicity: "Insert bird for sorrow," her speaker insists. While the poems in this book often operate as sanctuary, the speaker's signal turns siren, resulting in an eerie and emphatic alarm to alert us to the dangers of the conscious world. In "Parable of Grief," Olstein scripts violence onto the mundane; after regarding "snow-splashed grass" from her window, she levels this startling assertion: "When a bomb explodes in a marketplace every shred / of body must be searched for—flesh of watermelon, / fingernail, heart, stone." —*Cate Marvin*

Secondhand World, *a novel by Katherine Min* (Knopf): In this lucid and lyrical debut, Min offers the magnetic story of Isadora Myung Hee Sohn, an estranged Korean-American teenager struggling to understand just how it is that she, the lowly daughter, has managed to survive her ill-fated younger brother and the murder-suicide of her two parents. Offered in bracingly short chapters, the novel creates a fluid world in which monstrous changes come and go. "It's a secondhand world we're born into," Isa tells us. "What is novel to us is only so because we're newborn . . ." Min has a great talent for making the extraordinary seem like the ordinary fabric of life, while at the same time weaving a tale that is smart, assured, and completely gratifying. —*Fred Leebron*

Sanctuary, *poems by Adrienne Su* (Manic D): Do not allow the clarity of address in this striking second book to distract you from its many demands: Su's approach is risky in its sheer honesty and fierce by way of simplicity. The topics she addresses are as challenging as the formal rigors she undertakes and sustains with belying ease. Philosophically true, intellectually conversant, the speaker of these poems faces head-on the many implications of identity as an Asian American, and as a mother: "the written word / cannot compete with milk or tears." Tied by biological instinct and imaginative impulse, Su's poems beautifully address the conflicts inherent in writing and being. —*Cate Marvin*

Permanent Visitors, *stories by Kevin Moffett* (Iowa): In this funny and acutely perceptive debut collection, Moffett has an eye for the tragic that is also comic: a mother's unexpected death from a bad oyster is followed by the widower's hosting of a party of "challenged" youth; an émigré's desire for sex with "gazebo angels" runs counter to the sterile campus that houses the Institute for Advanced American Furtherance. In every story the voice is assured and yet keeps us off-balance. Overall, there is a wonderful symmetry between reckless storytelling and the momentary compensatory gesture, just as Moffett's characters are beginning to navigate the chaos of a strange but universal language. —*Fred Leebron*

Books Recommended by
Our Advisory Editors

New Books by
Our Advisory Editors

Margot Livesey recommends *Openwork*, a novel by Adria Bernardi: "An exquisitely written, vividly inhabited novel that follows the lives of three generations of Italian families." (SMU)

Elizabeth Spires recommends *Even the Hollow My Body Made Is Gone*, poems by Janice N. Harrington: "Like a hammer to gold, Harrington's richly lyric voice shapes her poetic material into unforgettable 'sung stories.' One of the marvels of this book is its convincing and tender reanimation of lives lived in a black community in the rural South that have long since vanished. Harrington knows, finally, that in the face of death, 'only the song remains. Only ruminant memory / taking our lives in its tough mouth.'" (BOA)

Gerald Stern recommends *Mistaking the Sea for Green Fields*, poems by Ashley Capps: "I love the scorching details of Capps's poems, as well as their withering honesty, their modesty, their crazy imagination, and their cunning. And I love their moral stance and their gracefulness." (Akron)

Rosanna Warren recommends *Letters from Aldenderry*, poems by Philip Nikolayev: "Fiendishly bright, world-savvy, word-savvy, large-hearted poems that tilt at lyric sentimentality ('Autobiography no longer saves') but keep an ancient faith: 'miniature illuminations mostly faded but some / still quite bright amid the frozen parcels of speech / the old quill is dead now but the books are alive.'" (Salt)

Madison Smartt Bell, *Toussaint Louverture*, a biography: A masterful portrait of the man who led the first—and only—successful slave revolution in history. (Pantheon)

Jane Hirshfield, *After*, poems: A luminous investigation into incarnation, transience, and our intimate connection with all existence. (HarperCollins)

Alice Hoffman, *Skylight Confessions*, a novel: An elegant new novel charting the history of one family whose lives are forever changed by the loss of their mother. (Little, Brown)

Howard Norman, *Devotion*, a novel: A haunting examination of romantic and filial love in the vast open spaces of Nova Scotia. (Houghton Mifflin)

Gary Soto, *A Simple Plan*, poems: A new collection that returns to the themes of place, childhood, and kinship with the down-and-out in Fresno. (Chronicle)

Ellen Bryant Voigt, *Messenger*, poems: A glorious arrangement of selections from six previous volumes, culminating in a series of new poems. (Norton)

Kevin Young, *For the Confederate Dead*, poems: A passionate pilgrimage embracing the contradictions of our "Confederate" legacy and the troubled nation where it still lingers. (Knopf)

CONTRIBUTORS' NOTES

Spring 2007

MARJORIE AGOSIN is a Chilean-American poet, editor, and human rights activist. She is the Luella Laneer Slain Professor of Latin American Studies at Wellesley College. She has received numerous awards for her poetry and human rights work, and has authored more than forty books of poetry, memoirs, and essays, as well as two plays.

CHARLES BAXTER is the author of *Beyond Plot*, forthcoming this summer from Graywolf. He has written four novels and four volumes of stories, and has edited or co-edited several books, including *A William Maxwell Portrait*. He teaches at the University of Minnesota and lives in Minneapolis.

MARIANNE BORUCH's most recent work includes *Poems: New and Selected* (Oberlin, 2004) and a second collection of essays on poetry, *In the Blue Pharmacy* (Trinity, 2005). She teaches in the M.F.A. program at Purdue University.

DAVID BOTTOMS's most recent book is *Waltzing Through the Endtime* from Copper Canyon Press. He is Georgia Poet Laureate and holds the Amos Distinguished Chair in English Letters at Georgia State University in Atlanta.

CLARE CAVANAGH is the Herman and Beulah Pearce Miller Research Professor in Literature at Northwestern University. She has translated ten books of Polish poetry and prose, and is currently working on an authorized biography of Czeslaw Milosz.

YIORGOS CHOULIARAS is the author of six volumes of poetry in Greek. Translations and reviews of his work have appeared in *Agenda, Grand Street, Harvard Review, Modern Poetry in Translation, Poetry, World Literature Today,* and elsewhere. Currently he is the director of the Press and Communications office at the Greek Embassy in Washington, D.C.

NICHOLAS CHRISTOPHER has published eight poetry books, including *Crossing the Equator: New & Selected Poems, 1972–2004* (Harcourt), just out in paperback; five novels, including *The Bestiary* (Dial), published in June; and a study of film noir, *Somewhere in the Night*, reissued in 2006. He is a professor in the School of the Arts at Columbia University.

VICTORIA CLAUSI's publications include a chapbook of poems, *Boarding House.* Her poems and reviews have also appeared in various journals and anthologies, including Henry Holt's *Roots and Flowers; Poems and Plays; Lumina;* and *Ploughshares.* She is Assistant Director of the Writing Seminars at Bennington College.

LYN COFFIN is a widely published poet, fiction writer, playwright, and translator of Czech literature. She has published seven books, including *Human Trap-*

pings (Abattoir) and *Crystals of the Unforeseen* (Plainview). She lives in Seattle.

MICHAEL COLLIER's most recent book is *Dark Wild Realm* (Houghton Mifflin, 2006). A translation of *Medea* (Oxford) also appeared in 2006, and a collection of essays, *Make Us Wave Back* (Michigan), will be published in 2007. He teaches at the University of Maryland.

JOSEPHINE DICKINSON has two poetry collections in the U.K., *Scarberry Hill* and *The Voice,* and her American debut collection, *Silence Fell,* was published in March by Houghton Mifflin. She lives in Alston, a small Cumbrian town high in the Pennines.

STUART DYBEK is a past guest editor of *Ploughshares.* His most recent book of poems is *Streets in Their Own Ink* (FSG).

ROBIN EKISS is a former Stegner Fellow. Her work has appeared or is forthcoming in *Poetry, TriQuarterly, Agni, The Kenyon Review, The Black Warrior Review,* and elsewhere. She lives in San Francisco with her husband, the poet Keith Ekiss.

GARY FINCKE's most recent poetry collection is *Standing Around the Heart* (Arkansas, 2005). *Writing Letters for the Blind* won the 2003 *The Journal*/Ohio State University poetry prize, and his most recent collection of stories, *Sorry I Worried You,* won the Flannery O'Connor Prize and was published in 2004.

CHRIS FORHAN was recently awarded an NEA fellowship in poetry. He is the author of *The Actual Moon, The Actual Stars,* which won the Morse Prize and the Washington State Book Award, and *Forgive Us Our Happiness,* which won the Bakeless Prize. He teaches at Auburn University.

ALLEGRA GOODMAN has written two story collections, *Total Immersion* and *The Family Markowitz,* and three novels, *Kaaterskill Falls, Paradise Park,* and *Intuition.* She is the recipient of a Whiting Writer's Award and a fellowship from the Radcliffe Institute for Advanced Study. She lives with her family in Cambridge, Massachusetts.

XIAOLU GUO studied film at the Beijing Film Academy and has worked as a novelist, essayist, and filmmaker. Her most recent novel in English is *A Concise Chinese English Dictionary for Lovers.* She also directed and produced *How Is Your Fish Today?,* which was an official selection at the 2007 Sundance Film Festival. The translators for her story, Rebecca Morris and Pamela Casey, live in London.

JUDITH HALL is the author of four books, including *To Put the Mouth To,* selected for the National Poetry Series, and *Three Trios,* translations of the poet J II. She has received awards from the NEA and the Ingram Merrill and Guggenheim foundations and serves as poetry editor of *The Antioch Review.*

PATRICIA HAMPL is the author of the memoirs *A Romantic Education* and *Virgin Time.* Her most recent book is *Blue Arabesque: A Search for the Sublime.* This fall, Harcourt will publish another memoir, *The Florist's Daughter.* She is Regents Professor of English at the University of Minnesota and on the permanent faculty of the Prague Summer Program.

PATRICK HICKS is the author of *Traveling Through History, Draglines, The Kiss That Saved My Life,* and *Finding the Gossamer.* He currently lives in Sioux Falls, South Dakota, where he teaches creative writing at Augustana College, and is an advisory editor for *New Hibernia Review.*

BOB HICOK's fifth book, *This Clumsy Living,* is just out from University of Pittsburgh Press.

GARRETT HONGO's work includes two books of poetry, three anthologies, *Volcano: A Memoir of Hawaii,* and *The North Shore,* a forthcoming volume of poems. The recipient of a Guggenheim Fellowship, two NEA grants, and the Lamont Poetry Prize, he teaches at the University of Oregon, where he is Distinguished Professor of Arts and Sciences.

MARIA HUMMEL is a Stegner Fellow in Poetry at Stanford and the author of the novel *Wilderness Run.* She recently received an award in nonfiction from the Barbara Deming Memorial Fund, and has published poetry in *New England Review, PN Review,* and *Hayden's Ferry Review.*

BEENA KAMLANI's fiction has appeared in *Identity Lessons* and *Growing Up Ethnic in America* (Penguin). She has received fellowships from Yaddo and Ledig House, and won a Tennessee Williams Scholarship at Sewanee and a fiction grant from the Connecticut Arts Commission. She lives in New York, where she is completing her first novel.

MARIA KOUNDOURA's book, *The Greek Idea: The Formation of National and Transnational Identities,* is forthcoming this year. Currently she is at work on a book on global cities and citizenship, and editing a collection of essays on taste. She teaches literature and cultural theory at Emerson College.

RYSZARD KRYNICKI is a poet, translator, and editor. His most recent volume is *Kamien, szron* (2004). He lives in Krakow, Poland, where he and his wife, Krystyna, run the publishing house A5.

PHILIP LEVINE divides his time between Brooklyn and Fresno. Later this year, Sarabande will publish a new version of *Tarumba: The Selected Poems of Jaime Sabines,* which he co-edited and translated with the Mexican poet Ernesto Trejo.

BRONISLAW MAJ is a poet, critic, and essayist. He teaches contemporary Polish literature at the Jagiellonian University in Krakow, Poland.

COREY MARKS's *Renunciation* was a National Poetry Series selection. His recent poems appear in *New England Review, Southwest Review, TriQuarterly, The Virginia Quarterly Review,* and *Legitimate Dangers.*

CATE MARVIN's second book of poems, *Fragment of the Head of a Queen,* is forthcoming from Sarabande this August. She is an associate professor in creative writing at the College of Staten Island, City University of New York.

JAMES MCCORKLE received the 2003 *APR*/Honickman Award for his collection *Evidences.* He is an editor of the *Greenwood Encyclopedia of American Poets and*

Poetry (2006); recent poems have appeared in *The Colorado Review, Conduit, Crazyhorse, Fiddlehead,* and *Harvard Review.*

MICHAEL MILBURN teaches high school English in New Haven, Connecticut. His book of essays, *Odd Man In,* won Mid-List Press's First Series Award in Nonfiction and was published in 2005.

EUGENIO MONTEJO is the author of twelve books of poetry. He has also published two books of essays and four volumes of heteronymic work. He received the Octavio Paz prize in 2005 and was awarded Venezuela's National Prize for Literature in 1998.

LAURA ROCHA NAKAZAWA, a native of Montevideo, Uruguay, is a Spanish translator and interpreter working in the Boston area. She has translated some of the poetry of Marjorie Agosin into English, in particular *Among the Angels of Memory.*

MURIEL NELSON has two collections of poems, *Part Song* (Bear Star, 1999) and *Most Wanted* (ByLine, 2003). Her work has been nominated twice for the Pushcart Prize and has appeared in *Ploughshares, The New Republic, The Beloit Poetry Journal, The National Poetry Review, Northwest Review,* and others.

KIRK NESSET is the author of two books of short stories, *Mr. Agreeable* and *Paradise Road,* as well as *The Stories of Raymond Carver* (nonfiction). The recipient of the Drue Heinz Literature Prize in 2007, a Pushcart Prize, and grants from the Pennsylvania Council on the Arts, he teaches creative writing and literature at Allegheny College.

DEBRA NYSTROM's most recent book of poems is *Torn Sky,* from Sarabande Books. Her work has appeared in *Slate, APR, The Yale Review, The Threepenny Review,* and elsewhere. She teaches creative writing at the University of Virginia.

JOYCE CAROL OATES is a recipient of the National Book Award and the PEN/Malamud Award for Excellence in Short Fiction. Author of *We Were the Mulvaneys, Blonde,* and *The Falls,* which won the 2005 Prix Femina, she is the Roger S. Berlind Distinguished Professor of the Humanities at Princeton University. Her new novel is *Black Girl/White Girl.*

JIRI ORTEN was one of the great European poets of the twentieth century. In the summer of 1941, he stepped off a street corner in Prague, and was struck by a Gestapo ambulance. He was refused admission to a nearby hospital because he was Jewish and died a few days later. He was twenty-two.

JACQUELINE OSHEROW's most recent collection of poems is *The Hoopoe's Crown* (BOA, 2005).

MARITA OVER won a Gregory Award in 1992 and is published widely in the U.K. Her publications include *Other Lilies* (Frogmore, 1997) and *Not Knowing Itself* (Arrowhead, 2006). She lives in Cockermouth, Cumbria, where she is training to be a psychotherapist.

SUE OWEN taught as the Poet-in-Residence at Louisiana State University and now lives in Cambridge, Massachusetts. Her fourth book of poetry, *The Devil's Cookbook*, is forthcoming this spring from LSU Press. Last fall in Scandinavia, she read her poems that have been translated and published in Stockholm and Helsinki.

ELIZABETH POWELL's work is forthcoming or has recently appeared in *Post Road, Slope, The Mississippi Review, Green Mountains Review*, and *Alaska Quarterly Review*. Her first book of poems, *The Republic of Self*, was the winner of the 2000 New Issues Book Prize. She teaches at the University of Vermont.

LEN ROBERTS's ninth book of poetry, *The Disappearing Trick*, will be published by the University of Illinois Press this summer. BOA Editions published his translations of the great Hungarian poet Sandor Csoori in a volume titled *Before and After the Fall: Selected Poems of Sandor Csoori*, in 2005.

JOHN RYBICKI teaches creative writing through Wings of Hope Hospice to children who have gone through a trauma or loss. His first book, *Traveling at High Speeds*, is available from New Issues Press. A new collection, *We Bed Down into Water*, is forthcoming from Northwestern University Press this fall.

CAROLINE SANDERSON was a poet who died several years ago. She previously published poems in *The Partisan Review*.

PHILIP SCHULTZ's most recent book of poems was *Living in the Past* (Harcourt, 2004). The poem in this issue is from his new book, *Failure*, due out from Harcourt this fall. He founded and directs The Writers Studio in New York City.

VIJAY SESHADRI is the author of two books of poems, *Wild Kingdom* and *The Long Meadow*, and many essays, articles, and reviews. He lives in Brooklyn and teaches at Sarah Lawrence College.

JIM SHEPARD is the author of six novels and two story collections. His fiction has appeared in *Harper's, The Atlantic Monthly, Esquire*, and *The New Yorker*, and he is a columnist on film for *The Believer*. A third story collection, *Like You'd Understand Anyway*, and a collection of film essays, *Heroes in Disguise*, will appear in 2007.

JASON SHINDER's poetry books include *Every Room We Ever Slept In, Among Women*, and a forthcoming collection from Graywolf Press. He teaches at the graduate Writing Seminars at Bennington College, and is founder/director of the YMCA National Writer's Voice and the Gibson International Music Initiative.

RON SLATE's book of poems, *The Incentive of the Maggot* (Houghton Mifflin, 2005), was nominated for the National Book Critics Circle Award and the Lenore Marshall Prize. He is the chief operating officer of a biotech startup and lives in Milton, Massachusetts.

ANN SNODGRASS's recent work appears in *TriQuarterly, Harvard Review, American Letters & Commentary*, and *Field*. She teaches at MIT. The poem in this issue refers to Cees Nooteboom's poem "Basho" as translated by J. M. Coetzee.

SUSAN STEWART is the Annan Professor of English at Princeton University and a Chancellor of the Academy of American Poets. Her most recent book of poems, *Columbarium*, won the National Book Critics Circle Award for 2003 and has recently appeared in an Italian translation by Maria Cristina Biggio.

DAN STRYK's five collections of poems and prose parables include *The Artist and the Crow* (Purdue). Forthcoming are *Dimming Radiance* (2007) and *Solace of the Aging Mare* (2007). Recent work appears in *Shenandoah*, *The Ontario Review*, *The Mississippi Review*, *Harvard Review*, *New York Quarterly*, and *Witness*.

MAXINE SWANN's stories have received an O. Henry Award, a Pushcart Prize, and been included in *The Best American Short Stories*. Her first novel, *Serious Girls*, was published in 2003. Her second novel, *Flower Children*, will appear this May. She has lived in Paris and Pakistan and currently lives in Buenos Aires.

WISLAWA SZYMBORSKA received the Nobel Prize in Literature in 1996. She lives in Krakow, Poland.

DANIEL TOBIN is the author of *Where the World Is Made*, *Double Life*, *The Narrows*, and *Second Things* (Four Way, 2008), as well as a book of criticism on Seamus Heaney. He edited *The Book of Irish American Poetry from the 18th Century to the Present*. He is Chair of the Department of Writing, Literature, and Publishing at Emerson College.

DAVID WAGONER has published seventeen books of poems, most recently *Good Morning and Good Night* (Illinois, 2005), and ten novels, one of which, *The Escape Artist*, was made into a movie by Francis Ford Coppola. He served as chancellor of the Academy of American Poets for twenty-three years and edited *Poetry Northwest* from 1966 to 2002.

JOHN WALKER has exhibited at the Museum of Modern Art in New York, the Venice Biennale, the Tate Gallery, and the Phillips Collection. He lives in Boston and Maine, and is Director of the Graduate School of Painting and Sculpture at Boston University. He is represented by Knoedler Gallery in New York and Nielsen Gallery in Boston.

CHARLES HARPER WEBB is the author of *Amplified Dog* (Red Hen, 2006), which won the Saltman Prize for Poetry, and a book of prose poems, *Hot Popsicles* (Wisconsin, 2005). Recipient of grants from the Whiting and Guggenheim foundations, he directs Creative Writing at California State University, Long Beach.

GEORGE WITTE is the author of *The Apparitioners* (Three Rail, 2005). New poems are current or forthcoming in *Boulevard*, *Prairie Schooner*, and *Southwest Review*. He works as the editor in chief of St. Martin's Press.

VALERIE WOHLFELD's 1994 collection, *Thinking the World Visible*, won the Yale Younger Poets Prize. Her work has appeared in *The Antioch Review*, *New England Review*, *Journal of the American Medical Association*, and elsewhere.

KEVIN YOUNG is the author of five poetry books, most recently *For the Confederate Dead* (Knopf), and editor of *John Berryman: Selected Poems*, *Blues Poems*,

Jazz Poems, and *Giant Steps: The New Generation of African American Writers.* He is Haygood Professor of English and Creative Writing and Curator of the Raymond Danowski Poetry Library at Emory University.

ADAM ZAGAJEWSKI is a poet and essayist. His most recent volume, *Music I Have Heard with You,* is forthcoming from Farrar, Straus & Giroux. He divides his time between Krakow and the United States, where he will begin teaching on the Committee of Social Thought at the University of Chicago next fall.

∾

GUEST EDITOR POLICY *Ploughshares* is published three times a year: mixed issues of poetry and fiction in the Spring and Winter and a fiction issue in the Fall, with each guest-edited by a different writer of prominence, usually one whose early work was published in the journal. Guest editors are invited to solicit up to half of their issues, with the other half selected from unsolicited manuscripts screened for them by staff editors. This guest editor policy is designed to introduce readers to different literary circles and tastes, and to offer a fuller representation of the range and diversity of contemporary letters than would be possible with a single editorship. Yet, at the same time, we expect every issue to reflect our overall standards of literary excellence. We liken *Ploughshares* to a theater company: each issue might have a different guest editor and different writers—just as a play will have a different director, playwright, and cast—but subscribers can count on a governing aesthetic, a consistency in literary values and quality, that is uniquely our own.

∾

SUBMISSION POLICIES We welcome unsolicited manuscripts from August 1 to March 31 (postmark dates). All submissions sent from April to July are returned unread. In the past, guest editors often announced specific themes for issues, but we have revised our editorial policies and no longer restrict submissions to thematic topics. Submit your work at any time during our reading period; if a manuscript is not timely for one issue, it will be considered for another. We do not recommend trying to target specific guest editors. Our backlog is unpredictable, and staff editors ultimately have the responsibility of determining for which editor a work is most appropriate.

Mail one prose piece or one to three poems. We do not accept e-mail submissions, but we now accept submissions online. Please see our website (www.pshares.org) for more information and specific guidelines. Poems should be individually typed either single- or double-spaced on one side of the page. Prose should be typed double-spaced on one side and be no longer than thirty pages. Although we look primarily for short stories, we occasionally publish personal essays/memoirs. Novel excerpts are acceptable if self-contained. Unsolicited book reviews and criticism are not considered.

Please send only one manuscript at a time, either by mail or online. Do not send a second submission until you have heard about the first. *There is a limit of two submissions per reading period, regardless of genre, whether it is by mail or online.* Additional submissions will be returned unread. Mail your manuscript in a page-size manila envelope, your full name and address written on the outside. In general, address submissions to the "Fiction Editor," "Poetry Editor," or "Nonfiction Editor," not to the guest or staff editors by name, unless you have a legitimate association with them or have been previously published in the magazine. Unsolicited work sent directly to a guest editor's home or office will be ignored and discarded; guest editors are formally instructed not to read such work. *All mailed manuscripts and correspondence regarding submissions should be accompanied by a business-size, self-addressed, stamped envelope (S.A.S.E.) for a response only. Manuscript copies will be recycled, not returned.* No replies will be given by postcard or e-mail (exceptions are made for international submissions).

Expect three to five months for a decision. We now receive well over a thousand manuscripts a month. Do not query us until five months have passed, and if you do, please write to us, including an S.A.S.E. and indicating the postmark date of submission, instead of calling or e-mailing. Simultaneous submissions are amenable as long as they are indicated as such and we are notified immediately upon acceptance elsewhere. We cannot accommodate revisions, changes of return address, or forgotten S.A.S.E.'s after the fact. We do not reprint previously published work. Translations are welcome if permission has been granted. We cannot be responsible for delay, loss, or damage. Payment is upon publication: $25/printed page, $50 minimum and $250 maximum per author, with two copies of the issue and a one-year subscription.

THE NAME *Ploughshares* 1. The sharp edge of a plough that cuts a furrow in the earth. 2 a. A variation of the name of the pub, the Plough and Stars, in Cambridge, Massachusetts, where the journal *Ploughshares* was founded in 1971. 2 b. The pub's name was inspired by the Sean O'Casey play about the Easter Rising of the Irish "citizen army." The army's flag contained a plough, representing the things of the earth, hence practicality; and stars, the ideals by which the plough is steered. 3. A shared, collaborative, community effort. 4. A literary journal that has been energized by a desire for harmony, peace, and reform. Once, that spirit motivated civil rights marches, war protests, and student activism. Today, it still inspirits a desire for beating swords into ploughshares, but through the power and the beauty of the written word.

EMERSON COLLEGE

NATIONAL
ENDOWMENT
FOR THE ARTS

massculturalcouncil.org

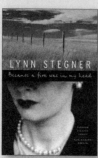

Paper Tiger
A Novel
BY OLIVIER ROLIN
Translated by William Cloonan

This prize-winning novel by one of France's most acclaimed writers tells, through protagonist character Martin, the elegiac story of a whole generation's coming of age.

"*Paper Tiger* is a brilliant novel that explores the complex intertwining of idealism and politics and violence, a critical theme in the early twenty-first century. —Robert Olen Butler, author of the Pulitzer Prize–winning novel *A Good Scent from a Strange Mountain*

$17.95 paper | 978-0-8032-8999-4
$40.00 cloth | 978-0-8032-3955-5

Because a Fire Was in My Head
BY LYNN STEGNER

Kate Riley is an unusual heroine, a beautiful, ambitious woman who rejects the conventional roles of women in her 1950s rural community. The premature death of her beloved father, coupled with a corrosive relationship with her mother, prompts Kate to flee her hometown in desperate search of happiness and approval. The story takes us through a succession of lovers, and of children born and abandoned, as Kate makes one bad choice after another.

"With exquisite precision, Lynn Stegner has captured Kate Riley's life in all its shadows and specters. A harrowing book, beautifully told."
—Bret Lott, author of *Jewel*

$24.95 cloth | 978-0-8032-1139-1
FLYOVER FICTION SERIES

University of Nebraska Press
800.755.1105 | www.nebraskapress.unl.edu | *publishers of Bison Books*

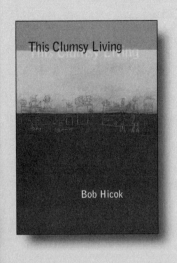
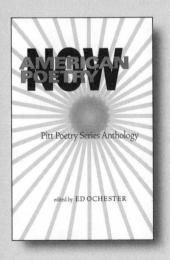

Announces its 48th Annual

BEST POEM CONTEST

www.stlouispoetrycenter.org

POSTMARK DEADLINE: MAY 31, 2007

First Prize: $2,000

& Publication in *MARGIE/The American Journal of Poetry*

Second Prize: $250　　Third Prize: $100

Finalist Judge: Stephen Dunn

"Winner of the Pulitzer Prize in Poetry"

GUIDELINES: 1. Submit 3 unpublished poems & a $15 entry fee payable to The St. Louis Poetry Center. (60 line limit per poem). Additional poems may be submitted for $5 each additional poem. 2. Enclose a single cover letter with your name, address, phone & poem titles. No names should appear on poems. 3. Simultaneous submissions are acceptable. Only send copies. Poems will not be returned. Include SASE to receive contest results. 4. All poems will be considered for publication. 5. Mail entry and fee by POST-MARK DEADLINE MAY 31, 2007 to:

The St. Louis Poetry Center
567 North & South Rd., #8
St. Louis, MO 63130
www.stlouispoetrycenter.org

Dorothy Sargent Rosenberg Annual Poetry Prizes, 2007

Prizes ranging from $1,000 up to as much as $25,000 will be awarded for the finest lyric poems celebrating the human spirit. Entries are due November 6, 2007. The contest is open to all writers, published or unpublished, who will be under the age of 40 on that date. Only previously unpublished poems are eligible for prizes. Names of prizewinners will be published on our website on February 5, 2008, together with a selection of the winning poems. For further information and to read poems by previous winners, please visit our website: www.DorothyPrizes.org.

- Entries must be postmarked on or before November 6, 2007.
- Past winners may reenter until their prizes total in excess of $25,000.
- All entrants must be under the age of 40 on November 6, 2007.
- Submissions must be original, previously unpublished, and in English; no translations, please.
- Each entrant may submit one to three separate poems.
- Only one of the poems may be more than thirty lines in length.
- Each poem must be printed on a separate sheet.
- Submit two copies of each entry with your name, address, phone number and email address clearly marked on each page of one copy only.
- Include an index card with your name, address, phone number and email address and the titles of each of your submitted poems.
- Include a $10 entry fee payable to the Dorothy Sargent Rosenberg Memorial Fund. (This fee is not required for entries mailed from outside the U.S.A.)
- Poems will not be returned. Include a stamped addressed envelope if you wish us to acknowledge the receipt of your entry.

Mail entries to: Dorothy Sargent Rosenberg Poetry Prizes
PO Box 2306, Orinda, California 94563

Prize winners for the 2006 competition, announced February 5, 2007:

$10,000 prizes to Marla Alupoaicei, Paula Bohince, Allen Braden, and Gillian Wegener.
$7,500 prizes to Pilar Gómez-Ibáñez and Dove Rengger-Thorpe.
$5,000 prizes to K. Ballantine, Danielle Cadena Deulen, Robin Ekiss, Tess Jolly, Allison Joseph, Eric Leigh, Erin Murphy, Felicity Plunkett, and John Poch.
$2,500 prizes to Kimberly Burwick, Xochiquetzal Candelaria, Chloe Green, Mihan Han, David Livewell, Christopher Locke, Lisa Ortiz, Rachel Richardson, Emily Rosko, and Jennifer Whitaker.
$1,000 prizes to Kelli Russell Agodon, Douglas Basford, Timothy Donnelly, Julie Dunlop, Vicki Goodfellow Duke, Scott Gallaway, Heather Hartley, Anne Keefe, Jennifer Koiter, Dawn Lonsinger, Tolu Ogunlesi, and Alexis Orgera.
There were also fourteen Honorable Mentions at $100 each.
Thank you to everyone who entered and congratulations to our winners.

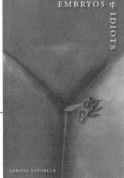

NATIONAL POETRY MONTH ❀ APRIL

2007

Visit www.poets.org
to find out about new spring poetry titles and more.

CHAIRMAN'S CIRCLE: Con Edison • Merriam-Webster
National Endowment for the Arts • *The New York Times*
Poetry Foundation • Random House, Inc.

BENEFACTORS: Alfred A. Knopf • Assoc. of Writers & Writing Programs
Ausable Press • Coffee House Press • Ecco / HarperCollins
Farrar Straus & Giroux • Harcourt • Houghton Mifflin
Library of America • Louisiana State University Press
Northwestern University Press • Penguin

PREMIUM SPONSORS: Alice James Books • American Library Association
Bennington Writing Seminars • BOA Editions • Bright Hill Press
CavanKerry Press • City Lights Books • Consortium • Copper Canyon Press
Council of Literary Magazines & Presses • Curbstone Press • The Drawing Center
Four Way Books • Geraldine R. Dodge Poetry Festival • Graywolf Press
Hanging Loose Press • Housing Works Used Bookstore • Kelsey St. Press
Marymount Manhattan College • Milkweed Editions
Modern Language Association • National Council of Teachers of English
Oxford University Press • New Directions • New Issues Press
Oberlin College Press/FIELD • Persea Books • Poets & Writers
Robinson Jeffers Tor House Foundation • Sarabande Books
Scribner • The Stadler Center for Poetry • University of California Press
University of Chicago Press • University of Georgia Press
University of Massachusetts Press • University of Pittsburgh Press
W. W. Norton • Wave Books • Wake Forest University Press
Wesleyan University Press • White Pine Press

The Academy thanks *Ploughshares* for being a Media Sponsor of NPM 2007.

BOSTON REVIEW

ANNOUNCES ITS TENTH ANNUAL
POETRY CONTEST

judge
SUSAN STEWART

first prize
$1,500

deadline
JUNE 1, 2007

PARTIAL RULES Submit up to five unpublished poems, no more than 10 pages total. Any poet writing in English is eligible, unless he or she is a current student, former student, or close personal friend of the judge. Manuscripts must be submitted in duplicate, with a cover note listing the author's name, address, and phone number; names should not be on the poems themselves. A $20 entry fee ($30 for international submissions), payable to BOSTON REVIEW, must accompany all submissions. Postmark deadline: June 1, 2007. All entrants will receive a one-year subscription to Boston Review. Send entries to Poetry Contest, BOSTON REVIEW, 35 Medford St., Suite 302, Somerville, MA 02143 **COMPLETE RULES ONLINE AT BOSTONREVIEW.NET**

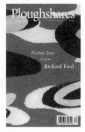